Books by KB Fisher

Of Storm and Shadows
Promoted with Tenure
Admit Two

OF
STORM
AND
SHADOWS

KB Fisher

First Edition: November 2024

Paperback ISBN: 979-8-9880200-4-2
eBook ISBN: 979-8-9880200-5-9
Library of Congress Control Number: 2024920205

For the lives lost and changed
by HURRICANE KATRINA

ACKNOWLEDGMENTS

To say that this novel was a challenge to write would be an understatement. Thanks to the brainstorming, late-night research, and honesty of my wife Carissa, I succeeded in completing the work. Nothing will ever replace our back-and-forth.

The same goes for my editor, Dylan Garity. Somehow, you manage to understand the stories in my head. Your continued support and guidance are invaluable. Thank you.

I grew up in Slidell, Louisiana—and I was a teenager there when Hurricane Katrina forever changed the lives of those living on the Gulf Coast.

Although by no means a factual account, this book explores many of my experiences during the storm, generally speaking—or at least what I remember from what seems like so long ago.

I lived between my parents' homes on Live Oak Lane and in Olde Towne. Luckily, I evacuated to northern Mississippi at the last minute and was able to escape the brunt of the storm. That is, until we returned to the aftermath.

My parents' homes took on several feet of water and were changed beyond recognition. Katrina left us with memories that will remain until our final days. The hurricane, in part, serves as the backdrop of this novel.

With that said, the story herein is a mystery thriller and is not meant to support or refute anyone's lived experiences at the time, although some of the locations are factual. As devastating as the storm was for the residents of Slidell, myself included, I chose Katrina as the backdrop of this novel because such a significant moment in Louisiana's history should be remembered. I also believe it serves well the tension of a good thriller.

My hope is that the story herein entertains you in a unique way. Hurricane Katrina, although devastating, was a time in my life that marked a new beginning as a Louisiana native.

Please enjoy this work for what it is: a *fictional* mystery thriller.

—KB Fisher

September 15, 2024

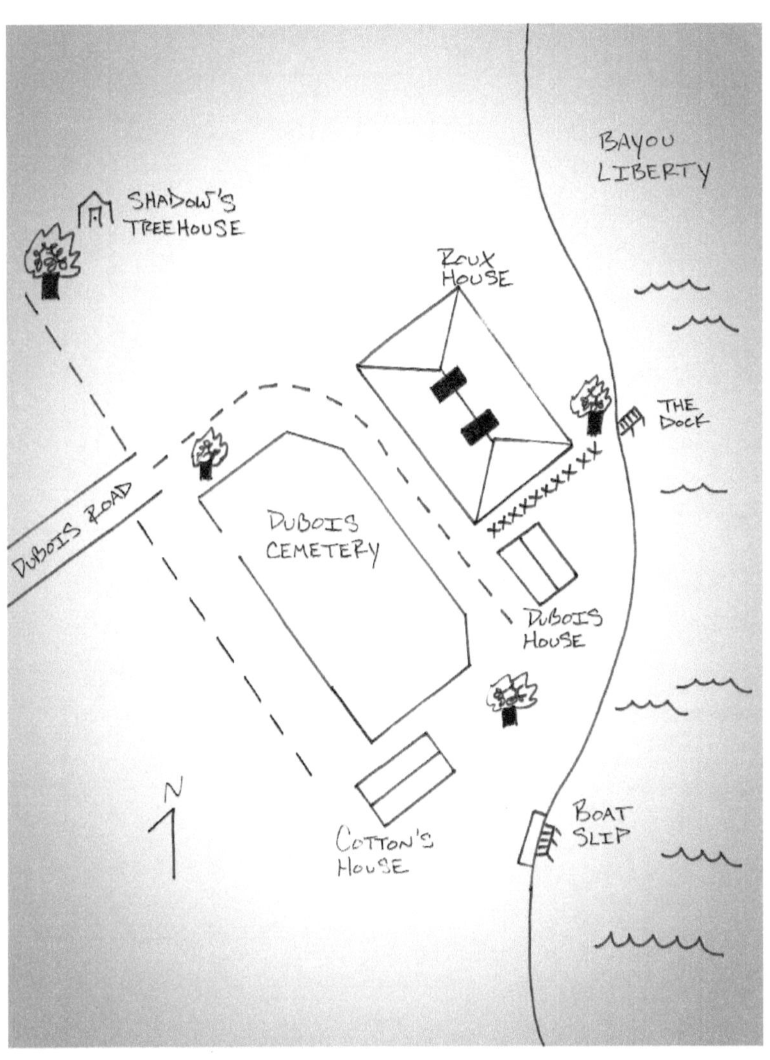

BAYOU LIBERTY
SHADOW'S TREEHOUSE
ROUX HOUSE
THE DOCK
DUBOIS ROAD
DUBOIS CEMETERY
DUBOIS HOUSE
COTTON'S HOUSE
BOAT SLIP
N

part one

Lance

ONE

August 29, 2005

This was bound to happen sooner or later, living on the bayou. Out here, muddied waters are a way of life, a character in and of themselves that seep into the farthest corners of your being—often for the better, but sometimes worse.

Standing in the center of my living room, I watch the murky tide push its way beneath the front door and across the wood floors. It comes in a rapid line of waves, each surge more forceful than the last. Before now, I thought I'd break down at the sight of water flooding my home. But I'm unable to pry my attention from the strangeness of it, like a body part twisted the wrong way, a big toe broken at a right angle to the foot.

Clearly, the sandbags on the other side of the door are pointless.

The water splashes against the toe of my boot just as the lights go out—no flicker, no off and on again. Only black. The kind of darkness that hides your hand even if it's an inch from your face.

Wind cuts across the corner of the house, the whistle as shrill as a barreling train. It's an eerie howl, accompanied by what I can only guess is the snapping of cypress trees and oaks. The popping sounds like the marsh on opening day of duck season. Only now, instead of a dry cold, the air is filled with a thick, low-pressure moisture as the AC goes quiet.

This isn't the first hurricane I've stayed for. I'm not sure what it is in particular, but this isn't anything like the ones that have come before.

I step back as lightning flashes through the dining room window, illuminating the water that breaks against the baseboards and swamps the hallway. The crack of thunder shakes the home to its bones, pulling my attention back to the urgency of the moment. Unless I plan on treading water, it's time to get up to the second floor.

I shuffle to the kitchen and run my hand across the counter, feeling for the flashlight I know is there, the bayou filling my boots with a thick warmth. A timer crawling up my leg. I grab the light and thumb the switch, then shine the beam on the front door.

The window to my right erupts into a shower of jagged, wet shards that blanket the side of my face. I crouch and fall against the banister, lifting my arm to shield my eyes. My blood skips a beat.

So much for the first floor.

Walking up the stairs, I look back and shine my light through the square hole in the wall, out to the row of dog ears between our homes, the boards crushed by an uprooted tree. The tide is rolling inland below bands of rain, as if the bayou itself is being resurfaced, reinvented. My eyes strain, but I fail to see Lauren's home beyond the splintered fence line.

Life's so-called problems cower once I realize my childhood home—at least, the way I've always known it—will never again be the same. Good thing my office is still dry.

I walk into the room and look out of the second-floor window. Sparks backlight the rain. I flash my light in the direction of her home, hoping to get a flicker in response, any reply at all. As hard as I look, I see nothing but a shifting wall of gray.

My flashlight blinks out, and the dark sweeps in again.

If I can feel my way into the hall, I know my old man kept

some spare batteries in the closet, right up until the day he went missing. Before I have a chance to reach for the wall, though, I pause. The darkness is sharpening my other senses. Otherwise, I'm not sure I would've heard it—the scream from outside, muddled by rain pelting the tin roof. At least it sounded like a scream; I'm not entirely sure.

I wait it out, listening for the sound to repeat itself. I hope I'm wrong, that she's okay and the noise was nothing more than the squalls of beating rain. I tap the flashlight against my hand, expecting it to turn on again all by itself.

Who am I kidding?

I reach out and feel for the doorway, then walk into the hall and open the closet door. The raw smell of bayou wafts from the living room below as the swashing water thuds against the kitchen cabinets, slamming them open and shut, over and over again.

The new batteries work. I rush back into the office, then shine the light out the window toward the mangled fence. Still, I see nothing. I drop my head and listen for another cry, but it doesn't come. I move to the other window, which looks out to the cemetery at the end of the cul-de-sac. It's all the same—more rain carried by more wind.

Our houses are the only two at the end of the road, between the graves and the water. Our families have lived side by side for the better part of a century. We inherited our estates from our fathers, although I'd be lying if I said our families were in any way neighborly. It's funny how some things are gone forever in the blink of an eye, and others never seem to change, no matter the circumstances.

Then I hear it—the nightmare climbing closer.

Back in the hallway, at the top of the stairs, I watch the water crash against the fifth step, playing with the idea of the sixth. It moves without a second thought. I sit down on the top step and think back to the last time she was here. The way she used to smile from her navy eyes.

This all happened so fast. If I'm being honest, I wanted to leave the moment we got the evacuation order. I was ready to. The car was packed, windows boarded, sandbags in place. But I couldn't leave her. Not by herself, not again.

The water breaks over the sixth step.

As much as I want to be angry at what's happening, at this storm and the chaos that's sure to follow, I can't. Living here alone brings with it a gloom that no storm can touch. With every interaction, she reminds me of what could have been. Every now and then, I catch a glimpse of the memories in her wistful smile. A hint of something that remains between us but for some reason refuses to be acknowledged.

As I sit here, drowning in the memory of how I once knew her, I keep hearing the last thing she said to me, only yesterday, over the gate by the mailbox. It plays on loop in the front of my mind, drowning out the noise of the shifting rain. "I'll be fine, Lance. There's no point in starting to worry about me now."

Then Lauren walked away—and I let her.

TWO

August 29, 2005

T he eye of a hurricane is a tease.

It's evening. Intermission has come and gone, and I'm standing back at the top of the stairs. Earlier, the chaos paused for a fleeting moment, just long enough for me to look around and soak it all in. Long enough to see water covering everything that was once considered a safe haven. The wind slowed to a mere threatening breeze, and the rain died down to a lingering drizzle, but it didn't last for long. The eye passed hours ago, and now it's all ramped up again for another round.

The scream—or whatever it was that I heard this morning—hasn't returned. The surge continues to push the water inland, as if the storm has no understanding of what it means for enough to be enough.

I slide the toe of my boot over the edge of the top step as I look out across the bottom floor, which is completely submerged at this point. "Don't even," I say, watching another ripple flow toward me and over the living room below, like a miniature tidal wave. The ripple continues into the hallway, and the ashen carpet absorbs it beneath my shoe.

"Touché." I nod in surrender.

I walk back into my office and look out the window at Lauren's home. I can see it now, but the ground floor is under water, as if it were built in the dead center of the bayou. In less than a day, this storm has completely changed our neck of the woods—in a way that even the best fiction couldn't touch.

Three bangs rattle the porch door at the end of the hallway.

Not random thuds from the debris floating in the water, but what sounds like a rhythmic knock.

"Lance! Ya in there?"

I walk into the hallway, the carpet squishing beneath my feet. When I open the door, I see Cotton standing on the other side of the screen. His pirogue is tied to one of the porch posts. He's soaking wet, and a beat-up wooden paddle rests on his shoulder.

"What in the world are you doing outside?"

"Ya know me, buddy boy," he slurs, "I got stuff to do." He holds up a gallon of melting daiquiri with an oversized straw protruding from the top. "White Russian?"

Then I remember—Cotton plays by his own rules. If there's one thing he's taught me over the years, perhaps by mistake, it's that rules are for the city life.

I can't help but chuckle, but that's Cotton for you. In his own little world. Hell, having to take his pirogue to get over here was probably nothing more than a mild annoyance. Forget the choppy waters and fading hurricane.

I hold up a bottle of water. "Thanks, but I'm pacing myself."

His speech slips and slides from the corner of his mouth. "Yeah. Ya always were a lightweight." He points at me, the jug dangling in the same hand. "I can tell ya right now—those ain't ya daddy's genes." He leans against the inside of the doorframe and rests the drink on top of his gut. His tongue searches for the straw as his eyes shut. Finding it, he takes a sip.

I step aside. "Why don't you come in, out of the rain."

Cotton lives next door but near the front of the cemetery— Lauren is on one side of me, and he's on the other. His home is on the main road and farther away than hers is. He's been around since I was a little kid, for as long as I can remember. He and Dad were best friends.

He steps inside. "I ain't gonna stay long, my boy. Just figured I'd stop by and see if ya need anything. Check in on ya and see if ya still breathing." He takes another drink.

I feel bad even asking, but it looks like the weather is starting to fade. This time, perhaps it will stop for good. "Actually, there is something you can do for me."

He raises the drink with one eye open. "Aight, then. Give it to me straight."

We walk out and onto the porch that wraps around the entirety of the second story, the decking covered by a few inches of water. The waves from our feet disappear into the splashes of rain.

I point to the Roux house. "You hear from Lauren at all?"

He forces his eyes open, looking out across the yard, at her house, then back at me. He shakes his head and offers up a disapproving but lighthearted smirk. "After all these years, ya still a stubborn little shit, ain't ya?"

I assume he's referring to the fact that Lauren has kept me at arm's length ever since she returned home a few weeks ago.

"Have you known me to be anything else?"

He takes another sip and taps the paddle on his shoulder as he sways a little. In all the years I've known him, I don't think I've ever heard Cotton say *no* to a favor—no matter how absurd the proposal. He'd give a complete stranger the shirt off his back, if he was wearing one at the time.

He nods at the hallway behind me. "Grab a jacket. It's a little wet."

I snatch my coat from the rack just inside the door, and we get into his green, wooden boat. It barely has enough room for the two of us.

We don't make it far before we come to the fallen oak tree

at the property line, the one that wiped out the fence. The boards have since been swept away by the incoming tide like they were nothing. The bottom half of the tree is still submerged, but the myriad of branches above the water are enough to block our path. We get out and shimmy our way up one of the larger limbs, then pull the boat over the branches and drop it into the water on the other side.

Cotton seems more concerned with keeping his daiquiri dry than the fact that his boat is getting dented to hell and back.

The brief journey next door, a distance of a hundred feet or so, takes us the better part of twenty minutes. It's like nothing I've ever seen—like someone took a pair of shears to the top half of the woods. Complete trees are missing, and most of the ones that remain are snapped like toothpicks. A truck that I don't recognize is floating over the cemetery. The tide is carrying anything and everything it can get its hands on: trees, bits and pieces of homes lost to the wind, dead animals, personal effects, capsized boats. A baby doll with blond hair and denim overalls floats a few feet from the edge of our boat—and that's only what I can manage to make out in the dying rain.

The withering storm washes away the sweat the instant it pours from my face.

We reach the second-floor balcony of Lauren's home. Cotton ties us off to one of the posts, and then we climb over the railing. The tide is stronger over here. The water rushes over the porch below our shoes, and I struggle to hold my footing.

I open the screen and bang on the door. "Hey, it's Lance!"

No answer.

I turn to Cotton. He sips his daiquiri and gives a single shallow nod to the door. "Try again."

I knock louder. "Lauren, it's me. Can you come to the door, please?"

Still, nothing.

Cotton walks to the nearest window and tugs at it from the bottom, but to no avail. "Yeah, little girl got it sealed up tight."

I walk to another window and peer inside before knocking on the glass. "Lauren? It's Lance."

"What ya so worked up over anyways?" Cotton says. "The water ain't even gone down, and ya getting all twisted up over the same ole girl. Yet again." The natural grit in his voice accentuates his skepticism.

Cotton sets down his daiquiri on the porch swing, which is somehow still hanging. He walks to the railing and pulls a crumpled cigarette from his pocket. Lighting it, he takes a drag, then abandons it between his lips as he unzips his camouflage coveralls with his back to me. He starts peeing between the rails before turning his head toward me. The smoke drifts back into his face and disappears over his stained, yellow-gray mustache.

I move to another window and peer inside. "I ain't worked up over anything. She needs someone to check on her, just like you came and checked in on me."

The cloud of smoke floats toward me. Cotton shakes and zips up.

"Can you see in here at all?" I ask, pointing to the pane of glass.

He walks toward me. "What in the world are ya doing?" Cotton asks, squinting through the glass. He takes the cigarette from his lips and sips his daiquiri. "Maybe she doesn't wanna be bothered."

"It's too dark. I can't see anything."

"Here." Cotton pulls his flashlight from the inside of his jumpsuit and holds it out.

I grab the light and shine it through the window, into what looks like a sitting area or library. I see no one, but I'm not sure if that's good or bad. The one thing I can make out is an old, golden lamp sitting on an end table just inside the window. A black-and-white handkerchief is tied to the base of it. I adjust the light to a sharper, narrower beam.

"What the hell?"

Before I realize that I've said it aloud, Cotton speaks. "What is it?"

"You remember the night that you and Dad waited up for me? That night I got home really late from the date that I swore never happened? Y'all hit the porch lights the second my feet touched the steps." I stand up straight but keep the beam of light focused on the lamp on the other side of the window. "Dad knew that he busted me."

Cotton swirls the jug and smiles from under his overgrown mustache. "Yeah. I remember that one. Ole man caught ya red-handed, though he didn't make a fuss about it. He knew what ya were up to. More than anything, he was just glad ya were getting out." He takes a drag and pushes the smoke from his nose.

"I remember it clear as day." I gesture to the lamp with the beam of light.

Cotton takes one more drag, then flicks the butt out into the rain, where it sinks beneath the tide. "Y'all were kids, my boy. Ya talking about something that was ages ago."

The rain is a few drops from done. The breeze carries a light mist as dusk sweeps over the bayou. I run the sleeve of my jacket across the window, erasing the falling lines of water to get a clearer view of the other side.

He leans down beside me and looks through the window. "Besides, what does some handkerchief have to do with anything?" he says.

It isn't the handkerchief itself that grabs my attention but what makes it unique. It takes a second for it to register, for me to place the familiarity of it in my memory.

That's when I notice the blood stains in the paisley design. The stains that I know to be Lauren's blood.

"Nothing, really," I say. "Other than the fact that it was mine."

THREE

May 1988

I was hoping that Lauren had gotten my note. If her father had found it, I was in deep shit.

I waited for her in Dad's flatboat, at the dock behind our homes. I checked my watch. The note had said 4 p.m., and it was three minutes till.

I had folded the paper as small as I could and tied it to the rope that hung from the oak tree over the water—at the end of our property line, abutting the dock I was waiting at. I saw her out there almost every day. Sometimes she brought a book, and other days she was with her cousin Brody, who I thought might be one of her only friends. At least, she was the only person I had ever seen with Lauren.

The gnats were getting bad, and the heat was smothering. Her father had probably found it.

I checked my watch again. It was four on the dot, and she wasn't there.

We hardly knew each other, except in passing. Our families had the whole "vague neighbor" thing going on, but we rarely spoke, much less formally met. I could have been a weirdo for all she knew.

He definitely had found it. He was probably watching me sit out there like some stalker, waiting for his one and only daughter to show up so I could drag her out in the middle of nowhere for her to never be heard from again.

It was after four, and I was drenched in sweat.

Who in the world went on a first date with someone they

barely knew, in a boat of all places—and in the Louisiana heat on a summer evening? What was I thinking? *Hey, here's a random note from the kid next door. Meet me behind your house so I can take you somewhere.* I should've known better. It was Psycho Killer 101.

I stood up and stepped onto the dock, but right as I did, she was there at the edge of the pier. She glanced over her shoulder to her home, then back to me.

Maybe he hadn't found it.

"Hey," she said.

I wasn't sure what to say, so I raised my hand in greeting like some sort of fool.

"Sorry I'm running late." She held up a wicker basket. "I brought snacks."

I could feel myself cutting a smile at the mere fact that she was there, but it didn't occur to me to say something in response. I stepped down into the boat and offered up my hand so she could do the same.

She climbed in. Her dress was the color of pure cotton, stopping just above her knees. The neckline cut straight across the top of her chest, leaving my imagination to its own devices.

She sat down on the seat in front of me and placed the basket on the damp but hot floor between us. "Where we headed?"

The wind ruffled her wavy, shoulder-length hair. Strands of honey brown blew across her face, but she stared at me as if the wind were absent. Her eyes were a deeper and purer blue than I had ever seen, matching the evening sky with a type of perfection I wasn't used to.

I turned around and pulled the cord, starting the motor, and spoke as I turned back. "I thought we'd go fishing."

She looked down at the fishing poles and did this cute thing with her mouth—half smile, half pursing her lips to one side.

Her chin dimpled. "You gonna teach me something, Lance Dubois?" Her speech rode a fine line between flirtation and sarcasm.

I pushed off the dock and pointed us in the direction of the Bayou Liberty bridge. We crept down the bayou just fast enough to steady her hair as the wind blew from behind us.

"If you don't mind," I said, "I'd like to."

Her eyes fluttered in what looked like approval, and we continued along, twisting and turning among the hardwoods that bent over the shoreline, sometimes close enough to touch.

A short time later, we reached the Bayou Liberty bridge. Without a doubt, it was the most unique place in town. It was simple but exceptional all the same. The gray-painted steel crossing was supported by a large concrete piling in the center, where the short span rotated and allowed boats to pass in either direction.

My dad Marcus was the bridge operator in a small control room on the south end of the bridge. His office was nothing more than a wooden shack that baked out in the open, under the direct sunlight.

On the north end of the bridge was the boat launch and docks, run by Catch-em—an elderly man who was never much for small talk. Regardless of whether or not you bought bait or ice or whatever else at the launch, his version of "thank you" was always some form of "catch 'em"—"catch 'em good, catch 'em for me, catch 'em big," and so on. His family had owned and operated the launch for as long as it was open, as far as anyone knew.

As we approached the bridge, two horns sounded from the other side, followed by what I knew to be the same from Dad, sitting in the control room. The bridge began to open.

Lauren looked back at me. "We're staying over here, right?"

I shook my head.

"*Right?*"

The bridge opened, splitting the bayou in two. A blue-and-white KingFisher idled toward us from the other side of the bridge, and I drove us through the temporary passageway.

As we passed the concrete piling, Lauren lay down in the boat and pulled her arms and legs in tight. She had a fearful look about her, which confused me more than anything else.

"What are you doing?" I asked. She lay in the fetal position on the floor, hugging her knees.

"Isn't your father working? Over there?" She pointed to the tower without much movement at all. "Isn't he the operator?"

I laughed and waved at the control room.

"It's fine," I said. "I promise."

She inched her head up from behind the edge of the boat, then waved in a slow, tentative motion. Dad tipped his hat to us as we passed. Once we were through, he sounded the horn again, and the bridge was pulled to a close by the long, rusted cables that splashed in the water. I waved back.

"I think we're all clear," I said to her in a playful tone.

Lauren rolled onto her back and began a slow laugh that built up to what looked like a sense of relief. She lay in the darkness of my shadow as the sun shone from behind me, and she closed her eyes and beamed with another uneven smile. The water rocked in hollow swashes against the side of the boat.

Then we pulled up to the last of the six docks. "Tie us off, will you?"

She crawled onto the deck and wrapped the rope from the boat cleat around the wooden piling at the end of the pier. Dusting her hands together, she looked to me for approval.

"Perfect."

"Stopping already?" she asked.

"If we're going fishing, we need bait. No?"

We walked to the service window, where Catch-em was looking out to the launch, sipping his black evening coffee. As usual, he was wearing his signature black-and-white chevron newsboy cap, which had faded to a washed-out gray.

"Mr. Lance," he said in greeting. "What can I do for ya?"

"Hey, Catch-em. Twenty minnows will do."

He set his coffee on top of the stack of newspapers behind the window. "Alrighty, then. That's four dollars."

I handed over the four ones, and he walked out of the shed and toward the live well. His pet wood duck, Woody, was perched on the rim of the bait box, rinsing his webbed feet in the spraying water. One day not long earlier, the bird had shown up at the bait station with a broken wing, looking for food. Catch-em had befriended him, and they'd been inseparable ever since.

Catch-em plunged the net down into the school of minnows and brought a few of them to the surface. Woody hopped along the edge of the live well, extending his neck, looking for a handout. "Boy, I done told you once today"—Catch-em shooed him away, and the duck flailed to the ground with his one good wing—"your greedy ass has your own pail." He pointed to a metal tin in the corner, then placed the fish into a small white bucket that had passed through more hands than I'd seen days. He handed it over with a wink and a nod.

"Be sure I get my bucket back, now," he said. I looked down and saw a few more minnows than what I had ordered.

"Yes, sir. We won't be long."

We turned and walked back to the boat.

"Catch 'em big," he said once he was back behind his window in the makeshift office.

I waved in return. "Will do!"

I dropped the trolling motor at the bow of the boat, which pulled us along the shoreline at a steady pace. The salmon rays of sunlight cut across the tops of the trees, behind them a cloudless sky. Lauren sat on the back seat with her hands in her lap, peering down at the bucket of lively minnows.

"You ready?" I asked.

"Ready? For what?"

I put us on a straight course ahead, avoiding the stumps and lily pads along the shoreline. Then I grabbed one of the two fishing poles from the floor of the boat.

"Fishing, of course." I pulled the hook from the bottom eye of the pole and held out my other hand. "Hit me."

She raised a single brow and spoke flatly. "Do what?"

"Hit me. Hand me a minnow."

Another of her laughs filled the air. That time, it was a "yeah, right" type of chuckle.

"No?" I said.

"Um . . . I'm all for learning how to fish"—she gestured to the water—"but baiting one of those guys"—then to the bucket—"that's gonna take some convincing."

I sat down and plunged my hand into the pail, removing one of the squirming fish. Her eyes went wide, and she pulled her arms in close.

"Straight through the lips, and they keep on swimming." I pushed the hook down through the fish's mouth and hung the bait in front of her to see. "Your turn."

She gazed into the bucket before looking at me once again. Her nose flared.

"It's a requirement of the date," I said in good fun. "You don't wanna upset me now, do you?"

"Oh, so this is a date, is it?" She cinched her lips, holding back the smile beneath.

I pulled the hook from the other pole and held it out. "Here."

She snatched it from me. Then she crept her other hand into the bucket, holding it above the water as if she were waiting for the bait to hook itself.

I jumped forward and shouted, "Watch it!" I followed it up with a laugh as she jumped back and slapped my arm.

"You idiot!"

But she leaned forward, and her hand was back in the bucket in no time. She snagged one of the minnows and fashioned a crazed look of resentment, her jaw clenched, arms stiff.

"Hook him. You better hurry," I said.

The minnow slid from her grasp and splashed into the water. We looked over the edge of the boat at the same time, then at each other.

"Lauren zero, bait one," she said.

She grabbed another minnow and brought the hook to its mouth.

"You got it," I said in a soft exhale.

She pushed the hook through the two gasping lips of the fish, but it fell onto the floor of the boat. Her hand jerked away, and a drop of burgundy splashed to the deck between us.

"You okay?"

I grabbed her hand and turned it palm up. Her grip eased, and we looked up at one another. For a moment, the cut was irrelevant—a passing mishap that paled in comparison to our touch. A breeze interrupted the moment and pushed the boat inland, against the shore. I killed the motor. The shade found us at rest amid a hanging screen of blue-green moss.

I pulled a handkerchief from my back pocket and tore a thin strip from its edge.

"It looks way worse than it is," she said, the drops still falling to the floor of the boat. She squeezed one eye shut as I tightened the wrap.

Perhaps at the same time, we noticed the bandage was wrapped around a certain finger.

"Don't you think it's a little soon for such a serious commitment?" she said.

I dropped my head and closed my eyes, the only way I knew how to deal with the awkwardness—a feeling she seemed to embrace. Maybe it had been a bad idea. Maybe I should've offered to bait it for her. The boat rocked, and I heard the sound of a cast. I looked up to see Lauren holding her pole. She looked me dead in the eyes and shrugged.

"What?" she said. She adjusted herself on the seat and sat up straight, rolling back her shoulders. "It's cute that you wanna teach me." Then she popped the cork with a flick of her wrist.

FOUR

August 29, 2005

s night falls and the water begins to recede, the violence of the tumultuous storm transforms into a sinister gloom.

Cotton adjusts the spread of his Maglite against the home. "What do ya wanna do, my boy? She clearly ain't answering the door."

"Yeah. I can't say that I'm surprised."

"Y'all still at it after all these years, huh?" He tucks the flashlight under his arm and sets fire to another cigarette. The fiery glow at the end of the stick burns quick in the lingering breeze.

"It's complicated."

"Ain't it always?" He takes a final sip of his long-melted daiquiri, the remaining drops gurgling through the straw. Then he looks at the jug with defeat and tosses it to the side. Another drag from the cigarette. "As much as I don't care to, we could head on over to Shadow's place. See if he's heard from her." The wind carries the stream of smoke from his nose through the beam of white light and beyond the porch.

"If we can make it that far."

He shines his light in the direction of the cemetery at the center of the cul-de-sac—not far from Lauren's balcony where we're at now, or my place next door. The path to the graveyard is submerged beneath a few feet of brackish bayou and crowded by fallen trees and a slew of debris, floating violently at will.

Cotton is under no obligation to help me find Lauren. He could be sitting at home, worried about himself and what he's going to do after everything subsides, but he isn't. He's here, with me. It doesn't surprise me, though. With how close he and Dad were to one another, he's treated me like a son since day one. Hell, Dad once told me that Cotton was the only other person in the hospital the day I was born—camo jumpsuit and all.

He's never said it outright, but I think he feels a sense of responsibility to look after me, now that his best friend is no longer around.

"It's gonna be a bitch, but I think we can make it," he says.

Shadow is Cotton's estranged brother. They're rarely seen together, cut from a different cloth. I could only describe their relationship as awkward tension, perhaps because Shadow approaches life as if he were an only child.

Over the last hundred-plus years, all of the property surrounding the cul-de-sac has been owned by the same three families—and all three dysfunctional.

Cotton grabs the rope to the pirogue and pulls it to the stairs that lead up to the balcony. We climb in and paddle toward the cemetery, which takes us far longer than it should. The water is low enough that our path is blocked by the fence surrounding the graveyard, so we follow it to the cemetery entrance at the front of the cul-de-sac. We stop under the large live oak tree at the entrance to the grounds. Other than being stripped of its moss, it appears untouched by the wind.

Cotton shines his light at the metal sign on the chain-link fence, just above the water line: *Dubois Cemetery EST. 1821*. The edge of the light catches another sign off to the side, leaning against the oak tree and holding back a pile of detritus. *This is a cemetery of Slidell, Louisiana! It is the final resting place of our family members and loved ones. IT IS NOT . . .*

The bottom half of the sign is masked by litter floating on

the surface of the water.

"Let's take a minute," Cotton says. "Ole boy needs a breather."

"Sure. We ain't far."

The rain is gone, and the tide is retreating at a surprising pace. As Cotton sweeps his light over the cemetery, a timid battlefield surrounds us in every direction. A stark juxtaposition of sight and sound fills the air around us—the land we once found familiar is destroyed beyond recognition but quiet to a fault, save the occasional gust of wind in the distance that evokes a squirrel's bark. A handful of headstones protrude from the water and hold back mounds of debris. A coffin, surfaced from the storm surge, sits against one of the mausoleums, the inside of the tomb visible through the shattered panes of stained glass.

"So this is what hell looks like," Cotton says.

I speak into the dark. "No. The devil himself couldn't come up with something like this."

No sooner have I spoken than a thud sounds against the pirogue.

I shift in my seat and grab the fence. "What was that?" We rock from side to side.

Cotton shines his light down into the boat, then up at the oak tree. "Wind, my boy. Lots of wind."

My sight is on par with a temporary form of blindness. I'm granted only moments of clarity wherever Cotton happens to point his flashlight. Why didn't I bring my own?

The thud returns and glides against the side of the boat. And by my ear, it's no breeze.

"That ain't the wind, Cotton."

He runs the beam of light from the bow down the lip of the pirogue and toward my legs.

Something moves between my feet. Against my boots.

He shines the light between us, illuminating the dull black scales of the cottonmouth wrapped around my ankle.

"Don't. Move." His speech is calm but firm.

"Cotton" is more of a title than it is a nickname—a designation bestowed upon him by his ability to brush off the bite of a water moccasin like a bothersome itch. Somehow, perhaps from being bitten too many times, or due to a freak genetic anomaly, the venom has little effect on the man. His ego included.

How it affects me, on the other hand, I have yet to find out.

The snake looks into the light, then turns its head straight at me. Cotton inches his hand toward it.

"Cotton . . ."

"Shut. Up."

The scales bump across the laces of my shoe as the venomous head advances between my legs. I grit my teeth, and the words barely escape my lips. *"Do. Something."*

Its tongue flicks against the inside of my thigh as the tail tightens around my calf.

Cotton shoots out his hand and snatches the snake just behind the head. It releases me and flashes its white mouth in the beam of cloudy light.

"Took you long enough," I say with a hint of nerves, disguised as sarcasm.

"Patience, my boy. All ya need is some good ole patience."

Before I can process what's happened, I hear a scream from the woods beside us, across from the cemetery. Cotton jerks his light in that direction.

"That wasn't just me, then?" I ask.

"Nah. I heard it too, my boy."

Then it comes again—a voice echoing from the timber that protrudes from the standing water like fingers from a grave. The snake flops against the inside of the boat, its head held firmly in his grip.

"Cotton," the voice calls with a hollow tenor.

The name doesn't come from the water around us, or from the houses down the street, but from the mangled trees above.

———

Cotton crushed the head of the snake with his paddle and tossed it in the water by the oak tree, which we've just left after taking a breather. I have a feeling he would've let it go if I wasn't with him.

Shadow calls to us from up ahead.

As we approach Shadow's treehouse, what remains of the former dwelling can hardly be called a house at all. A blue tarp covers a decent-sized, jagged hole in the roof that sits beneath a fallen limb, which looks like it's ready to fall to the ground at a second's notice. The one and only window is shattered, and the porch railing is gone altogether. Most of the wooden shingles that decorated the front of the home are missing, exposing the weathered and waterlogged plywood beneath.

One of Mr. Roux's pirogues—Lauren's, I suppose, now that her father passed away—is tied to one of the supports under the treehouse's deck.

Aside from being the cemetery caretaker, Shadow has been the Roux family handyman ever since Mr. Roux inherited the house next door to my dad. Mr. Roux was so impressed with what Shadow had done for the cemetery and my own family that he convinced Shadow to trade teams. He still cares for the Dubois cemetery, but other than that, he's devoted to the Roux family through and through.

"You really gonna try and save that crap?" Cotton shouts as

he holds out his paddle and catches us against what's left of an adjacent tree, just off the edge of the treehouse. He shines the light on his brother.

Shadow is sorting through a pile of something at his feet. "Not all of us can hoard our shit in some fancy house, b-b-b-bro."

Their disdain for one another picks up right where it left off. Every time. Shadow is the younger brother but looks a few decades older than Cotton. The top of his half-bald peak shimmers as the long, gray-and-white hair around the sides of his head blows in the wind. A clear, disposable poncho flaps over his muddy jeans and plaid shirt.

He spits out some of the tobacco stuffed behind his lower lip. The juice drips from his unshaven chin.

"Yeah, whatever," Cotton says. "We ain't stickin' around." He points over his shoulder. "You hear from Lauren at all? She ain't answering the door."

Shadow looks around, holding up a lantern in one hand and lifting his other palm. "D-d-d-does it look like I'm having a party out here? How the hell would I know where Lauren is?" His right eye begins to twitch and slams shut at a faster rate than usual—a tick that he's never been able to get a hold of.

Cotton nods to the pirogue tied to the supports beneath his brother's feet. "Well, I'm guessing you ain't find that boat while you were out for a stroll."

Shadow waves a hand at us. "And who the fuck are you? Slidell PD?"

Cotton looks at me and shrugs. "It was worth a try." He lights a cigarette and folds his arms.

In a way, I feel bad for Shadow. All he has is this run-down treehouse. Everyone's homes are screwed, now. But when you live in an already-shoddy, makeshift thing up in a tree, a hurricane might as well be a kick in the nuts. According to Cotton, the Roux family built and maintains the treehouse contingent on Shadow's ability to keep up with his side jobs for Mr. Roux—and now Lauren.

"Well if you hear from her, can you let us know?" I ask.

Shadow laughs and licks his lips, his tongue reaching to the tip of his nose. His few remaining teeth are layered with the brown sludge seeping from his gums. "I'm perfectly fine, thanks for asking. I'll be sure to drop what I'm doing and get right on it."

Cotton jumps back into the conversation. "Oh give me a break, Shadow. Don't act like ya ain't gonna be over at the Rouxs' place the second this water goes down. Shit, you probably already have been, by the looks of it." He points to the Rouxs' boat with the beam of light.

"Goddamn hurricane ain't even got both feet out the door, and you're up my ass 'bout where I been and ain't been." He waves the lantern. "F-f-f-fuck off."

Cotton narrows the beam of his flashlight and shines it straight into his brother's eyes. "Best of luck with your renovations." Then he whispers. "Little shit."

Shadow scowls, and his eyes weld shut in the blinding light—but the right one still twitches.

FIVE

May 1988

"Kill it," I said into the wind.

Lauren shut off the spotlight on the bow of the boat as I turned off the motor. We drifted forward with enough momentum to reach the pier—out of sight, out of sound.

The canary moon provided us with just enough light to see the edge of the dock. The boat slowed to a steady crawl, and then Lauren caught the piling and pulled us in.

"Got it," she said in a cautious voice. She tied us off.

I walked to the front of the boat and sat next to her on the bow. We looked at our homes, divided by the wooden fence along the property line. The rope swing dangled from the oak tree in the moonlight and hung motionless over the water at the end of the fence. Its hazy reflection floated hardly out of reach of the fraying knot, inches above the bayou.

To the left, my house appeared dark and lifeless. To the right, hers was vibrantly lit, the sound of chatter leaking from an open window.

The gnats had faded with the day's heat, but the butterflies, perched at the top of my stomach, lingered.

She turned toward me and lifted her shoulders, then dropped them at a timid pace. "I guess this is it, then."

"I guess so." I handed her the wicker basket.

Neither of us said it, but I suspected we were both thinking it: she had snuck out to meet me there hours before, and the sound of her parents in the house, her father in particular, meant that it was time to face the music. Unlike my own dad, Mr. Roux, the ex-mayor of Slidell, didn't seem like the type of parent who was keen on his daughter spending time alone with some boy— even if I was the neighbor's kid.

Still, I suspected we both felt that whatever earful she was about to get from her father was well worth the time we had spent alone.

She leaned in and gave me a peck on the cheek. I stood and lent her my hand to step up and onto the dock. I didn't want to push my luck, but I couldn't help it. "Maybe we can do this again?"

Looking down at me from the pier, she chose not to respond at all. Instead, she looked to her house with a slouch and hesitant eyes. She forced a smile and walked home.

I waited there in the boat until she made it through the back door. Once the shouting started, I figured it was best for me to do the same. As I passed the fence, I caught a brief glimpse of Mr. Roux, framed in a dim, gilded light. His voice rose in volume but sank to a deepened pitch, one cutting phrase at a time.

Part of me felt bad for Lauren. But to be honest, I didn't regret our time together. She was a chance I was willing to take, plain and simple.

As I stepped onto the porch, I did my best not to wake Dad, but apparently he and Cotton had plans of their own. The floodlights flickered on, and I was caught with my fishing poles and tackle box in hand. The humid night air dripped from my face.

"You do any good?" Dad asked.

"I sure hope so," said Cotton. "From the looks of it, he been working a lot more than some jig." He craned his neck and acted like he could see over the fence. "Ain't that right, my boy?" He winked and took a swig of the frozen, white drink from the gallon milk jug in his hand.

They were sitting in their usual chairs on the porch, rocking in synchrony. Cotton always said what Dad was thinking. They were like two sides of the same coin—one unable to exist without the other, and there was no coming between them.

"Just a few trout," I said. "Nothing worth keeping, though."

Cotton chuckled under his breath. "Trout, huh? Is that what they're calling 'em nowadays?"

Dad grinned and stood up. He grabbed me by the back of the neck and tested my pressure point. He'd insisted on checking it on a regular basis, ever since he found it by accident a few years back. "Kids your age are meant to test the waters, son. I'm just glad you're getting your feet wet."

Cotton slurred from his rocker. "My boy's getting a lot more than just his feet wet."

"Lauren Roux, huh?" Dad asked.

I pulled back the corner of my mouth, assuming it was a rhetorical question.

"That's good," he continued. "You just make sure you're being smart about things. Yeah?"

Before I could respond, the silence of the night was broken by the crunch of gravel from the road out front. Where Dubois Road ended and the cemetery began, the path turned into a gravel driveway that wrapped around the back of the cemetery and led to the Roux and Dubois homes, dead-ending just past our house.

If it weren't for the silhouette of his hunched posture and the way the wind caught his thinning, sickly hair, it would've been difficult to see Shadow shuffling from the drive toward the front door of the Roux house.

Cotton stood up and leaned against the porch post, sipping his daiquiri, looking next door as his brother disappeared behind the backlit fence.

Dad turned toward him. "You good?"

Cotton nodded as his tongue searched for the straw. "Uh-huh."

"How come he never comes around?" I asked.

Although they lived across from one another, Cotton rarely spoke about his brother. I never saw Shadow anywhere other than his treehouse, next door at the Rouxs' place, and the cemetery. Cotton, on the other hand, was a wending man, helping out anyone and everyone he could. He was retired from running his own trawling company, shrimping out in Lake Borgne and Lake Pontchartrain, mostly. But he ran around just as much after he retired as he had when he was working for himself.

"Sharing the same last name ain't always everything, my boy. Sometimes, blood is just . . . blood."

I set the poles against the house and took a seat in one of the rocking chairs. Cotton continued looking out at the driveway, although Shadow was probably inside the Roux house at that point.

"So that's you and him?" I asked.

Cotton was always the talkative type, except when he was deep in thought. It wasn't clear whether it was the booze or the memories, but he went quiet. I was curious, so I figured I'd prod a little.

He pondered the question for a second, either because he was ashamed or saddened by the fact that his brother might as well have not existed. "That's what?" Or maybe it was resentment.

"You and Shadow—y'all just share a last name? That it?"

"Something like that." He took a sip of the daiquiri and looked up at the perfectly defined moon, like a sticker on black paper. "Ya live next to someone long enough, ya eventually see the type of person they really are, whether ya want to or not." He looked back at me. "And ya ole man and I have lived next to Edward Roux long enough."

Dad sat down in his chair and took a swig of his Budweiser. "I think maybe what Cotton is trying to say is that the Roux family has a reputation."

"And?" I said.

"The name Shadow came from our mother, a nickname. He used to follow her around like . . . well, like a shadow. Anywhere she went, he was right there with her." Cotton swirled his drink and looked down into the jug with one eye, nodding along. "Ever since Mom and Pop died, lil' brother found someone else to latch on to."

"So . . . what?" I nodded to the house, peering at us from the other side of the fence with its enormous, bug-eyed windows. "I thought the Roux family had a good reputation."

"Of course they do," Dad said, "but the way people are behind the fence don't always match the costume they wear out in public."

"I don't get it."

The three-story home towered over our own. We lived in a modest cottage, but it was nothing compared to the Rouxs' place. The top floor alone was bigger than our entire place. It wasn't until then that I began to wonder how two families, so inherently different from one another, had lived next door to each other for so long yet hardly spoke.

Perhaps we were two families familiar enough to know to stay out of each other's way.

Cotton gurgled the last of his drink through the straw, then tossed the carton in the trashcan. "That's alright, my boy. That's *al*-right." He placed a cigarette between his lips. "You and Lauren are neighbors." He lit it and pulled a breath through the roll of paper. "Ain't nothing wrong with testing the waters."

"Just remember," Dad said, tossing his beer can into the trash, "to make sure that you see people for who they are. Not their reputation or some last name."

"And Shadow?" I asked.

"Yeah," Cotton said. He walked into the yard and flicked the still-lit butt over the fence. The rich, yellow light of their home radiated from between the dog ears like a hazardous portent. "Let's just say Shadow didn't get the memo."

As much as I loved Cotton, I had a feeling he was blowing the whole "family reputation" deal out of proportion.

Dad, too.

SIX

August 30, 2005

The stench of bayou muck jerks me awake.

I hardly slept, and I'm sticking wet with sweat from head to toe. The paper-thin blanket is glued to my body like cling wrap to a processed chicken. I pry open my eyes, and an unfamiliar silence charges the space around me: no air flowing from the AC unit, no buzz of the lights, no hum of the fridge. Only the faint hiss of a chainsaw off in the distance.

Even the birds dare not speak.

I push the blanket onto the floor of the office and swing my legs over the side of the futon. My neck is jacked, and the tension headache resting at my brow squeezes with a taut persistence. I look over at the alarm clock on the nightstand, but it's blank. All I see is the ghostly outline of four eights, separated by an empty colon. Checking the time on clocks that have ceased to work should be fun. A new pastime, perhaps?

I walk into the bathroom across the hallway and flip the light switch inside. It takes me a second to realize that the entire house is nothing more than a lifeless shell—something I should've gotten used to over the last twenty-four hours.

I take a leak in the dark, but the sound of urine splashing into the water feels too loud. Based on the deepened echo of the stream, I'm dead center, so I move it an inch to the side to hit the muted porcelain instead. I shake and push the handle on the side of the fixture.

Mother. Fucker. No water, either.

But I knew that yesterday, too.

I move to the sink and reach for the fixture, then pause. Nope. No, no. From the looks of it, this entire day should be fun—getting caught off guard by the mundane litany of tasks that are now without meaning.

Katrina one, Western civilization zero.

Out of habit, I walk to the stairs and start to take the first step before realizing that if I'm going downstairs, boots are a requirement. I'm walking back into the office when I hear a knock at the front door. Kneeling on the futon, I look out of the open window and down at the porch. It's Cotton.

"Hey, I'll be down in a minute."

He raises a cigarette in response. "No rush, my boy."

I slip on a fresh-ish pair of jeans and the white shrimp boots from yesterday. Then I walk down the stairs, holding my arms against the walls so I don't bust my ass on the several inches of mud covering the stairwell and living room floor. I grab the handle to the front door and pull, but Katrina is one step ahead of me—she always has been.

The door is warped and swollen like a dead fish that's sat out in the sun at a blistering time of year. Hell, it even smells like one.

I hear Cotton from the other side. "Yeah, I don't think ya getting through there."

A wet breeze flows steadily through the hole in the wall, outlined by jagged shards of glass, formed by the giant branch that dodders against the side of the house. I'd rather not climb through a death trap, so I open one of the windows that hasn't been busted and climb through there.

"Well, shit. It took ya long enough," Cotton says.

"I'm lucky I got out at all. Damn house is one giant labyrinth."

I look back at my home in the daylight for the first time

since the storm ended. The water has mostly subsided, but a few feet remain standing near the bayou itself, not far from the house. The sheer task of walking will take some thought if I'm looking to go anywhere at all. The ground is covered in a solid sheet of mud and littered with the cause of nightmares to come: dead animals, slaughtered trees, and a miasma that I suspect is only familiar to coroners and first responders.

The house itself looks like shit from the waist down—the top floor is untouched, save for a few missing shingles and the piles of litter covering the porch. The bottom floor more closely resembles Chernobyl ten years after the fact.

"I guess The Dirty Dell has officially earned its name." Cotton lights up as we take in the scenery.

I fold my arms. "And all it took was a one-night stand." I'm not proud that our town is nicknamed after a sexual position, but hell, you've got to have fun with it once in a while.

Cotton turns to look at Lauren's house. He blows the smoke from his nose and narrows his eyes with a ponderous brow. "Any word from ya girl?"

"No. It's driving me crazy, to be honest."

He looks out to the cemetery, his hands on his hips, cigarette smoldering between his lips. Then he glances back to Lauren's and rolls the filter between his teeth. Without a word, he walks next door, climbing over the debris between our homes.

"What are you doing?" I ask.

He pauses and looks around, sitting on a tree trunk as if it's just another day in the neighborhood. "If ya still ain't heard from her, then we need to try again."

"Cotton, your place isn't any better off than ours. You got your own stuff to worry about right now."

"Oh, please. This disaster ain't going nowhere." He waves

a hand. "Come on. If you're worried about her, then so am I."

———

I throw my entire body against the front door, shoulder first. It doesn't budge. I step back to get a running start.

"What do ya think ya doing?" Cotton says.

I charge forward and bounce off of the door like some sort of rag doll. "Damn thing must be swollen worse than mine." I wince and grab the edge of my shoulder. Somehow, the sidelights are intact.

Cotton shatters the adjoining window with his Maglite. "Or maybe it's a metal door with a deadbolt." He gestures for me to climb through first. "After you, my boy."

We climb through the tall, slender opening and step down onto the muddied floor.

In all the years I've lived next door to the Roux family, I've never been inside their home. From the outside looking in, I pictured something far different from what I see now. I imagined it being along the lines of *MTV Cribs*, but it's nothing like that at all. It's huge, but something's different—a little off. Maybe it's the mud and sagging drywall that's skewing my idea of what it should be.

I cup my hand to my mouth and call out. "Lauren?"

We walk from the dining room into the kitchen, taking it all in. A sofa sits against the island at the center of the room, and the fridge is face-down near the base of the staircase, where it must have come to rest after floating in the storm surge.

I look to what I think is the living room. The sodden ceiling has fallen to the floor, exposing the joists and insulation that make up the second floor above us.

Cotton puts his hands in the pockets of his coveralls and

puffs on the cigarette as he looks around. "Hello?" he says through the smoke.

I look up at the ceiling in the living room, enthralled by what the water has done.

He follows my gaze. "What is that?" he asks. He walks toward me, sidestepping the furniture that's been shuffled around and overturned every which way.

We stand side by side, gazing at the nails protruding from the ceiling joists, holding slivers of insulation that dangle like soggy cotton candy.

"What is that?" he asks again.

"What's what?"

Cotton steps closer to the corner of the room, putting his vision to work. He looks at me as if he wants to ask me something, but he says nothing.

Then I notice it. I step forward, unsure of what I'm seeing at first—or at least what it's doing inside.

"That." He points with his cigarette.

What looks like a small white camera the size of my fist dangles from the corner of the ceiling by a single red wire, knocked loose by the fallen drywall. I step back, then turn to the kitchen.

Cotton stares at the corner of the ceiling and adjusts his mustache, unable to look away from it.

As I walk from room to room—back into the kitchen, then to where we entered through the dining room—the chaos around me fades like one of those signature shots in the turning point of a Hollywood horror film.

"Cotton . . ."

The camera seems to hold him there in some sort of trance.

"Cotton!"

He walks to me and leans his head back toward the living

room. "That ain't normal, right?"

I look to the corner above the front door. "And that?"

Another camera looks down over the foyer.

"Come on," he says. "Let's check upstairs."

As eager as he was to come over here, I have a feeling that Cotton is having second thoughts about being here any longer than we need to be—I know I am. We struggle to peel our attention from the oddness of the cameras as we walk to the staircase.

"You ever notice those before?" I ask.

"Never been inside the place."

That can't be right. He's lived two houses down this whole time—surely he's been inside of the Roux home. I can't imagine Shadow working for Mr. Roux and Cotton never being in here.

As we reach the second floor and walk down the hallway, I finally realize what it is that I couldn't place in the mess below— what was erased by the storm. The house is the definition of minimal living. Not a single picture or piece of art adorns the eggshell walls.

"Hello? Lauren?" I intend to shout, but it comes out hesitant. Still, my voice bounces between the naked walls.

We walk down the hallway and into a study, where I see the lamp and handkerchief next to the window. The room is empty other than several bookshelves lined with encyclopedias and history texts. A desk with no chair sits at the center of the room—nothing more and nothing less.

"Talk about clean," Cotton says.

"Forget clean. This is something else altogether."

We're turning to walk out of the room when I hear a thump through the walls, followed by what sound like squelching footsteps. I rush out into the hallway and turn toward the other end of the home. The water rose just high enough to cover the carpet on the second floor, like it did over at my place.

I look down and see several lines of footsteps, different shapes and sizes layered atop each other, running back and forth down the center of the hallway. We follow them to the other side of the house. Suddenly, the cameras in the corners of the rooms below us seem normal, compared to what we see.

The tracks disappear—straight into the mirror at the end of the corridor.

SEVEN

May 1988

T he dock out back sat on the property line and was considered neutral ground.

Dad and Mr. Roux had gotten into it on more than one occasion about who had built it—the Roux family or our own. It was that old. I could recall both men spewing the same argument:

Our family built that dock, so I'd appreciate it if you stopped leaving your boat tied up there.

Oh, the dock is yours, is it? Well it shouldn't have been built on my property, then. Get rid of it!

Of course, no one destroyed anything. Over the years, it evolved into the physical manifestation of the tension between the families, the dividing line between the more and less fortunate.

He never admitted it, but I could see that the whole situation surrounding the dock ate away at Mr. Roux from the inside out. Dad, on the other hand, got a kick out of using it as his own personal cattle prod, jarring his neighbor with one nonchalant use of the pier after another.

And it worked, too.

"Come on, you little pussy," Rowan said, like the encouraging teenager he was. He took off his shirt and widened his arms in the sun, flexing his anorexic biceps and puffing out his chest like he was fifty pounds heavier than he was. "She ain't gonna come to you, if that's what you're waiting for."

I hadn't told my friend about the fishing trip. For some

reason, keeping it a secret felt good—like Lauren and I had something no one else did. Something that everyone else was completely oblivious to.

He ran off the back porch and screamed at the top of his lungs as he reached the dock. "Rooowan booomb!"

Lucky for Lauren, he caught enough air that his feet barely missed her head before he grabbed the rope and swung out over the bayou, flipping backward and then hitting the water with a resounding smack. Rowan himself might have missed her as she sat on the dock, but the splash wasn't as considerate.

I walked down to the water and across the decades-old, weathered planks. "Sorry about the idiot," I said to her. "We're still waiting on the test results."

She looked up and dimpled her chin, her book freckled with shriveled dots of moisture. "Well, I hope you have an answer soon."

I sat down next to her. Our feet dangled over the edge of the pier.

With Rowan being the good friend that he was, he had been pushing me to make a move on Lauren for years, even though she hardly spoke to us—or anyone, for that matter. He poked at us every chance he got, and that day was no different.

"Aw, look at y'all," Rowan said. He cupped his hands and splashed our legs with the warm, tinted water. "Just two peas in a pod."

"Better than two peas for a brain," said Lauren.

Rowan stuck out his tongue and closed one eye, shielding its stone color from the onslaught of the afternoon sun. His other eye, the one laced with a deep brown, bobbed at the surface of the water. Only once had I teased him about the condition—the hetero-something-or-another, they called it— and he'd had a damn near full-on meltdown. Rowan didn't take kindly to criticism, so I'd left it alone ever since. That was one part of having a friend like Rowan: you learned to appreciate what buttons could be pushed and which ones should be left alone.

His parents were never home, so he practically lived at our place. Dad didn't mind, though. He had told me several times that I needed to venture out and get some more friends—especially those who stuck around. Cotton was one of the only people who came around on a regular basis, so I think Dad knew what it was like to have that one person you could rely on. For whatever reason, he thought Rowan was that guy for me.

The slap of a screen door echoed across the water. All three of us looked up at the second-floor balcony of Lauren's home. White railings and columns in the foreground, reddish brick behind them.

Her father walked out onto the porch, smoking his pipe in a gray three-piece suit, per usual. Lauren raised her hand as if she were greeting someone for the first time, but he just stood there, puffing with one hand at his side, staring at us. Unreadable from head to toe.

As upstanding as Mr. Roux's reputation was, it didn't line up with what I had seen over the fence, nor with the way his daughter acted when he was looking on.

"What's with your old man, anyways?" Rowan said. Unlike me, Rowan didn't come with a filter.

"What do you mean?"

He thrashed his arm like he was drowning, calling out to the man on the balcony in a sardonic greeting. "Ahoy from below!"

Rowan didn't give a shit. He never had. His specialty was pushing buttons—in particular, ones that were already beaming red.

"That." Rowan pointed to Lauren's father, who looked

down at us like we were invalids holding his daughter hostage. "I know he's your pops and all, but damn. He ever do anything other than stare people down?"

"Chill out," I said, catching him off guard with a warning splash.

"He's not as bad as you think," Lauren said. "He just cares, that's all."

"Cares? Cares about what?" said Rowan. "Who blinks first?"

That time, I hit him with a silent look of my own.

A worn screech of rusted springs rang out from the porch on the other side of the fence. We looked over and saw Dad sitting down in his rocking chair, popping open his beer and sipping the white fizz as it fell to the ground. He looked up and over at Mr. Roux and lifted his beer in greeting. The man blew a line of smoke from the balcony but said nothing, offered no gesture in return.

"Yeah," said Rowan. "He's one big teddy bear. Ain't he?"

The men continued peering over the line of dog ears, each relishing his guilty pleasure of choice. Then, almost on cue, they turned to the three of us, as if the only reason they were out there was to supervise us. It was a peculiar thing, watching them watch us.

The rope swing wasn't anywhere near as tight as the air between the homes. The men looked over the fence yet again. Mr. Roux turned his pipe upside-down and knocked it onto the porch railing like a gavel from a judge. The ash, caught by the wind, floated to the fence and over the property line.

Mr. Suit-and-Tie curled a single finger at his daughter, which apparently was enough for Lauren to close her book and stand up.

"Seriously?" Rowan said. "That's it?"

"What's wrong?" I said. "What is it?"

Lauren dusted her backside and looked up at the balcony, shielding her eyes from the sun with the warped paperback. Her father turned around and walked inside.

"Sorry," she said.

"What did we do?" I asked.

She made it from the dock to her side of the fence, then turned and walked backward. "Don't worry about it."

I wanted to believe her. I tried to.

But the shadow cast by the looming home amid the otherwise tranquil day seemed to devour her as she turned and walked inside.

EIGHT

May 1988

Once Lauren had left the dock as abruptly as she did, the darkness of her home crawled nearer to the water's edge. The unmoving gaze that I felt eating away at the back of my neck each moment I turned away from the house as I floated there told me it was time to head home. But Rowan stayed in the water, alone, with not a care in the world.

From the empty cans sitting on the counter, I could see that Dad had a good buzz going from the six-pack he had finished while I was out. The moment I walked inside, he was headed out the door with another sixer in hand.

"I'm heading next door to help Cotton out with some upkeep on his boat. You up for it?" he asked.

"Of course."

We walked over to the two-bedroom log cabin where Cotton had lived alone for the better part of his adult life. For whatever reason, that was the way he wanted it—just him, his sailboat, and a few crab traps strung from the boat slip with a blue roof out back. I would often hear people say in passing that they wanted a simple life, but Cotton lived it. He was by far the most content man I had ever known.

Dad snapped a beer can from the pack as we approached the boat slip. Cotton was hosing down the bow of the boat. "Think fast," he said, tossing the drink to Cotton without a proper warning.

I was guessing it wasn't the first time Dad surprised him in such a way, because Cotton caught it with hardly a glance. Then he turned the hose on Dad for a split second, darkening his jeans against his pencil-thin frame.

"I see ya brought a fresh pair of hands," Cotton said. "Grab the brush and get on up here." He pointed to the extended scrub brush next to a bucket of soapy water.

Dad had told me that Cotton acquired the sailboat years earlier, before he retired from the trawling business and sold his shrimp boat. There weren't any similar sailboats on the bayou. Most of our neighbors farther down the water owned ancient, dinged-up flatboats or pirogues that served no greater purpose than to get from A to B, or at most older sailboats that were much the same—held together by a layer of rust, hidden by a fresh coat of paint. Cotton's boat was nicer than that. It was all-natural wood, and he maintained it like a family keepsake. From the look of it, the boat was worth more than his house.

I grabbed the scrub brush and stepped onto the bow. The cabin of the boat was small, with just enough room for two people, although Cotton had set it up to where he could have lived out of it at a moment's notice if he needed to.

He popped open the beer and held it out over the side of the boat, letting the froth fall to the blanket of green algae on the water's surface. Dad grabbed the hose and took over rinsing the remainder of the boat.

"Where'd you get this thing from, anyway?" I asked.

Cotton stepped onto the dock and took a seat in his faded, dried-out lawn chair. He pulled a loose cigarette from the front pocket of his coveralls and placed it between his teeth. "It was my ole man's boat." He searched for a lighter but came up short. "Left it to me in his will."

"I know you've had it for a while, but you never told me that," said Dad.

"Uh-huh." Cotton removed the unlit cigarette from his mouth and leaned his head back, closing his eyes, seemingly not willing to get up and search for a lighter. "Left me the cabin, too. The two of us got really close after Mom died."

Dad turned around and looked at the house. "Sounds like you made out pretty good, then. All things considered, I mean."

"Oh yeah. I was still a young one when he passed. Had the house to myself, paid off and everything, before I even knew what hit me."

"I thought you moved out here by yourself?" I asked.

He opened his eyes and looked at me as I put the brush back into the bucket. I stepped onto the dock so Dad could go behind me with the hose.

"Nope," Cotton said. "My parents lived in that cabin ever since my grandparents passed. The whole cul-de-sac's the same way. Ask ya pops." He pointed to Dad with the cigarette, popping it with his thumb to free the ashes, although it still wasn't lit.

"Uh-huh. The Dubois clan, Cotton's folks, and the Roux family have all been out here for generations."

I grabbed the lighter from the edge of the barbeque pit and handed it to Cotton. "So the cabin was given to you? What about Shadow?"

Cotton clicked the lighter and set fire to the paper. "Ha. Shadow . . ." He looked at the cigarette as if wondering where it had come from. "What about him?"

My dad cut in. "That's not something you need to be asking, son."

"What?" Cotton spoke with a defensive edge in his voice. "Don't start with that bullshit. The kid can ask whatever he wants." He reached back and pulled another one of the lawn chairs next to his own. "Have a seat, my boy."

He leaned forward and plucked a beer from one of the plastic rings and tossed it in my lap. I glanced at Dad, but to my surprise, he didn't object. He did give me a look, though, like he was waiting for me to object for him.

"Thanks, Cotton," I said, "but I don't think I'm old enough to be—"

"Ain't old enough? Old enough to what? Have a beer with ya ole man and ya neighbor? Ya got some hair on ya balls, don't ya? Ya gotta be what—nineteen, twenty by now?"

Dad looked at Cotton, then back at me.

"Seventeen," I said.

"Well, shit." He pointed to the beer. "That'll put a little pep in ya step. Put some hair on ya chest."

I popped the top and sat back in the chair. If Dad had a problem with it, I think he would've made more of an effort to stop me.

"Like I was sayin'"—he gave my father a sideways glance—"ya ain't ever gotta be worried about asking me anything, my boy. I'm an open book. Live life as an honest man, and ya ain't ever gotta worry about keeping up with ya lies." He took a drag. "What were ya asking me about again? Oh yeah. Shadow."

It was my first beer. To be honest, it tasted like ass—like a flat, watered-down soft drink, only worse. Dad turned off the hose and dropped it in the grass.

"My ole man left me the house and the boat in his will, which he had written up after our mom passed. There was a bunch of other crap, too, but that was the bulk of it. As far as my brother goes, that will is part of the reason he turned out the way that he did."

"What do you mean?" I said.

"Well, I was left the house and the boat, and was made executor of the will, which left me in charge of all the money.

Shadow?" He turned in his chair and looked out to the woods across from the cemetery. "Shadow was left that little sliver of land over there." He raised his index finger. "Along with one dollar."

Dad grabbed a beer for himself. "One dollar?"

"One. Dollar."

"What made your dad do that?" I said.

"Well, if you've ever spoken to Shadow, I'm sure ya can tell that he's all about himself and only himself, and he's been that way ever since he was a little kid. Ain't no fault of his own, I guess. But once Mom died, he told our dad that whenever he got around to writing up a will, he wanted to sit down and tell Dad what he wanted—once my pops was good and gone."

"Jesus Christ," Dad said.

"Yeah. Just imagine losing ya wife, and all ya kid can manage to talk about is what ya gonna give him when *you* die, too." He dropped what little remained of the cigarette into an empty beer can, then placed it on the dock and stomped it with his foot. "Needless to say, Pops had a plan for him alright. He was sure to give him some of the estate, but it was gonna be on his own terms. And that's exactly what happened."

The wind began to pick up, and I could feel that the cool humidity was well on its way.

"So what does that have to do with you?" I said. "I mean, wasn't that between him and y'all's dad? Why does he hold that against you?"

"That's just how some people are, my boy. If there's one thing in life ya can't control, it's how other people treat ya, regardless of what ya do or don't do. I do my best to be a decent brother, but I draw the line at being involved in any way with Ed Roux." He stabbed his thumb over his shoulder.

The whole thing between Cotton and Shadow was

unfortunate, really. I could barely imagine what it would've been like to have a brother who resented me because of my relationship with our own father.

"Well, it's a nice boat," I said. "Hopefully, you can keep it in the family for years to come."

"Here," said Cotton. He reached down, deep into the inside pocket of his jumpsuit, and pulled out a keychain with one gold and three silver keys. The light from beneath the boat slip reflected from the metal, bright white amid shifting shadows as the mosquitos circled above us. He removed one of the keys and tossed it into my lap.

"Woah, woah, woah," Dad said. "What are you—"

"Calm down, ole man. It ain't what ya think. It's a key to the cabin door of the boat." Cotton's nose flared, and he slapped me in the chest with the back of his hand. "There. Now ya have somewhere to come and relax if ya need to get away." He nudged me with his elbow. "Know what I mean?"

I didn't know what to say, but I could feel my dad's eyes burrowing into the side of my skull. Already, I sensed an unease between them, but I couldn't refuse the key. Cotton had no one else to present with such a gesture. Hell, our relationship might have been the closest thing he ever would have to a son—surely, Dad was able to see that.

Who in their right mind would have refused such a thing?

NINE

August 30, 2005

Where the hell is she?

Cotton and I searched the entire house earlier, but no Lauren. As worried as I am, he's reassured me that she has family nearby, which I was already vaguely aware of. I hope she was able to leave at the last minute, although she insisted on staying; or maybe someone got to her before we did, and she left once things started to die down. Either way, I need to know where she is, and that she's okay.

There were several types of shoe prints on the second floor of her house, running up and down the hallway. So if I have to guess, she's with someone.

After we left Lauren's house earlier, Cotton ran back home and grabbed his chainsaw so we could start clearing the driveway and Dubois Road. It looks as though a handful of pencils were dropped from the sky by some careless onlooker—only the pencils are three-ton trees that were all laid down in the same direction with no consideration for what lay beneath them. Cars, homes, roads, powerlines—they all withstood the same fate.

We started with the driveway and worked our way past the Roux house to where the once-gravel drive turns into the main road at the front of the cemetery. Before going any farther, though, we've decided to take a break. There's no point in rushing. Not with something like this.

Cotton is kind enough to have cut us each a seat from one of the trees we felled, and now we're sitting beneath the oak at the entrance to the graveyard. I've heard of the "calm before the storm," but the kind of quiet here, next to the several coffins that ogle in my direction, sifted from the ground by the tide, is unlike anything I've known.

Cotton glances down the driveway. "Well, it's a start."

We've cut a path just big enough for a small vehicle to squeeze through, but there's a slew of debris that needs to be cleared before anyone can inch their way down the trail—not that anyone will be driving back here anytime soon. The several blocks between us and Thompson Road, about half a mile away, need to be cleared first, which I imagine will take some time.

I look back at Lauren's house. "Yeah. I guess so."

The chatter of chainsaws and generators hums in every direction.

"I'm sure she's fine. Didn't she tell ya not to worry?"

I'm trying not to, but every which way I look, it doesn't feel right. Something sour claws at the top of my stomach.

"Yeah, she did. But she hasn't been back in town for more than a few weeks, Cotton. I mean, she has enough on her plate as it is. And now this?"

The smell, even with us sitting outside in what should be fresh air, is well-nigh more than I can bear. The slop beneath my feet bakes in the thick Louisiana heat. I lean forward and drip a rope of spittle from my lips in an effort to rid my mouth of the acridity.

It fails miserably.

"I know ya talked to her right before the storm hit, but other than that, ya been able to see her much since Roux died? Since she came back?"

"Not as much as I'd like to. I've been trying, but every time we start to have a conversation, all she can manage to talk about is how I left town. How I left her *and* my dad. I mean shit,

Cotton, we were teenagers. That was . . . how long ago now?"

He lets out an irritated huff and hangs his head down low. "Really? How in the world she figure that ya left ya pops? Come on, my boy. We both know that ain't how it played out. Ya getting all twisted up over someone who don't know her ass from a hole in the ground. I ain't got nothing against the girl, but that's a pretty shitty thing to say about him."

He isn't wrong, but to me, it's all too familiar.

"It isn't just that, Cotton. You were living right here back in '96, when Josephine hit. You telling me this doesn't remind you of how Dad just up and—"

"No. It doesn't. Don't do that to yaself." He leans back against the fence. His eyes turn down and run across the mud.

"Besides," I continue, "every time I walk over there, guess who shows up?"

"Well, that doesn't surprise me." He hits my leg with the back of his hand. "Just don't let all this make ya feel any which way about ya dad. You hear me? I'm sure Lauren's fine." He speaks with a tone that suggests he's willing to entertain my curiosity. "And ya ain't left no one. Not then, not now."

"But I did leave."

"No. Ya spent some time away to help out ya family." He leans in. "And ya daddy talked ya into it. He's the one who sent ya out there because he couldn't afford to leave town himself. Ain't no shame in that."

"Yeah, well. Until I find Lauren, it's all the same to me."

"I think ya getting ahead of yaself. This storm ain't but a day old, ya hear me? Everything'll come together. Okay? Ya pops would—"

"Hello!"

I hear the voice from behind us, down the street near Cotton's home. We turn and look. A young woman in blue jeans and a white T-shirt—one with a red cross stitched into the left side of the chest—is standing in the middle of the road.

She holds her hands at her sides, expressionless. "Food and water?" She steps forward, but several powerlines are snaking across the road, hiding among a pile of branches and other debris.

We stand up in what seems like choreographed timing. "That ain't a good idea," Cotton says in a nonchalant way.

She steps closer. "Do what?"

"There's power lines," I say. Then I turn to Cotton. "You think they're live?"

"I doubt it, but ya'd be a fucking idiot to find out."

I speak to myself as we walk closer. "If she's all the way back here, didn't she just cross a million other downed telephone poles?"

The woman stops and looks down at her feet, as if seeing them for the first time. Then she looks back up at us. She has a camouflage backpack on her shoulders, and she's holding what looks like a black duffel bag. "Got some MREs. Bottled water, too." She holds up the bag. From the looks of it, she's the one who needs the water.

"Um, yeah. Sure," Cotton says, audibly uncertain of what's happening. "You ain't getting through there, though." He points in front of us to the several trees lying across the road, as well as the telephone pole hanging over the street like some sort of obvious ambush, itching to fall.

The woman looks around and retraces her steps, balancing between the fallen limbs. Her feet squish deep into the layer of muck. "Over here?" She points to a log at the edge of the ditch, all of which is filled to the brim with a brown paste that floats atop what water has yet to fall.

She drops the duffel bag to the ground and squats next to

it. Cotton and I look at one another: *Where did she come from?*

She pulls out a few brown pouches and sets them on the log, balancing them in what seems like an unnecessary effort in the middle of such chaos. Then she does the same with the water bottles, hovering her hand over them as if to keep them from falling. The woman crouches again and peers into the black bag, pointing at it while mumbling to herself. Her eyes dart from side to side. She zips the bag and stands up.

I look at Cotton, and he looks at me. The woman turns on a dime and steps away, playing hopscotch with the powerlines and other perilous trash scattered over the road.

Somehow, she walked all the way back here. Alone.

TEN

June 1988

The key to a successful crabbing trip was being patient and having a reliable helper attached at the hip. As it turned out, Lauren was both.

I had my doubts that she would sneak out again, but when I asked her to tag along on one of my trips to the Bayou Liberty boat launch, I had barely gotten the question out before she agreed. Rowan was tied up for the day, and running both nets and string at the same time was nearly impossible by myself. So, things worked out.

The docks were empty, and we were lucky enough to have the six piers all to ourselves. At most, we could cover two or three of them at a time—depending on how good the crab were running.

"So, what's the plan?" Lauren asked.

We walked onto the last pier, then sat with our legs hanging over the edge, our feet teasing the water below. I grabbed the pack of chicken wings from the plastic bag, along with a spool of string.

"Well, we'll get some lines out first, then we'll throw out a few nets. One of us pulls, and the other scoops."

The day was beautifully placid, the sun a perfect sphere on the surface of the water. Lauren shielded her eyes from the reflection with an open hand.

"Here." I removed my sunglasses from the front of my white undershirt and leaned over, placing them over her eyes. Her hair curled beneath the black frames. I could no longer see the blue behind the shades, but there was no need. Those dimples, I had an inkling, would have always been enough.

I pulled out a line of string and stretched it from hand to hand, three times over, and cut the end with my pocketknife. Then I wrapped the line around the bend in one of the wings and tied it in an unforgiving knot.

"I wasn't sure you'd wanna get out with me again." I tied the other end around the piling at the middle of the pier and tossed the wing over the edge. "From what I could hear, your dad didn't seem too pleased after you got home from our fishing trip. Or the other day in the back yard, with me and Rowan." I gestured to the pack of chicken as I cut another piece of line. "Your turn."

She grabbed one of the wings and set an impressive knot deep against the bumpy, slimy skin. "Father is just misunderstood. That's all."

I tied the line to an adjacent pole, and Lauren slung the chicken out over the water. The line snapped taut, and the wing splashed into the bayou.

There was something attractive about pursuing things I knew I couldn't have—and from what I had gathered living next door to the Roux family, Lauren was one of those things. I couldn't help it, though. For all the time I'd known *of* her, I knew virtually nothing about her—but that was what I was hoping to change.

We walked to the next pier and set another pair of lines to the pilings in the middle of the dock. The nets were meant for deeper water, at the end of the landings.

"You worried about Edward Roux, Mr. Dubois?" She spoke as if she knew something I didn't.

"Should I be?" I picked up one of the round nets and gave it to her. "Here. I'll get it set up." She held it out while I secured another chicken wing to the center, then tied the line to the last piling. She threw it out a few feet off the end of the dock, and we turned to the other side.

"Maybe I'm the one who should be worried," she said.

"Ha." I tried to come off as teasing as possible. "You? Worried about my dad? Oh, please. Maybe if my mom was still around, sure. But Dad isn't anything to be worried about." I lifted my chin to the control booth at the foot of the bridge. "Only thing he's concerned with is whether he has some company on the patio when he isn't working."

"And your mother?" she asked.

Surely, she had heard, but maybe she was asking as more of a courtesy. I was itching to ask what she had against "dad" and "mom," but I decided against it—even though the formality of "mother" and "father" made me twitch a little.

"She passed away from cancer years ago," I said. Her expression faded a bit. "One more reason he needs the company." I pointed to the first line we had set, which was stretched firm and beginning to walk across the bottom of the bayou. "And yours?" I asked. Somehow, I didn't know. At least, not the details.

"Same," she said. "Freak car accident."

We rushed over to the line and got on our knees, peering over the edge of the dock. Our faces shone back at us in the water, side by side. I grabbed the scoop net and readied my hand.

"Grab the string and pull it in as slow as you can. You'll feel him on the end, pulling back a little."

She grabbed the string and pulled it in, two fingers at a time. The thread ran across the water, collecting a line of algae along the way.

I dipped the net into the water a few feet from the line, and it disappeared into its own reflection.

"That quick enough?" she said.

"Nice and slow."

I could start to see the faint outline of a blue crab beneath the surface of the water, its legs paddling frantically. I pulled the net up to the surface as slow as I could. Once the crab caught wind of the situation, it was too late. We had him. I pulled the net out of the water with a jolt.

"Hell yeah," I said, in what was probably too high of a pitch.

I raised the kicking and pinching crab to eye level between us, the skin of the chicken wing hanging through the holes in the net like the half-eaten, soggy flesh that it was.

Lauren raised her hand, and we high-fived—but she didn't let go. She pulled me in close, holding my fingers tight between her own.

"Dinner zero, us one," she said.

Then she kissed me on the cheek—with those sultry lips.

———

"Well, well, well," Cotton said as Lauren and I walked up to the porch, carrying the ice chest between us. "Look what the cat dragged in."

"Y'all up for a boil?" I said. He and Dad were rocking in an off-cadence rhythm in their chairs, looking out over the late-evening bayou.

"That depends," Cotton said. "Ya gonna need more than a half dozen if ya coming around here talkin' about a boil."

They stood up and walked to us. Lauren opened the lid to the ice chest and stepped back, our catch on display for the gawking that ensued.

"Well damn, son," Dad said, his jaw all but dragging across the grass.

Cotton responded by patting his coveralls, searching for that missing smoke. He reached inside the jumpsuit and pulled out a bent cigarette, jamming it between his teeth. It looked as if it had been plucked straight from a black-and-white cartoon classic. "Why don't ya grab the burner, ole man." He peered down at the mass of crawling blue. "I'll get these cleaned up and ready to go."

"Roger that," said Dad, turning to Lauren. "You good with a knife?"

"I can be."

"Alright, then. We should have some lemons and onion in the fridge if you wanna get going on those. Think you can handle that?"

"Yes, sir."

"There's a few heads of garlic in the cabinet above the stove, too."

Cotton and I grabbed the ice chest and carried it beneath the patio, setting it down next to the hose on the side of the house. Dad walked inside. No sooner had Cotton turned on the water than we heard a voice from behind us. "I think it's time you get on home, little g-g-g-girl."

We turned around to see Shadow, gripping Lauren by the arm. She pulled herself free of his grasp and looked at him like she couldn't catch a break, her expression withered. It looked like she had been half expecting him to show up.

Shadow looked over his shoulder, to the Roux house on the other side of the fence, then back at us. His eyes darted between us, and his tongue slid across his few remaining teeth as he fashioned a broad, slimy grin.

"Come again?" Cotton said. He dropped the hose to the ground.

His brother stepped toward us and pointed at Lauren. "Mr.

Roux says it's time for his girl to get on home." Shadow spit the dip from his mouth without so much as a flinch. The juice dripped from his chin.

"Watch yaself, brother," Cotton said. "As far as I'm concerned, Mr. Roux can fetch his own daughter."

Dad walked out of the house carrying the rusty burner and propane tank. "Can I help you?" he said, setting them down on the porch.

"It's okay," Lauren said. She looked up to the third-floor window of her house—a silhouette was framed there in a backdrop of shifting yellow. "It is late. Perhaps I should get home."

Dad stepped between us. "I think you stumbled onto the wrong side of"—he paused and looked around—"well . . . you're in the wrong place." Dad was a pencilly five-foot-eight, but he spoke like a lofty six-six.

If I hadn't known any better, I would've thought Lauren was being defensive. "Really, Mr. Dubois. It's nearly dark out." Her mouth twisted into a seemingly jovial shape. "Father likes to have me home by a certain time. That's all."

Shadow batted an eye at my dad. For a moment, it looked like he was pushing the man's buttons on his own property. I had to be imagining it. "Yeah, *Mr. Dubois*. That's all." Then I realized—he had no control over it. The eye appeared to have a mind of its own, with its haphazard, maniacal tempo.

Cotton stepped forward and placed his hand behind her, his other held out in front of them, toward her home. "Come on, Lauren. I'll get ya home, now."

I looked up to the window of the Roux house, but the figure was gone. All that remained was a pale stream of smoke, circling in the abandoned room.

ELEVEN

June 1988

S plinters of glowing light from between the dog ears dimmed and reignited as the three of them strode toward the house, under the half-shaded moon.

I turned back to the porch. Dad was looking over the fence at the Roux house, deep in thought, his arms folded and his jawline tense. He leaned over and snatched a beer from the ice chest on the porch, shaking his head. Then he popped the top and shrugged. "Neighbors, huh?" He slurped from the can.

The sputter of a boat engine sounded from the dock out back.

"I'll be back," I said.

"Don't worry about it. I got these covered." Dad plucked the hose from the ground and picked up where Cotton had left off, rinsing the catch.

I ambled through the darkness of the back yard, toward the bayou. The smokey, oiled scent of a struggling motor wafted toward me.

No matter how hard I fought to avoid it, it found me—the unease of feeling watched. The darker it got, the more I felt it: the shadow panting at the back of my elbow. And that house over the fence.

Maybe spending time with Lauren was a bad idea, but I liked bad. I liked the idea of *her*—the pull of something that was off-limits. Hell, if she wasn't worried about spending time on the Dubois side of the fence, then why should it have bothered me?

Sometimes, bad was good.

What was there to fret about, anyway? The rich daddy who sucked on his pipe and didn't talk? Or the hired help who couldn't string together a proper sentence? I wasn't sure which one was more laughable.

As I approached the dock, Rowan was tying his boat to the pole.

"What was all the commotion about?" he said, tossing the remaining line into the boat.

"Beats me, dude. Me and Lauren just got back from crabbing, about to set up a boil, when shit hit the fan. Shadow thought he'd just show up out of the blue and drag Lauren back home."

Rowan sat on the piling at the start of the dock and looked to the right of the fence.

"Shadow? Showed up at *your* house? Holy shit."

"Yeah. I think 'holy shit' is appropriate."

The bayou chirped and croaked under the heaviness of the wet air, but if I listened hard enough, I could hear the exchange of voices growing heated from the other side of the fence. Rowan and I looked at one another as the talking grew forceful, more anxious.

"Where's he at now?" Rowan said.

"Who?"

"Shadow."

"He's back over at the Rouxs' place. Where else would he be? Cotton ended up taking Lauren back home, but Shadow was right there with them, stuck up their ass the whole way."

He looked next door, then back at me. Rowan stood up and began walking to the other side of the fence with his head hung low, like he was treading beneath the still-spinning blades of a chopper.

He waved me forward. "Come on."

"Rowan." I crept forward and yanked at his sleeve, pulling him down. "What the hell are you doing?"

He brushed his shoulder and adjusted his T-shirt, though it was more of a tattered rag. "What does it look like? I wanna hear what the fuss is all about. Don't you?"

"Hell no. You wanna get shot? It's bad enough Lauren's been with me all evening. You wanna make it worse?"

He sprang to his feet, but I pulled him down again.

"Besides, what's your obsession with them anyways?" I said.

"With *them*?" He spoke as if he were overly offended, but I knew he was screwing with me. His sarcasm knew no bounds. That was Rowan. "I ain't obsessed with no Roux." He craned his neck over the bushes at the back of the yard. "Now, that Shadow fucker—that dude's something else. Maybe I'm just fascinated by wacked-out nutjobs." He crossed his eyes and hung his tongue from the corner of his mouth. "D-d-d-don't ya wanna know why I is duh way I is?" He curled his top lip and licked his teeth.

I popped him in the cheek with an open hand.

"What the fuck, man?" He spoke like the slap was something out of left field, but he should've seen it coming.

I could've tried to stop him from going any further, but it was a moot point. Once Rowan had his mind on something, that was it. Like a squirrel fixated on a shiny gum wrapper—nothing and no one was going to stand in his way.

Even if that meant we might get peppered in the ass while being run off of the Roux property.

"Now," he continued, "you gonna help me bust this thing open, or you just gonna sit here and rub one out behind the bushes?"

He tucked his arm between his legs and rolled forward on

his shoulder, then crawled on his hands and knees like some sort of armed forces vet on a bad acid trip. I wanted to slap the shit out of him once more, but by the time I considered it, he had belly-crawled to the back porch of the Roux house and was crouched behind their four-wheeler.

Again, he waved me forward, and of course, I followed.

"I swear to God, Rowan. If we get caught, I'm gonna beat the living shit out of—" He cupped his hand over my mouth. His eyes grew wide and jerked to the side, his fingers tinged with pine.

The back door crashed against the house.

I heard Cotton starting in on someone. He spoke in a stiff tone. "Listen to me. Ya wanna be involved with Ed Roux, go right ahead. Ya ain't listened to me yet when it comes to this family. But ya don't need to be bringing his shit over to Marcus and Lance."

"Screw you," Shadow said. "You got n-n-n-no right coming over here with that shit. I w-work for Ed Roux because I have to. Ain't no one else around here willing to give me a chance, and he does."

I inched my head out from behind the back tire of the four-wheeler. Cotton and Shadow were face-to-face and awkwardly close.

"Like I said," Cotton continued, "you do what ya gotta do. But keep Marcus out of it. Ya shouldn't be over there—"

"Give me a break, Cotton. You wanna come over here judging me because I work for someone with a little pull in town? Someone who has connections? What about you?"

"What about me?"

"Marcus is the only person you talk to, Cotton. At least I'm over here working for the Roux family, bro."

"Working for him? Is that why ya running around after dark

searching for his daughter? What kind of work is that, Shadow?"

Cotton stepped back and looked out to the yard, shoving his hands deep into his coveralls. I ducked back behind the four-wheeler.

"When ya first started working for Ed Roux, it seemed like a good deal. He does a lot for ya, Shadow. I ain't gonna lie. But I also ain't stupid. Don't act like he ain't got ya doing more than just *working* for him. The man's got ya wrapped around his finger. Ya just too blind to see it."

The clamor from inside the home was starting to die down. Cotton and Shadow quieted their conversation and moved off the porch, deeper into the back yard.

Rowan and I inched our way around the four-wheeler, steering clear of their view.

"So what, bro?" Shadow said. "I do what I gotta do to keep my head above water. Is that so b-b-b-bad?"

I heard a spit, followed by the sound of leaves rustling beside me. A glimmer of moonlight hit my eye, reflected from the dip spattered across the ground near my foot.

"Is it bad that an ex-politician has ya keeping tabs on his daughter? I don't know, brother. You tell me."

No response.

"I ain't gonna keep blowing smoke up ya ass. It ain't worked before, and it ain't gonna work now."

The metallic flick of a lighter pinged across the yard, and light danced against the bark of an adjacent tree. Then the metal snapped shut.

"Just do me a favor," Cotton said. He paused, and I imagined him taking a drag. "Keep the damage to a minimum. They're just kids. Ed ain't gotta know where Lauren was."

Shadow grumbled. "It's a little late for that, b-b-b-bro. Who do you think sent me over there to begin with? You think someone like Ed Roux don't know what his only daughter's up to?"

"Oh, I bet he does—thanks to you."

Shadow inched closer to his brother. His face glowed a ghostly orange as Cotton inhaled, then expelled the smoke from his nose. "If Marcus knows what's good for him," Shadow said, "he'll keep that kid on his side of the fence."

Rowan and I looked at one another. Through the grayish moonlight, I saw for the first time a trace of unease in my friend's eyes.

TWELVE

June 1988

Just as my eyes began to give out under the weight of the day gone by, as night grew deeper, a rattle at my bedroom window sent me lurching to my feet. A bead of sweat traced the edge of my eye and ran down the side of my cheek.

I looked at the blurred numbers of the alarm clock on my nightstand. It was 11:55 p.m.

The sound returned—and grew louder, heavier.

I set my feet on the floor and let the one large shadow of the room close in around me, like a thick, squeezing blanket. Then I fixed my attention on the window that I knew was there but had yet to appear. One vague outline after another, my surroundings came into focus.

Another tap followed, accompanied by an ill-defined croon. "Lance."

I stood up and moved toward the window. I knew my room. Front to back. Every corner. Every creak of the original, fragile floor. But it didn't stop me from holding out my hand and bracing myself for what I couldn't see. Preparing myself for the emptiness in front of me.

"*Lance.*"

I stepped forward. A humid draft swept across the top of my hand as the windowsill came into focus, followed by the decades-old crack in the window.

"Let's go," said the voice.

Somehow, through the black of the night, two flashes of blue materialized on the other side of the pane.

"Grab some shoes," Lauren said. "Come on."

Before I could ask, she had turned around and was waiting for me against the railing.

Surely, after all that had happened that evening, I was deep in some dream. She shouldn't have been at my window. Not then. Not at all. I was still trying to work out what Rowan and I had heard behind the Roux house only hours prior.

If Marcus knows what's good for him, he'll keep that kid on his side of the fence.

It was beyond me what the hell that meant, but it didn't matter. Lauren shouldn't have been there, on my side. On the *other* side. Clearly, there was some hypothetical fence I had yet to see. Some divide between our two worlds I had yet to uncover. Yet there she was.

And that simple fact pulled me out of the house and beneath tranquil skies.

I slipped on my ragged Adidas and grabbed a flashlight. I opened the window but soon paused, one leg out, the other in. Even in the dark, the mere sight of her outline sent a pulse down my throat and pushed my stomach out of the plane from ten thousand feet. A forbidden-but-good twinge weakened my legs and excited me in a way that would've embarrassed me if not for the dark.

She held up what looked like the same wicker basket from that first perfect day together. "You up for an adventure?"

At midnight? *No.* With Lauren? *Of course.*

I eased the window shut behind me. "After you."

I couldn't help but place my hand on the small of her back. But the touch of her skin—which I hoped would linger with no end—was anything but small.

When Lauren suggested an adventure, I guessed it was going to be anything but the cemetery.

As we reached the bottom of the stairs, she grabbed my hand and didn't let go. She led us down the driveway and to the front of the graveyard, at the break in the fence, then stood motionless with my hand in hers, swinging the basket. "What's a good spot?" she asked.

I was trying to wrap my head around the whole sitting-with-the-dead thing. As far as I was concerned, just outside the fence would have been ideal. So, I offered up an uncertain frown.

"Okay, then." She gestured to one of the mausoleums at the center of the yard. "This one it is."

She pulled me forward until we reached a large brick tomb, covered in a thin layer of plaster that was intentionally crumbling from the edges of the structure—like a modern-day German smear. A skinny wooden door at the front of the crypt was flanked by a strip of frosted red glass on either side. Above the door, just below where the roof formed a tall peak, was a weathered, lichen-covered sculpture of a melancholy woman, a shawl draped over her head.

"Isn't it gorgeous?" Lauren said, setting down the basket and pulling a tall white candle from inside. She set it down on the cement entryway to the tomb and lit it.

"Sit," she said.

We sat on the grass in front of the mausoleum. The yellow light flickered beside us.

"You come here often?" I said, half joking, half serious.

"What's wrong? You have something against the macabre, Lance Dubois?"

Only then did I notice my sunglasses hanging from the front of her shirt, the flame dancing in the lenses between her small but perfect breasts.

"The macabre? No." At least, not when I was with her.

Lauren removed two glass tumblers and a six-pack of

sweating Root beer from the basket. She handed me one of the cups, popped the top on one of the cans, then filled my glass with the dark, foaming drink.

"Sorry about earlier," she said. "Family can be . . . well, family." Then she filled her own glass. "This is my mother's grave. And, yes—I do come here often."

How did I not catch that? Of course her mother was buried there. Where else would she have been?

"Don't worry about it," I said. "And sorry about your mom."

"It was a long time ago." She lifted her glass to the front of the cemetery. "I'm sorry about yours."

I didn't care to talk about Mom. Not that anything negative surrounded her passing, other than the obvious. I just felt that some things were better left alone.

"You know this place pretty well, then," I said.

She smiled in a subtle way. "We do live here." She glanced over her shoulder to our homes, even though they were hidden under the middle of the night.

I allowed her words to linger for a moment, letting the thought of dead mothers pass.

"Somehow, I have a feeling your dad isn't the biggest fan," I said, doing my best to change the subject.

"Fan?"

"Of me."

She leaned back with her hand in the grass and sipped her drink. "That's nonsense. Father is only doing what fathers do best."

"Oh yeah? And what's that?"

She placed her drink to the side and sat up straight, looking me in the eyes. Unblinking. "Making their daughters' boyfriends paranoid." She pressed her plush, minty lips against mine. "It seems to be working."

"Boyfriends?"

Lauren whispered seductively in my ear as she climbed in my lap. "Uh-huh. That a problem?" She brushed her lips against mine again, then slid the tip of her tongue into my mouth, until we met in the middle.

"No. I don't mind at all," I muttered raggedly as I held her close, caressing the side of her face.

Even the way she kissed was forbidden. In a good way. And I wanted more. She tasted like a forewarning—and I liked it.

She leaned in to kiss me again, this time playfully nibbling at my tongue with her teeth. Then she paused as though lost in thought and pushed her hair behind her ear.

"You and I aren't that different, you know," Lauren said.

I fundamentally disagreed, from the outside looking in, but I took the bait. Anything to reel her back in. To taste her again.

"Yeah? What does the daughter of a mayor have in common with someone like me?"

"Someone like you?"

"Surely there's a reason we're neighbors and our families never talk."

"That's neighbors being neighbors, *neighbor*."

Maybe I could've phrased it better, but there was no denying it: her family had a reputation. An image. Her dad had an image. Hell, her dad *was* the family image.

"I know Father can be a bit much, but he's a good man. You'll see."

I sipped my drink. I certainly preferred it to actual beer. Or maybe I just preferred her—regardless of what I had in my hand. "Maybe we should get together, then. Hang out sometime."

Even through the candlelight, that dimpled chin gutted me. I almost leaned in for more, but I hesitated. I wanted her to want me. "We are 'hanging out,'" she said.

"I meant your dad. I should meet him. You know . . . officially. Not just from the driveway."

Her nose flared. "You sure do have a hard-on for fathers. Or is it just mine?"

"Just yours."

The truth of the matter was that I had a hard-on for neighbors named Lauren. And I was intrigued. The truth was, Cotton didn't *not* like anyone. The truth was that her whole family was an enigma, nothing more than town whispers that revolved around one man's last name. Around his previous political engagements, whatever those might have been.

On more than one occasion, I had waved at Mr. Roux from my side of the fence. He'd never waved back.

The truth was, I didn't know shit about her family, other than the vague one-liners from a third party here or there.

So naturally, I liked the idea of her even more.

"Hm," she said. "What if I like the fact that Father doesn't know you? At least, not really."

Then it occurred to me: what if that was what we had in common? What if the fact that Lauren knew she shouldn't have been there was what brought her over the fence in the middle of the night? What if she liked the wrongness as much as I did?

I hoped so.

In the still of night, a bell chimed. Only one ring.

"What was that?" I said.

Lauren snickered. "Really? You live right here, and you don't know?"

I had no clue.

She gestured with her chin to the corner of the cemetery. "Back in the day, they used to put a bell above ground, on the headstone of the graves, in case someone was buried alive. The bell was attached to a cord that ran inside the coffin. So if you were buried and still breathing, you had a way of communicating with the outside world."

One of Lauren's this-or-that expressions crossed her face, and I was unable to tell if she was pulling my chain. "I think you're full of shit," I said.

"There's only one left," she said, pointing across the way. "Of course, there's no cord attached to it, but it's the only bell out here. How it's still there a century later is beyond me."

"I guess they just don't make them like they used to."

Another chime sounded and echoed between the graves. Then another.

"What?" she said. I was guessing she could see the concern on my face, lit by the flame.

I looked around, mulling it over. "There's no wind."

"And?"

She leaned over and pressed her lips to the side of my neck, as two bells rang out—at the same time.

"Yeah, I'm out," I said. I stood up and knocked back the rest of my drink. "We should do this again sometime."

Lauren rolled to her knees. "I thought you were up for an adventure, Mr. Dubois?" Her grin deepened, her lips sleek in the shifting light.

I wasn't sure how many of them followed, but the two bells were drowned out by a number of others I couldn't count, and the graves became overshadowed by an ensemble of rings.

She sprang to her feet. "Wait up."

Hand in hand, we walked to the front of cemetery with not another word spoken. We exited through the break in the fence and turned the corner, where she pushed me against the live oak and, once more, gave me a taste of those mint lips.

THIRTEEN

August 30, 2005

"What ya in the mood for, my boy?" Cotton picks up two of the small, army-brown packages. "Spaghetti and meatballs or Cajun rice with red beans and sausage?"

The idea of eating dinner from plastic pouches, warmed by a self-heating packet, has me feeling like a toddler in a highchair with no choice in the matter. I can always head back to the house and see if there's any bread and peanut butter left that I brought up to the office at the last minute, before the kitchen went under, but my stomach grumbles at the thought of it.

"Surprise me," I say.

He hands me one of the packets. *MENU NO. 18: CAJUN RICE, BEANS & SAUSAGE* is printed on the front. *Meal Ready-to-Eat, Individual.*

We straddle one of the trees that lies across the road and peel open our dinner. Ready to eat, my ass. I remove the ten-piece puzzle and read the directions on how to piece it together.

"I hope this tastes better than it looks," Cotton says.

"Tell me about it."

From what I can garner, each meal comes with a few sides, a beverage base, an accessory packet, a spoon, and the "flameless heater" to warm the meal in the same box that it comes in. My side: peanut butter and crackers.

I mutter to myself. "You gotta be kidding me."

I tear open the green heater bag, slide the packaged meal inside, and pour some water up to the fill line. Then I fold it over and place it back into the box. By the time I prop it against a knot in the tree, I can feel the heat weakening the cardboard. The contents bubble inside.

"Look at you," Cotton says. "Chef Dubois."

He seems to be struggling with the process of "preparing" his ready-to-eat meal. "You need a hand with that?"

"Nah. Cold is fine by me."

"Seriously? You don't want some help heating it up?"

"I ain't the picky type." He tears open the package and shovels a heap of the lifeless spaghetti into his mouth with the plastic spoon. He winces as he chews it but wastes no time scooping another bite.

The drone of chainsaws in the distance has come to a halt, and the evening is mellow under the cloudy but harmless skies. A few minutes later, my food is ready, and we sit in the middle of the disheveled road and eat an early dinner. We've managed to clear most of the driveway, but as I look in the other direction, down Dubois Road, I realize how little we've accomplished.

I haven't ventured past the cemetery as of yet, but looking farther down the road toward Cotton's house, the landscape snaps into focus—like the image from a Polaroid after a few dozen shakes. A near-perfect line of trees are snapped from the waist down, forming roughly a fifty-foot lane that crosses the road, from the bayou to the other side of the street and as far as I can see. Then it hits me: hurricanes spin off other storms inside of them like miniature, hellish spawn. It must have been a tornado that swept past the house when the flooding started—the chaotic scream of a freight train barreling across the bayou.

Maybe there is a silver lining. At least Cotton and I still have our homes to repair. We at least have something to work with.

It looks like a few of our neighbors farther down the street are unable to say the same.

Cotton is lying back on the fallen tree. I finish my somewhat decent meal and am pushing the trash back into the cardboard box when movement catches my curiosity at the corner of my eye.

When *Lauren* catches my attention.

"Is that her?" I say.

Unmoved by my question, Cotton keeps his eyes welded shut. "What?"

"I think Lauren just walked into her house." I gesture in that direction.

That seems to get his attention. He sits up. "Do what?"

"I think that's Lauren."

I'm not entirely sure how confident I am in the statement, but I'll take anything I can get. It's got to be her. Or at the very least, someone who knows where she is.

I roll off of the tree trunk and walk up the driveway, leaving my trash behind. Cotton follows at my heels.

After a few paces, we're walking up the sidewalk to the front door of her home. Stupidly, I knock, as if there's some sort of privacy amid the madness. The door is still swollen shut, as we left it that morning; hence, the busted window.

I call out anyway. "Lauren? You in there?"

I turn the doorknob and push, but it's frozen solid, fixed in place as if it never existed. I lean over and peer through the broken window. "Lauren? Hello?"

I hear Cotton behind me. "Ya seeing stuff, my boy."

Maybe I am. More than likely, I'm not.

"Hello?" I step through the window and into the dining room. It's only been a few hours since we've been here, but the smell has evolved into something that forces my hand over my nose. Part sewage, part rot. Shielding my face does nothing for the stench that seeps into the deepest corners of my throat.

We walk into the kitchen, then do a quick sweep of the

living room. I see no one, only footprints covering footprints, tracked in layers throughout both of the rooms. I glance up at the corner of the living room, where one of the cameras was hanging only this morning.

The wire is cut. The camera is gone.

I turn back to the dining room. Surely the other one is there. Was I misremembering? Was it the corner of another room? As I step into the foyer, at the base of the stairs, someone's face is an inch from my own. Even in the aftermath of the storm, the smell of tobacco pours from Shadow's breath.

"What are you two d-d-d-doing here?"

Cotton walks up behind me. "What the hell are *you* doing here?"

"This isn't your property. If you know what's good for you, you'd turn around and—"

"And this ain't *your* property, either," Cotton says. He looks past his brother, to the staircase covered in a fresh set of footprints leading straight to Shadow's feet. "You wanna explain what you're—"

"I ain't gotta explain sh-sh-sh-shit, bro."

I step backward, one slow heel at a time, into the kitchen, keeping an eye in front of me. Once there's enough space between us, I turn and look up to the corner once again. Still, no camera. The spliced wire hangs there. Motionless.

I walk past them and back into the foyer.

"I work here," Shadow says, "and I suggest you leave."

Then the two of them speak in a way that fades to a silent nothing. Or at least, I'm distracted enough not to hear them.

It's gone—both of them. A single wire hangs from the corner over the front door. No camera. All that's left is me standing here, looking up, gawking at some cable in the midst of what is surely the worst natural disaster our town has ever seen.

With everything around me, all that I'm standing in—the muck suctioned to my feet, the stench sodden in the back of my throat, my body running on self-heating garbage, a home never again what it used to be—a fucking *wire* has me starstruck.

I step closer.

Even with the camera gone, I feel as if I'm being watched, followed, from the very same corner. And from the corner behind me, breathing at the back of my neck. As if there's no need for the cameras. No wires. No viewer.

It's this home.

Then I feel it, approaching from behind me.

"Let's go," Cotton says, and I flinch back into the moment.

"What? Why? You know where she is?"

"The little shit's right. This ain't our property."

I look back to the foyer. Shadow stands there with his hands at his side. Stiff. A lump behind his lower lip.

Cotton climbs through the hole in the wall. "Let's go."

I follow him, but the inkling follows me. We reach the driveway that connects my home with Lauren's. I stop and look back. The man hasn't moved. Shadow stands there, watching, waiting. I have no idea what for.

I turn and continue down the driveway—but it follows me. The idea of that house, steady at my elbow.

FOURTEEN

July 1988

I seldom went fishing to fish.

Rowan and I sat on the dock with our poles in hand, our feet hovering just above the water. Mosquitos dotted the surface of the bayou as the sun began to fade behind us, igniting the treetops into a flaming orange on the adjacent shore.

Sitting out there was our weekly happening during the summer. Unspoken of and unplanned, we would ride our bikes to the Bayou Liberty docks and buy some minnows from Catchem, then head back to my place for a few evening casts. It was nice to fish at home and avoid the buzz of the boat launch from time to time; living on the water had its perks.

The fish bumped against the inside of the metal pail between us.

Rowan cleared his throat. "So. You and Lauren get crazy yet?"

"Get crazy?"

The whiz of his line fizzed through the air, followed by the splash of a minnow hitting the water. His voice deepened. He leaned over and sang dramatically into my ear—about having the time of his life, and never feeling like that before. Then he stood up and placed the fishing pole between his legs, his voice climbing in pitch, swearing it's the truth. He held his pole with one hand while curling a finger toward himself with the other, although I knew good and well the finger move was several seconds earlier in the movie. "*And I owe it all to you—*"

I flicked him between the legs, and he fell into his chair with a well-deserved shrink.

Rowan was never going to let me live that one down.

A few months prior, he had decided to show up unexpectedly to ask me for help with checking some crab traps he had set the day prior. Dad wasn't home, so he had let himself in. Needless to say, the sight of Rowan opening my bedroom door while I was pleasuring myself to Jennifer Grey carrying a watermelon was something both of us would surely remember for years to come.

"Sit the hell down," I said. "And no. We have yet to dance, Rowan. Clean, dirty, or any which way."

"That's all you had to say, then. No need to bring my nuts into the mix."

We sat for a while longer, fishing but really thinking to ourselves. Basking in the dying sun. We were the type of friends who could sit for hours on end without saying a word to one another—and be perfectly content. It didn't matter that we hadn't had a single bite. Embracing the evening was our only goal.

"I know I give you a lot of shit about you and Lauren," Rowan said, "but I only do that because I think y'all are so much alike."

I popped my cork. The reflection of the orange ball wrinkled in the ensuing waves.

"Yeah, I know."

I could tell he wasn't all that comfortable initiating a humorless conversation, but he continued anyway. "How are things going so far? I mean, y'all gonna be official?"

"Hell, I have no idea." But I hoped so. Man, did I hope so. "Her and I aren't exactly cut from the same cloth, you know?"

The tinkle of keys sounded from behind us. We turned.

"Speaking of thread count," Rowan said.

Mr. Roux was walking along the side of his house and toward the gravel driveway, the fabric of his immaculate three-piece ivory suit shining in the evening glare. Strangely enough, he didn't get into his obnoxious, classic Rolls-Royce. Instead, he continued down the drive and past the cemetery.

"Where in the world is he going?" I said.

"Mail?"

"No. Their mailbox is right next to ours."

We looked at one another. Rowan cocked his head to the side and widened his eyes.

"No," I said.

"Oh, come on." He reeled in his line and set his pole on the dock. "You and I both know where he's headed."

He had that I'm-going-and-you're-coming-with type of glare. Getting nosy with my neighbors was becoming a repetitive thing with Rowan, but I admired that quality in him—his ability to run down his curiosity and take risks in life. If not for Rowan, I never would have pushed myself to get to know Lauren, or to ask Catch-em for that summer job the year before, or apply to the music program at UNO when everyone else had said I needed to pursue a "real career." His curiosity pushed him forward, and as a byproduct, it pushed me too.

Often straight into the path of other people's business.

I went after him. "What the hell, Rowan?"

We crept along my side of the fence to the front of the property and next to the two mailboxes, then moved with our heads down along the cemetery chain-link fence, until we reached the live oak at the entrance. We ducked behind the tree and waited.

It was like watching oil mix with water. Roux stopped at the trailhead to Shadow's treehouse. He looked left, then right. The smoke from his pipe blew back toward us. He adjusted his vest and stepped forward as if he were dressed for the occasion.

He wasn't. His pristine, brown-and-white Oxford dress shoes met the soil and subsequent puddles without pause. He walked into the woods, and we moved behind the trash cans at the edge of the gravel road.

Rowan lunged forward, but I grabbed his arm. "Again, Rowan—what's your obsession?"

He yanked his arm free. "Oh, grow a pair, will you?"

He led the way—and I followed, of course.

We kept a good fifty feet between ourselves and the dressed-up man. The path to Shadow's home was an overgrown trail, so remaining hidden was a simple task. We stopped behind an old, rusted barrel several feet into the woods, off the beaten path. Shadow was out front of his treehouse, tending to the several dozen homemade windchimes below the home, scattered about his version of a yard—another quirk that Rowan had claimed "needed looking into." In reality, it was one more reason for Rowan to be the prying teenager he was.

"Oh, come on," Shadow said as he turned and saw Mr. Roux approaching the treehouse. "I told you I'd be by later t-t-t-t-today."

Mr. Roux said something or another about not caring. It was difficult to hear him with his back to us.

The woods were silent, save the clanking of a few of the wind chimes—some made of wood, others fashioned from junk metal or plastic. Some were even glass. If my eyes weren't deceiving me, I would've said that a few of them were designed from the bones of small animals. Rodents, perhaps.

Roux walked about the property like he was in his element, with an Irish fighter's swank. Like he belonged there. Shadow cowered under the shade of the forest canopy.

Mr. Roux ran his finger through one of the hanging

decorations. "Still screwing with garbage, are you?"

The wooden chime clanked and clacked. Shadow retreated beneath the deck of his tree-bound home.

"A man's gotta have a hobby, yeah?"

The suit-and-tie stepped below the decaying platform. All I heard was "side job," followed by a drop in Shadow's posture, dragging his already low shoulders to a defeated slouch.

"Yes, sir. But isn't there another w-w-w-way to—"

"No."

Shadow stepped back, but Mr. Roux inched forward.

He removed the pipe from his mouth and shoved the stem of it into Shadow's forehead, tapping it several times against his cowering brow. He held the pipe there and blew a ring of smoke straight into the lesser man's face.

Then the boss spoke. ". . . tarnish *my* family name . . . and only daughter."

Shadow turned his head and spit. His gaze wandered as if he were incapable of looking back at the man in front of him. "I'm assuming I g-g-get my usual?" he muttered.

Mr. Roux grinned with the half of his mouth that wasn't holding the pipe. He looked around, up to the rotting floor of the treehouse deck. For the first time since arriving, he stepped back, chewing on his pipe. Puffing, chewing.

Rowan and I looked at one another—and Rowan mocked the two of them by holding up talking puppet hands and moving his mouth in a theatrical performance, minus the words.

I held up my hand like I was about to flick him again, and his puppets covered his mouth and groin.

Mr. Roux reached into the inside pocket of his coat and pulled out a white envelope, thumbing through the contents without removing what was inside. He slapped it against Shadow's chest.

Shadow removed the money and began counting. His gaze returned to Roux, and he paused with the cash in one hand as he dropped the empty envelope to the ground.

He held up the fresh, stiff bills. "You're cheap. You know that?"

"Cheap people beget cheap pay, my friend." Roux puffed another perfect ring into the man's face, the smoke breaking over Shadow's balding head. Neither man blinked. Roux turned over the bowl of his pipe and knocked it against the stairs of the home, and the ashes were caught by a fleeting wind.

He slipped the pipe into one of the hip pockets of his suit and turned away, one hand gripping his lapel, the other removing a gold pocket watch. He checked the time, snapped the watch closed, and continued walking at a casual pace.

He didn't make it far before pausing next to a sapling at the edge of the home—the one and only magnolia on the property. He placed the watch back into his coat pocket.

Roux looked the small tree up and down. He turned back to Shadow, then again to the tree. He lifted one of the green glass wind chimes, hooked to a low-lying branch. Then he dropped it to the dirt at his feet—next to his once-gleaming shoes.

The man spoke to the tree as if it were seeking advice. Like a friend in need, perhaps. "Most people in your position would be grateful."

He plucked one of the waxy, cream flowers from the tree and pushed it to his nose—then he strode down the soppy path once again.

FIFTEEN

July 1988

Thanks to Rowan, all I was able to think about was taking the next step with Lauren.

I didn't want to force it, of course. Hell, I was more nervous about it than I was excited. I was about to start college, and I still hadn't had sex. At least, not *sex* sex—not the kind that really mattered.

I sat in bed, staring at the key on my dresser. Cotton wouldn't have given it to me if he wasn't serious about me using it. Right?

Dad wouldn't be home until almost midnight, and Cotton was gone for the weekend, helping one of his old crew members set up a new trawling rig. Lauren had said she would stop by after dinner, and it was just past 7 p.m.

So I sat on the edge of the mattress, waiting for her to knock. Looking at the key. Waiting. Looking.

Maybe I was jumping the gun. Maybe she was the type of girl to hold out for the perfect betrothal. Maybe I should've been waiting for *her* to make the first big move.

What if I did make the first move—and she pushed me away? What if she *literally* pushed me away? What could be more embarrassing than that?

I looked down at my hands. The sweat shone like glitter across the ridges of my palms and fingers. Like I had grabbed one of those naff Valentine's cards in an endless sea of better options.

I looked at the alarm clock—7:05 buzzed in block numbers.

Then I turned back to the key.

What if she wanted me to make the first move? How could I have expected her to do it herself?

I slid my hands down the front of my jeans and over my knees, but the wetness returned to my hands in no time at all.

Worse yet, what if she had slept with someone when I hadn't? What if the whole thing came across as pathetic, desperate even? On the other hand, with everyone away, it might turn out to be our only chance. But what if Mr. Roux—

I heard the springs on the screen door before I heard the knock.

It was now or never. I bounded to my feet and swiped the key from the dresser, then slid my shoes on as I walked into the living room. I paced through the kitchen and reached to open the patio door. Orangish rays scattered through the thin and pallid curtain there. Her shadow—hair curling in an evening crossfire—stood on the other side of the door, perfect. Funny how I knew her from nothing more than a vague but flawless shape.

I opened the door, and she rushed me with that dimpled chin and a full-on hug, all but floating on the tips of her toes to reach me. The feel of her breasts against me, my hands around her waist, sliding to the small of her back—it melted me in that very spot.

She tucked her head into the crook of my neck and squeezed. Then she leaned back and ran her hand through my hair, kissing me like we'd been kept at bay for years.

"Well, hello to you, too," I said.

She answered with another kiss, one that lingered and was more deliberate.

"Come on." I grabbed her hand and pulled her from the doorway.

She spoke with a flood of anticipation. "Where we rushing to?"

Our hands swung between us, refusing to part ways.

We strode behind the house and into Cotton's back yard, guided only by the peach moonlight, our homes separated by nothing more than a lone towering pine tree. As we approached the sailboat, Lauren stopped in the yard, just shy of the dock.

Both the setting sun and full moon were visible in the sky.

"What's wrong?" I said.

"Is this okay? Are we even allowed over here?"

I stepped onto the dock and pulled the key from my pocket. I held it up between us. "According to Cotton, we are."

She glanced over her shoulder in the direction of her home, which had begun to fade in the late evening hours. I stepped into the boat and unlocked the cabin door. "I promise. It's fine." I held out my hand and helped her into the boat. It rocked only marginally as she took my hand and stepped down. The hull echoed under our feet, the bayou an orange-yellow glass under the early-night sky.

I took her hand and guided her into the cabin, where there was enough room for the two of us to stand and maneuver, shoulder to shoulder. A thin line of windows allowed a small cut of moonlight into the cramped room.

I spoke in a low voice. "Isn't it quiet?"

She reached out her hand, feeling the edge of the cabin, and sat across from me on the makeshift sofa. "It is."

I felt her hand grab mine, pulling me toward her.

We sat together, her legs draped across my lap for what seemed like hours but was likely thirty minutes or so. It was pure bliss, holding her so close for so long, no one knowing where we were or who we were with. We hardly talked, instead enjoying the silence of one another's company.

When she slid her legs from my lap, if only for the most excruciating of seconds, I thought the evening was coming to an end. Then I realized that couldn't have been further from the truth. She was merely moving—from her back to my lap.

She straddled me and lowered herself one slow inch at a time. I had no doubt she could feel it—how hard I was between us.

Her hips crept forward, pushing the warmth of her thighs against it. And a yearn escaped her lips against the edge of my ear.

From the look of it, I was wrong; neither of us was required to make the first move alone. We both could, and we were. I had brought her there, and from the looks of it, she had sensed why.

She kissed my neck and ran her tongue along the edge of my jaw, then bit my chin and pushed her hips forward once again. She ran her hands under my shirt and lifted it overhead. The weight of her stole from my lap as she stood up, and I felt the fabric of my shirt brush my leg as it fell to the floor.

I sat forward and grabbed her waist, kissing her navel and stomach before running my thumbs along the inside of her shorts. I rocked them from side to side, pulling them down until they fell on their own accord. As soon as they did, she slid off her lace boy shorts, and I slipped my shorts—briefs included—down to my feet.

"I don't have anything," I said. Admittedly, I didn't have a clue what I was doing, but what I needed and didn't have I was sure of.

She didn't speak at first, and she straddled me yet again. That time, I could feel the modest hair between her legs, brushing against me, sliding across the bottom of my stomach, then farther down to where we met.

"That's okay. Just tell me when." She grabbed me and

guided us together. Her legs spread farther apart on the couch, and we were as close as possible.

"Okay."

We went slow, as difficult as it was, being my first time and all. I held out as long as I could, but the way she felt, first time or not—her skin against mine, the two of us sweating, her breath in my ear—made it impossible to hold out any longer.

"Alright," I said, and she pushed herself up.

All I felt in that moment was the night air hitting my wet skin, as she grabbed me in her hand until the warmth dripped over us both. She knelt beside me with her mouth to my ear.

"Them zero, us one."

Only then did the shadow scurrying from beneath the boat slip draw my eye.

SIXTEEN

August 1988

What had happened inside that boat played on a perpetual loop in the front of my head, like Dad's vinyl *Led Zeppelin IV* with that notorious scratch halfway through "When the Levee Breaks." I was obsessed, and I knew it.

That was all I was left with, though. Like so many times before, Lauren and I were together, and then we weren't. That night on the boat was the last I had heard from her, but Lauren going radio silent wasn't anything new. She had gone MIA for days at a time—despite the notes I would leave at the rope swing out back, and the evenings I'd spend down at the water, sitting on the dock. Reading, "fishing," staring at the sun as it drowned in the adjacent shoreline.

But I always knew she'd be back.

Dad's phone had woken me up through the bedroom walls first thing in the morning, and he'd been in the kitchen ever since, talking to someone in a sad, private tone. I'd been sitting on the sofa since the sun had started to bleed through the glass and drip from the windowsill. Every now and then, I'd hear him sniffle, then he'd go silent. Whatever it was—whomever he'd been preoccupied with for the last several hours—I suspected it wasn't good.

Dad never got choked up over anything trivial.

I gaped at the TV in a sort of trance even though it was off, my reflection caught in the dark-gray mirror of the screen. The memory of Lauren straddling me, her wet body molded against my own, was enough to keep the gears turning in my head.

The beep of the kitchen telephone snapped me out of it. Dad sniffled once more, and I heard the phone meet its receiver on the wall. He walked into the living room and sat in the recliner across from me, but he said nothing.

"What is it?" I asked.

He fumbled around with the pillow behind his back. Then he fidgeted with the remote on the end table. I could see that he was taking his time. Stalling, perhaps.

"That was your Aunt Ninette." He paused. More touching of the remote. He looked up at the ceiling to keep the saline at bay. "Your Uncle Holden isn't doing so well."

"Isn't doing so well" wasn't all that specific, but I knew it was on the more serious side, given Dad's melting expression and complete dearth of eye contact.

I wasn't sure how anything could have been wrong with Uncle Holden. He was someone who took charge of the world. Someone who things happened *for*, not *to*. He was the one who everyone ran to when they couldn't handle life for themselves. What could possibly have been wrong?

"He's got cancer," Dad said. "Esophageal cancer."

Aunt Ninette was the polar opposite of Uncle Holden. He was her whole world, though. Hell, her universe—beautiful explosions and all. It was hard to think of her existing without her husband. Like a moon with no planet.

I was still trying to wrap my head around it, so I let Dad steer the conversation forward.

"It doesn't look good. Your aunt said they went to the doctor yesterday to get an update"—he shook his head and looked off at the corner of the room, bouncing his knee—"but it's already spread."

Up until that point, I hadn't lost anyone close to me. My eighth-grade teacher had died from cancer, but she was far older than Uncle Holden. Decades older. I'd go as far as to say it hadn't been a surprise when she passed away. But Uncle Holden was in his late forties. He should've had decades ahead of him; according to twentieth-century medicine, he was young.

Dad sniffled and blinked the water away. "But hey." I could tell he was trying to brush it off like it was just any old bad news, like he would have still had a brother in the foreseeable future. "I guess that's what happens when you attack life the way that he does."

The comment didn't need an explanation. I knew what he meant by it—as did anyone who knew my uncle. I'm pretty sure The Eagle's "Life in the Fast Lane" was written as a dedication to the way Uncle Holden lived his life. He smoked like it was a challenge, drank beer as if it were spring water, and ate what he pleased—extra ketchup a must.

"Aunt Ninette say anything else? They have a plan?"

"Yeah." A drop of sardonicism, or maybe livid sarcasm, diluted his sorrow. "'Make him comfortable' is what the doctors said, apparently."

"There isn't anything they can try?"

"It's too far along."

I could already picture Uncle Holden reasoning his way through the news. He was never one for self-loathing or regret— I don't think those ideas existed in his mind. I had once heard him lay out an argument for why working out and dieting were a waste of time.

I could still hear his raspy voice, as clear as day: *Now you tell me why I should get in shape and go on a diet. You want me to eat some trash food that tastes like cardboard and bust my ass working out so I can . . . what? Have more days to eat more shitty food and work out again? It don't make any sense, nephew. Sure—you'll live longer. There's no doubt in my mind. But if you dread every meal and waste your life away in a gym, what's the point? No food to savor, no time with my family on the ranch. No thanks. I'll take a short, feel-good, out-of-shape life over a long, stressful one any day of the week.*

I had yet to think of a decent response.

Uncle Holden was more interested in philosophy than he realized. Was it worth it? Living longer so that you could work toward living longer?

"Sorry," I said. "She say anything about how long he has left?"

"Months. A year if he's extremely lucky. But, more likely than not . . . months."

For the first time since he had sat down, my dad leaned forward and looked me in the eye. "I spoke with your aunt for quite a while, and there's something we need to discuss."

Dad never wanted to "discuss" anything. That word was reserved for special occasions, and he wasn't much for anything special unless it was truly warranted.

I pulled my legs up onto the sofa and got comfortable. "Alright."

"Your aunt and uncle are gonna need some help running the ranch with everything they have going on. Between the upkeep, booking hunts, the taxidermy, the hunts themselves . . . they have a lot to get done."

Uncle Holden and Aunt Ninette owned a guided hunting ranch in the Texas Hill Country, a few miles west of Austin. They had built the business from nothing, and it had grown into an absolute monster success over the past ten years or so. Their focus was to offer high-quality guided hunting for white-tailed deer mostly, but it had evolved into so much more: lodging and dining, mule deer and javelina hunting, taxidermy services. Everything. It was Uncle Holden's dream, and he was living it.

"Okay," I said, not sure where the conversation was headed.

"There's no way they can keep the business up and running with your uncle as sick as he is."

I couldn't believe Dad was seriously thinking about moving to Texas.

"Are you thinking about moving? So . . . what? You're just gonna up and sell the house?"

He shook his head and wiped the corner of his eye.

"I don't get it."

"This is home. I'm not selling our home, son. But in order for us to keep this house, I need to stay here and work."

Surely, he wasn't suggesting what I thought he was.

"What are you saying, then?"

He adjusted the pillow behind his back once more. "What I'm saying is that you're seventeen. As unfortunate as it is, with everything that's going on with your uncle, I think this might be an opportunity for you."

"An opportunity? An opportunity for what?"

"To help out with something that's bigger than sitting here in Slidell, waiting around for some degree four years down the road."

I hadn't seen that one coming. My dad, Marcus Dubois, was suggesting I skip out on college? What happened to "Get a degree, son. Learn to work with your head and not your hands."?

If I hadn't known better, I would have said he was trying to drown out the idea of losing a brother by doing something meaningful for his son. Something he thought was worthwhile.

"Think about it." He inched forward in the chair. "I already talked to Aunt Ninette. She insists that they need the help, and she said your uncle is willing to show you everything. And what he can't show you, she will. It's a chance for you to take over a family business later on down the road. Something that's a guaranteed success. Hell, it already is a success."

Admittedly, it wasn't a horrible idea. But how bad were things really, if they were looking to a teenager for help?

"You just said it yourself—I'm seventeen. I'm still a teenager. How in the world is a teenager gonna run a business like that with no experience? And why me? Surely, there's someone else they can ask."

He chuckled under his breath. "You wouldn't be *running* anything. You'd be helping your Aunt Ninette and learning the ropes of how the business works. So maybe, one day, you could take things over or, at the very least, be a part of running the company. It's helping out your family. And a large part of it would be manual labor that your uncle can no longer handle."

When he put it like that, it felt like a no-brainer. Who wouldn't have gone?

Dad got up and walked to the kitchen. "Just sleep on it, okay? I told your aunt you'd give her a call tomorrow, after you have some time to mull it over. It's a lot to think about."

And just like that, Lauren had taken a back seat in my head.

SEVENTEEN

August 31, 2005

It's morning. I stand naked over the copper clawfoot tub, staring at the few inches of nearly melted ice inside of it, racking my brain for another way I can rid myself of the filth crawling over my dried and cracked skin.

I've got nothing.

The reek of warm bayou, soaked into the floor beneath my feet, bakes in the Louisiana heat. Even with the windows open, every breath is flat-out horrid. I lift my arm and smell myself.

Goddamn, it's wretched.

I step into the frigid water and stand there, looking down at my grimy feet as they shed two days' worth of Katrina filth. If I knew that several days later I'd be taking a bath in melting ice—delivered in bags by a truck because running water no longer exists—I would've followed the damn evacuation order. But hell, hindsight is always twenty-twenty.

No one expected this. No one could have dreamt it up if they tried.

Another draft of moldy warmth hits my nose, but is it me or the soggy house, sloughing off in layers one floor below me? I grab the sides of the tub and lower myself into the bone-numbing water. The cold sends a shock between my legs and down through the core of my spine, but I remind myself how nasty the alternative is. How I would feel if I didn't bathe as soon as possible—if I can even call it bathing?

I wash as best I can with the few inches of water around me. By the time I'm done, the once-clear liquid is one shade shy of black—a stark apposition to my hardly clean skin. Just as I reach to pull the chain, connected to the rubber stop, I hear the slap of a screen door.

As I stand up and peer through the bathroom window, a figure, obscured by the dirtied pane, shifts on the balcony of Lauren's home.

I pull the stop to the tub and step out and straight into my shoes. Despite how cold the water was only minutes prior, sweat pours from my head. I grab my towel and dry off only enough to call it done, then slip my shoes through my shorts—but I trip as I rush to the back door. I regain my footing and walk onto the balcony as I pull down my shirt from overhead. My hair is soaked, and my clothes are already damp against my skin, wet from the Southern heat.

Maybe she's back to check on things?

I strain my eyes.

From what I can tell, it isn't Shadow. Cotton wouldn't go over there without me. It has to be her.

I wave but get nothing in return.

I push my hands back through my half-wet, half-oily hair and march down the stairs, then toward the Roux house. The waterline of the bayou is back to its usual self, minus the well-defined shoreline and standing trees. As I get closer, I realize it isn't Lauren; hell, it isn't a woman.

"Hey," I call out, walking to the stairs that lead to the balcony. "Can I help you?"

It's a kid—late teens, maybe. He stops at the edge of the balcony, leans forward, and looks down at me. "Hi."

"Can I help you?" I ask again.

"Yes. You seen Lauren around?"

I walk up the stairs and meet him on the balcony. From the looks of it, he too has had a hellish few days. His disheveled, dirty-blond hair is nothing more than a tattered bird's nest, his jeans are unkempt and caked in crusted mud from the knees down, and his shirt is stained with more than a day's worth of sweat. He adjusts the black backpack on his shoulders and looks around, pulling at his knotted hair in what appears to be a nervous habit.

"No, I haven't, actually. I've been looking for her myself." The kid looks familiar, but I can't place him. "How do you know Lauren?"

He runs the straps of the backpack through his bony, pale hands and looks at my house, then back at the Roux home. "She's my cousin." He holds out his hand. "I'm Cody." His whitish-gray, fishlike eyes meet my own. He doesn't blink.

"Lance." We shake hands. From the look of his thin, deficient skin, he's been hunkered down inside for more than a few days.

"Yes, I thought so."

I swear I know him. At the very least, I've seen him before.

"You ain't heard from her at all?" I say.

His hand is cold, and his grip is certainly that of a teenager. By no means am I a big guy, but his hand crumples under my own.

"Unfortunately, no." He points past my house and a bit skyward. "I live down at the end of Thompson Road, right past the Bayou Liberty bridge. We touched base once she got back in town a couple weeks ago, after her dad passed away, but I was starting to get worried with the storm and all. Especially with her being by herself."

"Same."

"As I'm sure you already know, she's a stubborn one. We tried to get her to leave, or at the very least stay with me and my parents, but she wasn't having it."

Aside from her mom and dad, Lauren had been rather reserved about her family before I left town all those years back. But then again, she was a teen herself at the time. The only other family I saw her with then was her cousin Brody, who lives at the end of Thompson Road as well. Or at least, she did.

"You aren't related to Brody, are you?" I ask.

He nods and points at me. "Yes. Brody is my mother," he says in a flat voice.

I look back to Dubois Road and the destruction beyond it, as far as I can see. The clamor of generators and chainsaws is gearing up yet again for another day of the neighborhood clawing its way back to some shred of normalcy—which is undoubtedly far from its grasp.

"It's quite a hike from the end of Thompson Road," I say. "You must have gotten an early start."

"Yes." He gestures to the road beyond the cemetery. "You're not missing anything. It's all the same as what you see right here. It's even worse once you get closer to the boat launch."

"I'm sure."

"You look around inside yet?" I say, glancing to the Roux home.

"Yes. She's definitely not here, which has me worried even more, considering she said that she was gonna stay behind and ride it out."

"Me and Cotton, our neighbor, had a look around twice already, but we don't know where she's at either. I was thinking she might be with your mom, or someone might have come and got her as soon as things started to die down."

"Maybe," he says. "I'm not sure who that would've been, though. Definitely wasn't us."

We walk down the stairs and onto the front porch. He sets

down his bag next to the broken window that leads into the dining room.

Then he continues. "The footprints upstairs, though. Someone else was here."

"That's what me and Cotton were thinking."

He leans against the house with his hands at his side, looking out at the cemetery.

"You said Cotton's y'all's neighbor?"

"Yeah."

"Where's he live at?"

I point to the other side of my home. "Right over there."

"Y'all ain't seen nobody else?"

"No, not really." Then I remember Shadow, who's inevitably around no matter what. "Actually, their groundskeeper, or helper, or whatever you wanna call him, lives right there on the other side of the cemetery." I point in that direction. "That's Shadow, Cotton's brother."

The kid looks that way.

"Where's your folks at, anyways? They at home?" I say.

He pauses, his attention fixated on the trail to Shadow's treehouse.

"Cody?"

He eases his way out of whatever thought he was in. "Yeah?"

"Your family at home?"

"Sorry. Yes, they're still there—worried, of course. I told them I would check on Lauren if it would make them feel better. It's an easy walk until you hit Live Oak Lane, then it's a nightmare getting around all the trees. Everyone's doing a decent job getting a lane cut down all the roads, though."

I feel bad for the kid. I can tell just by looking at him that he's not cut out for what we're going through, or for the hike he's had to make just to get here, much less getting back home.

"I tell you what, why don't you come on over to my place, and we can get you something to eat and drink. I got some water and MREs left over from yesterday."

He looks through the broken window and into the dining room, then up to the patio ceiling, as if he can see straight through to the second floor of the home. "What if she *is* here?"

"We've looked. No one's here."

He wipes the corner of his eye, but I can't tell if he's sweating or if the circumstances are toying with his emotions. Who sends their teenager into the aftermath of a hurricane, alone, to check on family?

"We can wait for her at my place," I say.

With some hesitation, as if he's forcing himself, he glances in my direction. "Maybe I should stay here."

His pale, sickly skin shimmers in the heat. His breathing turns rapid and shallow, and his legs look like they just might give out. He shoves the words from his mouth. "How well . . ." He pants and runs his forearm across his brow. "How well do you really know—"

The kid leans back against the home and eases himself to the muddy ground. He gasps for air through pursed lips, his eyes unmoving. He fumbles for his bag on the ground next to him.

"Hey, are you okay?"

He grabs the backpack and unzips the small front pocket, then pulls out an orange pill bottle. Two, maybe three pills rattle inside.

He breathes like a fish out of water, flopping on a sunbaked dock.

He struggles and fails to open the bottle. Then he holds the container out toward me and shakes it. I grab it and twist open the top, then hand it back.

He fishes one of the round pills from inside and slaps his palm against his mouth. His hands shake as he searches the bag again, but he comes up empty-handed—so he swallows the pill dry.

"Come on," I say. "Let's get you something to drink." I step away but stop and turn back.

He doesn't move. He doesn't flinch.

He just sits in the mud, his eyes wide—fearful and white, unmoved by the gnats drawn to the moisture on his face. The kid drags the backpack up to his chest and squeezes it with both arms. Slowly, he turns his head up to the ceiling.

The gnats touch and go at the edge of his eyelids.

"You go ahead. I'll catch up," he says.

EIGHTEEN

October 1996

Texas was another world.

Aunt Ninette was cooking dinner inside. I was sitting on the back porch of the ranch house, thinking about how I'd ended up so involved with the business of my extended family.

I had left Slidell eight years ago. After nearly a decade, the memory of Uncle Holden still lingered in the hallways of the home—in every chair of every room. The back patio where he had spent most of his time was damn near exactly the same: the European mounts of deer he had harvested on the property, hung at length above the inside of the patio screen; the smoker-barbeque pit in the corner, surrounded by half a dozen rocking chairs; the stainless-steel fridge, which Aunt Ninette kept packed to the gills with his go-to beers; and a laminated map of the ranch with all of the hunting stands labeled, framed under a glass tabletop at the center of the porch. The same glass that, somehow, was unscathed after hundreds of drunken clients had celebrated their successful harvests.

Uncle Holden's cancer had been far worse than anyone expected, his doctors included. He passed away just three months after I arrived at the ranch—but on his own terms, lounging on the sofa with his Natty Light and oxygen mask, smoking like the freight train that he was.

Aunt Ninette's teasing still echoed throughout the home. *Your stubborn ass is gonna blow yourself up, Holden. Are you too sick to see the goddamn oxygen tank? Your eyes failing now, too?*

And his response. *Shut the hell up, Ninette. Ain't nobody asking you how to kill me. I'm more than capable of doing that all on my own.*

The back-and-forth had been their own love language. *Oh, your dying ass loves me*, she would say.

He'd blow the smoke from his nose and over the cannula that delivered the much-needed air to his stubborn lungs. He'd hand me his empty beer can and rant about all the young, sexy women he would have preferred to be spending his dying days with. Then they'd kiss and curl up on the couch. Their banter and bickering was an honest type of love—playful spats I only hoped to one day share with a wife of my own.

Learning the ins and outs of the guided hunting business from Aunt Ninette had been rough at first; Uncle Holden hadn't had the energy for much at all, beyond his vague advice on guided hunting itself and how to work the food plots, both of which I figured out largely for myself. Not long after he had passed away, we hired the company's first outside employee—a young guy named Jake. He worked part time, and the three of us became a well-oiled team.

I heard the patio door open, and the footsteps grew louder from behind me.

"Here you go, hun," Aunt Ninette said, and she set down a plate of food. Her hand brushed my shoulder as she walked back inside. "Let me know if you need anything."

"Thank you."

The brisket sandwich steamed on a blue ceramic plate, next to the sweating and salted margarita. Aunt Ninette had spoiled me from day one.

After Uncle Holden had passed away, I imagined she needed someone to devote her time and attention to, someone to care for. As much as I had insisted that she didn't need to break her back day in and day out, serving me left and right, I eventually gave in. After a while, I realized that it was important to her, so I played along.

I took a sip of the margarita. The salt and lime mixed at the edge of my lips, and I closed my eyes as I savored the bittersweet end of another seven-day work week.

I thought back to the first six months. Tuesdays were slow because most hunts ended on a Sunday or Monday, so I'd head out to one of the box stands by myself.

Before living on the ranch, seeing that number and size of deer anywhere else would have blown my mind. And at first, it had. But after a while, it changed from an adrenaline rush to a unique kind of peace. Something I learned to covet. I'd sit out there for hours if there were no hunts on the schedule—thinking, writing in my journal, getting lost in the scenery and red-orange sunsets. Cactuses and dust could mesmerize, given the right backdrop.

In the beginning, I'd bring my rifle with me so Aunt Ninette would think that I was hunting, but after returning to camp enough times with nothing but stories for why I was empty-handed, she eventually caught on that I simply wanted to escape. And her questions had turned to smiles.

Eventually, Cotton had called and broken the news. I wasn't sure how he had found out, but Lauren was gone. Mr. Roux had sent her overseas to live with family. At least, that was what Cotton had heard. Apparently, she too had an aunt and uncle who were willing to take her in, only hers were in France. I couldn't prove it, and I suspected I would never know for certain, but I had my doubts that she'd moved willingly. She was far too content living in Slidell.

Just as I picked up the sandwich and the tang of barbeque hit my tongue, Aunt Ninette returned. She held out the home phone. "Telephone," she said.

"Who is it?"

She lifted her brow. "Mr. Daiquiri himself." Then she walked inside.

Cotton rarely called.

"Hello?" I said.

At first, there was silence. Then I heard a breath that was heavy with guilt, or perhaps worry. Either way, I was unsure of what the quiet meant, but I was no longer hungry.

"Hey, Lance."

Shit. I don't think Cotton had ever called me "Lance."

"Hey. Everything okay?"

Another pause. "Ya got a minute? You sitting down?"

I didn't need to respond. He wasn't waiting for me to get comfortable.

"It's ya dad, Lance. I think ya need to come on home for a while."

"What happened? What's wrong? Is he okay?"

His hesitation was uneasy, like pulling a knife out one inch of ill-sharpened steel at a time. He didn't sound like himself.

"I'm not sure, Lance. But ya need to come on home. Ya dad's gone missing."

Surely, my hearing had failed me.

Aunt Ninette must have heard me talking. She returned and sat next to me.

"What do you mean 'missing'?"

She put her hand over her mouth and leaned forward.

"He's gone," Cotton said. "I know ya got a lot going on over there, but ya need to make a trip home. Okay? Ya dad's been missing for nearly three days. Slidell PD is on their way over now, but it'd be nice to have ya here. There's no one else."

"But what happened? How do you know he's missing? There's no way that he—"

"Just come on home, Lance. I'll be here."

The look on my face must have been nothing short of get-me-the-hell-home, because Aunt Ninette grabbed the phone from my ear and began pacing the porch as she spoke with Cotton. As I sat there and thought about it, my mind jumped to the obvious. Suddenly, my shoulders fell, and I was sure it was all a mistake. It was too big of a coincidence.

I jumped up and grabbed the phone from Aunt Ninette.

"Cotton, what about the storm? Josephine just rolled through the gulf. He's probably just out helping someone. You know how he is when it comes to those storms. Hell, you too. I'm surprised you ain't out helping people right now."

"Lance, it wasn't that bad. The storm did some damage to the coast, but we're fine. Slidell is fine. At least, it is here. He's never been gone like this and not asked me to watch the house, Lance. He's just . . . gone."

Dad always asked Cotton to keep an eye out when he wasn't around. Always.

I sank back into the chair, and Aunt Ninette grabbed the phone once more. She said something or another to Cotton about getting me home. All I remembered after that was blindly jamming clothes into a bag and lying in bed, staring at the ceiling until my alarm went off several hours later. I left first thing in the morning, before daylight.

I felt guilty the entire drive—Dad was missing, and all I could think about was that I was returning home for the first time in eight years.

And Lauren wouldn't be there.

NINETEEN

October 1996

I drove behind the cemetery and past the Roux house, its shadow towering over the fence at the edge of the property. Stopping in front of my childhood home, I threw the car into park.

Cotton was right—it was as if Dad had just up and left without a trace. At least from my view inside of the car, the house looked no different than it had eight years ago. Like the ghostly shell of my upbringing, red door and all.

I stepped out and walked to the front door. I pulled my keys out of my pocket and, out of habit I suppose, without really thinking about it, grabbed the one on my keychain that had faded almost entirely from a blinding, finished nickel to an antiqued, dull brass. I reached to unlock the door.

But what if it was open? Dad never left the house unlocked.

I palmed the key and turned the doorknob—the open doorknob.

Then I pushed the slender and faded wine-red door and stepped inside. It smelled about right, like beer and, well, more beer, but no Dad. I flicked on the light switch in the den, and the room drowned in a warm and calming amber.

"Dad?"

Keeping with the times must have run in the family. Just like Aunt Ninette kept the ranch as Uncle Holden had left it, our home was no different from the way I remembered it all those years back. Dark, smokey, and a signature '60s motif—original, down to every tile and fixture.

As I made my way through the house, nothing really screamed "missing dad" other than the fact that nothing looked out of place, and he was nowhere in sight. Maybe that *was* something.

No sooner had I walked into the kitchen to check the wall calendar next to the fridge—the one Dad updated religiously—than I heard the rocks shifting beneath tires out front of the house. I moved to the window and looked out to the driveway, where that Rolls-Royce parked in front of the Roux house. The suit-and-tie, pressed and clean as ever, walking like a featured memory on the big screen in my head, sauntered from the car and disappeared behind the same old fence.

I went back to the calendar in the kitchen and scanned what Dad had listed for the month. Nothing jumped out as important at first, but what I did notice was that nothing was on the books for the last two weeks. I flipped back to the previous month, and the month before that. Not a single week had more than two days unmarked. He'd written down even the most trivial of tasks. The last note caught my eye: *fix dock*, scheduled exactly two Saturdays ago to the day. Not a word after.

Dad always said that the dock out back was neutral ground, something that didn't belong to the Rouxs nor the Dubois family alone. That left two people who might have known about the repairs—Ed Roux and Cotton. If Dad was planning on fixing the dock himself, he surely would've asked Cotton for help. It was possible that Mr. Roux was planning to fix it, but it was unlikely. If that was the case, why would Dad have it on *his* calendar? I thought manual labor was beneath Ed Roux, and I doubted people like him wasted their money on what could have been paid for by lesser neighbors, who'd end up doing it on their own anyway. And he never would have asked Dad for help.

I walked out of the kitchen and onto the porch. From there,

I could see it—the tattered dock and accompanying rope swing, hanging over the bayou, its reflection lifeless. Unchanged after all those years.

Dad didn't just up and leave. He had things to do. Drinks to sip. Fish to catch. Suns to watch as they plummeted beyond the reeds. Leaving without a word, leaving things unfinished—that wasn't like him.

Wherever he was at, someone knew.

I stepped off of the porch and walked to the driveway, then around the pair of mailboxes—one a new form of black steel, the other crumbling to a burnt-orange tarnish in the Southern humidity.

As I lifted the steel knocker on the tall double door, I realized that if Mr. Roux answered, it would be the first time we had spoken. All those years he had stood out back, watching from the porch of his three-story home, and we had never talked. Not once. Even my waving had gone unacknowledged.

What the hell was I going to say? What was I doing?

I dropped the metal against the door, and I could hear the three thuds echo from inside.

There was no answer, so I waited. As I lifted the knocker yet again, I heard a string of hollow footsteps, but the figure who approached the door could never have afforded a suit. I should've half expected it. The door opened, and there Shadow stood. He ran his forearm over the edge of his mouth.

He grunted, looking behind me to the driveway. "You lost, Lance Dubois?"

"Mr. Roux home?"

He lifted a beer bottle to his lips and spit. A thick liquid swashed inside of it, as he adjusted the lump behind his lower lip.

"What do you w-w-w-w-w-want?"

From the sound of it, some things really hadn't changed.

"I need to talk with Mr. Roux."

What I felt like saying was, *What are you doing answering the Roux door?* But I decided against it for obvious reasons.

"Sure," he said. "If you wanna tell me what it is you're d-d-d-doing here."

He stepped forward and bypassed the bottle altogether, spitting some of the dip onto the porch, a trace of spittle hanging carelessly from his chin. As he moved within arm's reach, I noticed that I was now taller than him, and I had a feeling that he realized it, too. I was no longer Lance the neighbor kid. He had to look up at me now. It seemed as though he wanted to say more, perhaps prod a little like he used to.

So, I stood there, and let what I had said simmer.

He licked his lips and opened his mouth to speak, but the sound of soles echoing off of the marble floor behind him cut short the moment.

"Now, now, Shadow," Mr. Roux said. His voice dragged, formidable and deep. "No need to give the boy a hard time."

He moved into the doorway, and Shadow stepped back. "What can I do for you? *Boy.*" His eyes painted me from head to toe, from my work boots up to my flannel shirt. His disapproval of my attire was evident.

"I'm looking for my dad. I was wondering if you—"

I stopped as he pulled that gold pocket watch from his vest pocket. "Well, go on," he said.

"And I was wondering if you've heard from him."

Shadow huffed in the background. Roux glanced over his shoulder and offered up a half-baked sneer.

"Now, why would I have heard from your father?"

It was Shadow's turn to smirk now.

Roux checked the time, then snapped the watch closed. He

kept it in his hand and massaged the metal with his thumb, rubbing it like a lucky charm.

"I don't know, you're his neighbor." I spoke with as much respect as I was being given. "Aren't you?"

It was strange—watching Shadow watch us, standing behind the man like he was some sort of disease-ridden watch dog, his mouth salivating at the opportunity to get the better of someone. Anyone.

"I'm not sure I like your tone," said Mr. Roux.

"Yeah," Shadow added. "It's the tone."

"Have you seen him?"

Mr. Roux frowned and shrugged a shoulder. "Not lately. What's it to you?"

"Cotton hasn't heard from him in a few days. I just got back into town, but I wanted to check with you first to see if y'all've seen him around before I talk to the police."

Shadow mumbled in the background. "Few d-d-d-days, huh. Hardly a missing person."

Mr. Roux stepped forward and onto the front porch. He dropped the watch back into his vest pocket. What he did next shifted the slightly off-kilter conversation to something more.

The man stood next to me and turned to face his house, the two of us looking at Shadow as he stood in the foyer. His shoulder grazed mine—and his hand lightly dusted his coat where it had touched me. Then he leaned his head toward me as Shadow watched us. Grinning.

"I do not know where your father is," he said. He looked at Shadow. "Isn't that right?"

"That's right."

"But what I do know"—he spoke as if he were shielding our conversation from someone behind us—"is that this is the last time you set foot on my property."

A hand grabbed my shoulder and squeezed.

"Yeah, it is," Cotton said, grabbing the back of my neck and pulling me toward him. We turned, and he walked me to the driveway.

"What are you doing?" I said lowly. "Have you talked to Roux? What if he's seen Dad?"

"Keep walking," Cotton said sternly.

I glanced back at the house. Mr. Roux and Shadow stood side by side on the porch, watching us as we ambled farther down the gravel driveway. Roux pulled his pipe from his jacket pocket. He bit down on the stem and struck a match. Once we passed the mailboxes, Cotton stopped and faced me.

"What are ya doing?" he said.

"What does it look like? If anyone other than you knows where Dad is, it's him." I looked back. They stood there, watching us still. "Or that pet freak of his," I added.

"You should know by now that ya dad and him don't speak. Ed Roux ain't the type of person ya accuse of—"

"I'm not accusing him of anything, Cotton. Don't you wanna find my dad?"

"Of course I do, but that's what Slidell PD is for, my boy. Ain't nothing changed with Roux since the day ya left. He wasn't someone ya threaten then, and he ain't—"

"I'm not threatening any—"

"And he *ain't* someone ya mess with now."

"Okay, so what do you propose we do?"

"I say we head on back to my place and wait for the police to get here. Last I spoke to them, they said they'd be here around now." He thought on it for a second. "Maybe bringing ya back here so quick was a bad idea."

"Really, Cotton? Really? Because the last we spoke, you said it yourself: there is no one else."

"Come on. Let's wait over at my place."

Just as we turned to walk behind the house and toward Cotton's back yard, another car pulled into the driveway in front of the Roux home. We turned back.

As the vehicle came to a stop, a middle-aged woman stepped out of the car and opened the back door.

"Who's that?" I said.

She caught a brief glimpse of us standing in the yard. Then her focus shifted to the several bags inside the car, which she started to remove.

"No idea. But she's been coming around for a while. She started showing up years ago—not long after ya left, actually."

Mr. Roux and Shadow watched as the woman removed two armfuls of groceries from the back seat. Neither of them moved, not an inch.

"I guess he got lonely in that big-ass house with no one but your brother around," I said.

"Beats me."

She kicked the door of her car closed as she hugged the bags, the contents nearly spilling to the ground. The woman walked to the house as Mr. Roux and Shadow stood on the porch, looking straight at us. Just before she reached them, a box fell from one of the bags and onto the ground.

Only then did Shadow react with a sideways glance at his boss, and a shallow nod sent him into the yard.

He picked up the box of Cocoa Puffs and shoved it back into the bag before grabbing the woman by the arm and attempting to escort her inside. The lady snatched her arm back and pushed a bag of groceries into Shadow's hands.

Mr. Roux looked on.

TWENTY

August 31, 2005

Ostensibly, I'm not the only one looking for Lauren. The kid wanted to hang back for a minute at the Roux house, so I'm waiting for him at home. I stand on the porch and contemplate where the hell she could possibly be, much like I did with Dad all those years back. It's too familiar. Too terribly familiar.

As long as Cotton and I waited, and as much as we worked with law enforcement to find Dad over the course of those years, he never came home. I waited, though. I helped Aunt Ninette with the ranch as much as I could from Louisiana; as much as I wanted to be in Texas and continue with what I had helped build, I couldn't talk myself into going back.

It's only been two days since Katrina rolled through, so surely there's a logical explanation for her whereabouts. Certainly, she'll turn up sooner or later. After all, she hasn't exactly been forthcoming with me since she returned a few weeks ago. I can't blame her. I didn't exactly give her a proper goodbye at the end of that summer.

That kid, Cody, looked like he was about to have a damn near nervous breakdown next door, so I grab some water and extra MREs I have sitting around upstairs, then return outside to wait for him. Or maybe he was simply wrecked from the walk over. Either way, I feel bad for him. Both that he was sent over by himself, and that his cousin is missing.

In a way, I feel bad for myself, too. My whole world is turned inside out, as is everyone's around me, and all I can think about is her. Not the one who "got away," but the one I left.

The blond hair, washed-out eyes, thin build—I swear I've seen the kid before. If he's Brody's son, I've probably seen him in passing somewhere. But where? When?

With the answer set to roll from the tip of my tongue, he walks into the yard and toward me. He's carrying his backpack, and his demeanor is seemingly reined in.

"You good?" I say.

"Yes." His voice remains bland. "How about that water?"

I hand him one of the bottles I got from the lady with the red cross on her shirt. We sit in silence for what seems like minutes. Then, the queries start in.

"So, what are you doing, anyway?" he says.

"Well, we were able to clear most of the driveway, so I guess at this point we're just waiting for—"

"No." The kid looks next door to the Roux house. He lifts his chin and keeps it there. "Lauren. What are you doing with my cousin?"

I don't get it. We're neighbors. What am I supposed to be doing with his cousin?

"I don't follow."

He glances around. "From the looks of it, you have a lot more to worry about than some neighbor."

But Lauren isn't just "some neighbor." She's my . . . present—the fleeting splinter of time where the future, which I can't touch, meets the past, which is never more. More nights than not, that summer is the topic of my most lucid of dreams.

"Me and your cousin go way back. Turns out, we're a little more than neighbors." I don't realize how strange that sounds, until I say it. "Well, once upon a time. Maybe."

"More than neighbors, huh?" He finishes the water, crushes the bottle, then hands it back to me. "That's an interesting turn of phrase."

His eyes lock with mine, demanding more.

"But that was a long time ago," I add.

"Hm." He points to two of the MREs on the ground between us.

"Sure," I say.

"Sounds to me like it might not be all that long ago, Lance." He places the packages into his bag and zips it tight. "Yes?"

Before I can process what he said, he starts walking back to the Roux house. Just before he reaches the gravel drive, he turns around. His gaunt fingers grip the straps on his shoulders. "I think I'll wait for Lauren next door. If I know my cousin, she'll be back soon."

Cody turns away and strides to the Roux house once again, amid the fallen trees and endless debris. He walks through the chaos as if it's something of an afterthought.

What the hell was that?

As odd as the kid is, I hope he's right. It's only been two days, but still, no Lauren. As much as I hate to admit it, I need to start worrying about the obvious: minute by minute, my house is devolving into an uninhabitable purgatory. I can't leave even if I want to, given the state of the roads, but I can hardly bear staying. Even the second floor, which the water barely touched, is unendurable two days later.

Maybe Lauren should be the last thing on my mind.

I don't get it, though. She's been back in town for several weeks, and she's hardly given me a chance to speak with her. I guess I can't blame her. I know all too well what it's like to lose a father—even if he was someone like Ed Roux. I get it.

The second my foot hits the bottom stair to the balcony, I hear it—the kid shouting from the balcony across the way.

"Hey! Get over here!"

I can't hear all that he says next, but I do hear "Lauren."

"Hurry!"

I drop my water and run to the house without a second thought. I step through the jagged hole in the dining room wall of the Roux home, then turn to the stairs.

"Up here!"

We checked the second floor. And the third. What the hell did—

"Lance!"

I slip on the top step, my hands sliding across the damp there, as my knees hit the floor.

"Over here." I hear him behind me, in the hallway.

I regain my footing and turn the corner.

Never in a million years could I have expected it. I freeze, hesitant in the middle of the corridor, the kid panting at the other end. I look past him, then again at his frenzied and slack-jawed face, those white eyes now burning wide.

He stumbles over his words. "What do . . . what—what do we do?"

I run past him to the other end of the hallway—to where the thin floor-to-ceiling mirror is shattered. A deceptive door.

The suffocating padded walls envelop me as I step inside of the dark room. To my right is a square of broken CCTV monitors, to my left a set of metal lockers. On the ground: Lauren, with her golden-brown hair strewn across the cement floor. Blood is smeared across her face. I kneel beside her, and as I do, she props herself up and onto her forearm.

"It's about time you showed up," she says.

And that's when it hits me.

part two

Lauren

TWENTY-ONE

August 27, 2005

F ather is beside me.

I take a seat in the wooden chair next to his recliner, as I always do once I clean the kitchen after breakfast. The television screen is empty, save the reflection of my dress and the hem that has inappropriately inched its way up my thigh. I slide it down so that it rests below my knee. My shoulders appear forward, so I roll them back and correct my posture; it always needs fixing.

I glance in Father's direction, hoping he appreciates my effort—but the television is off for a reason. The remote sits on the end table, on the other side of his recliner. I stand up and walk to the far side of his chair and grab the clicker. As I turn back, I see that Father is slouching, too.

His black-and-gold urn is leaning, so I set it straight in the corner of the leather chair.

Father always stressed the importance of watching the morning news. "How can you attack the day if you don't know what you're up against?" he'd say. It's part of my routine, now, even though I'm not crazy about it.

I sit down and turn on the news, pulling my shoulders back again. The first channel I land on is the "god-forsaken weather." At least, that's how Father used to phrase it—the longest-running lie that no one cares about.

I try another station, but the same advisory is on every one of them: *Hurricane Katrina, Category 3, MANDATORY Evacuation Notice for St. Charles Parish, St. Tammany Parish, and Plaquemines*

Parish. The message runs in a blue ribbon across the bottom of the screen, interrupting even the reruns on the non-news channels.

His laugh, even cremated—I can hear it like no other. "Mandatory evacuation," he'd say in a loathsome chuckle. "That must be for the Dubois clan. I guess that's what happens when you don't have a third floor." And he'd poke his finger at the ceiling.

I lean over and adjust the urn. Posture is more than an appearance. It's how the world treats you.

As I turn back to the television, the screen flashes to a satellite image, solid white bands circling over the Gulf. A perfectly defined eye at the center of the storm, spooling and spooling.

I hear the metal knocker drop against the front door, and the thud bounces from the marble floors. I flinch and look to the foyer.

Feet scurry above me, but they go silent at the top of the stairs.

"You there?" I hear a tentative voice from above. Then I look up to the corner of the living room where the small red light is blinking. In a way, it seems pointless now that he's gone.

"Yes."

It's not like you would answer the door if I wasn't.

I lean over the chair and place the remote back on the end table, facing it forward and aligned with the edges. "No . . . I'm not leaving," I say to Father.

Another slam of the knocker fills the room. As I walk to the door, he's peering through the frosted sidelights, the shadow of his hand cupped around the edge of his eye—a figure that is all too inquisitive.

"Lauren? Hello?" I hear from the porch.

My hand grabs the bronze handle, but I stop and adjust myself. I pull down my blouse so that my cleavage is front and center, and I drop my hair.

Another light blinks in the corner above the door. Watching.

The feet shuffle away from above, like a mouse through the attic.

"Sorry," I say, looking up, anticipating Father's disapproval. I lick my lips and push my breasts higher in my bra as the light blinks next to the black lens, watching the foyer from above. No one is at the other end, now. I draw a deep breath and reach for the handle yet again.

I open the door, but Lance looks surprised that I did. I put on my best I'm-busy look and lean against the inside of the doorframe.

"Hey," he says.

"Hi," I hurry out.

He glances past me and into the kitchen. "You got a minute?" He steps forward, but I move onto the porch and ease the door shut behind me.

"What is it?"

I'd be lying if I said it wasn't peculiar—parting ways without warning so long ago, and now he's standing in front of me, seemingly worried, like no time at all has passed between us. As if the passage of years is nothing more than a minor consideration.

I fold my arms behind my back and lean against the outside of the house. The humidity sweeps across my chest, and the wind rustles my dress. His eyes move down across me, below my chin.

"Did you hear about the storm?" he says. "Are you leaving?"

He isn't allowed to worry. Not anymore—at least, not about me. Besides, there's more than merely me to worry about now.

"And why would I do that?"

He only looks at me with those milky gray eyes. His ruffled, dirty hair blows in the same direction as the fabric across my thighs.

"It's supposed to get pretty bad," he says. "You're here alone. I'm just worried is all."

"Oh?"

"And besides," he continues, "you've only been back in town for a few weeks. I'm sure you've got enough on your plate as it is."

I force the corners of my mouth upward, but they fall soon after.

"I think I'll be okay, Lance. Really."

He steps closer. "At least let me help you out, get everything boarded up and ready for you. Surely, you can't do that all on your own."

"No, but Shadow's around."

He only nods and looks back, past the cemetery.

"Okay."

I turn to go back inside, but his hand catches my arm. "Hey," he says.

I look down at the way his fingers hold me, but he lets go. His touch is mostly resentment, tainted with a tinge of craving— but I know better, by now.

"I'm sorry about your dad. I know y'all were close."

I'm not sure how to respond to that, so I don't.

"I know you have a lot going on, with him passing away and all, but if you need anything, I'm right next door. I'm free if you need me. And Cotton's still around, too."

Oh, the irony.

"I know, Lance. Like you said—I've been back for a few weeks. I know."

He puts up his hands, palms out. "Okay. Okay." Then he points to his house. "I'm right here."

"Thank you."

I turn around and open the door. He bypasses the walkway altogether and strolls through the front yard, toward the fence. As I step inside, I decide to add a touch of reassurance to our interaction. I pause in the doorway and let the breeze mingle with my dress, lifting my skirt only enough to tug at what I'm sure he thinks is possible. Then I lean my head back out of the door, just enough for him to see me watching.

As I thought he would, he pauses at the fence and glances back. Once I'm sure that I've got his attention, if only for a split second, I step inside.

I lean back against the inside of the door.

Lance zero, Roux one.

TWENTY-TWO

July 1988

I could tell by the way Lance had fumbled his hands over my body that it was his first time, but that didn't matter. It was perfect—the sailboat, the moment, and everything else.

Together, *we* were perfect.

The second I left his back yard and rounded the fence, I was caught off guard by how dark my house was, save for a single ocher glow smoldering in father's study on the second floor.

After feeling my way along the fence, I stepped beneath the porch and attempted to open the back door, but it was locked.

Surely it wasn't that late. Were we together for that long?

As I slid my key into the door, I remembered the alarm. What other choice did I have, though? I grabbed the handle and pushed down on the lock with my thumb. The door broke open, and the cold air swept over the inside of my legs—a stark contrast to the heat of his body against mine only moments prior.

But . . . no alarm.

I eased the door shut, turned the lock, and tiptoed through the kitchen and up the stairs. The house could not have been quieter.

As I edged my way down the hallway and toward my room, I felt the sweat that had smeared between us drying on my neck and chest, tacky in the frigid indoor air. The saltiness lingered on my lips, along with the grip of his hand around my neck.

Before I crossed in front of Father's office, I stopped and

closed my eyes, running my tongue over my top lip. I could still taste him. The way his mouth—

"Get in here." The grit in Father's voice filled the hall, even at such a middling volume.

I rounded the corner and stepped into the room. Father was sitting on a stool at the corner bar. If I had to guess, I would've said that he'd left the alarm off intentionally, and that he'd locked the door on purpose too. He'd known I'd be home at one point or another. Based on the amount of smoke filling the room, he had been waiting for quite some time.

I already knew what conversation lay ahead, and it wasn't Father's glare, or his waiting up, that surprised me. It was Shadow—standing behind the bar with a towel slung over his shoulder, pouring Father a drink. A Jack on the rocks, by the look of it.

"Sit down," Father said. A demand, not a suggestion.

Shadow pushed the drink forward then stepped back, farther behind the bar, into the corner of the room and the darkness that lingered there. I could no longer see his face, only his hand, which reached into his shirt pocket and removed a can of dip.

Father swirled the drink on the bar top and drew a deep drag from his pipe, blowing the smoke over the glass that sweated before him.

He spoke while looking at the drink. "You have fun?"

Shadow mumbled to himself in the corner of the room. "I sure hope so." His hand grabbed a pinch of the dip and lifted it to his mouth, which was hidden deep in the black.

Of course, I couldn't answer the question—not without lying or coming off as haughty.

Father pushed the glass in front of me and took another drag from his pipe. "Have a drink," he said.

Just like that, the conversation I knew was coming—the one I so terribly dreaded, barreling down the tracks, full speed ahead, smoke and all—kicked off.

"Go ahead," he said. "Drink it."

The shadow in the corner of the room, behind the bar, grumbled with delight.

"No, thank you," I said as politely as possible. As much as I knew that that response was a mistake, deep down, I hoped he would let it go.

Father's mouth formed a mordant grin as he leaned forward, inching the glass farther in my direction.

"Drink."

I knew what was happening. Father didn't want me drinking any more than he wanted me smoking. Or dipping. Or lying.

Or sleeping around.

He pushed it again, with a single finger. "Come on," he said softly, as if coaxing a sheltered dog to eat for the first time in days.

Shadow lifted an empty beer bottle to his lips and spit. I still couldn't see his face, but the sound alone sent an uneasiness deep into the pit of my stomach. The woody, thick aroma of tobacco surrounded me in every direction.

I suspected Shadow didn't need to be there, but I knew Father well enough. I knew that whatever this was, the end goal was to teach me a lesson, part of which was the humiliation of having someone else in the room.

There was no way around it, so I grabbed the glass.

Father leaned back and bit down on his pipe, the smoke billowing from his flared nose. His were the only eyes I could see, but I felt the weight of both men, staring, bearing down on me as I lifted the glass to my lips.

All of us had our virginity—it was only a matter of

perspective. Lance was a virgin when it came to sex, Brody when it came to smoking, among other temptations. And me? Alcohol. I'd never cared to touch the stuff. Didn't plan on it, either. There was just something that rubbed me the wrong way about voluntarily dumping poison into my body. But hey, to each their own, I guess. If you're that gloomy . . .

Father knew it, too—my aversion to it.

I tilted back the drink. At first, it wasn't that bad. Once I swallowed, though, it was all over. I leaned forward and gagged, holding back the vomit that tore at the back of my throat worse than the drink itself.

Shadow huffed from the corner. "Serves you r-r-r-right." He spit.

Father leaned forward yet again. He pushed the glass closer. I looked up, but all I saw was a smoldering pipe through my blurry eyes and fallen hair.

"Finish it."

Shadow spoke in a lowly tenor. "Ain't that right."

"Come on," Father said. "Half down, half to go."

Hesitating would have been the worse move. Either way, I was drinking it. That I was sure of—as were they.

I grabbed the glass and knocked it back without so much as a sip first.

"Yeah. There we go," said Shadow.

Father grabbed the glass and turned it upside down, slamming it onto the bar. The ice shattered into melting shards over the two of us. "Sit up straight," he said in a taut, dry voice. "It's bad enough you can't hold your liquor."

"Ain't that r-r-r-right," I heard from the corner.

Father struck a match and relit his pipe. He waved out the flame, then tossed the smoking stick onto the bar before sliding the glass in Shadow's direction. Only for a moment did the man step out from the corner of the room. He pulled a fresh glass from behind the bar and poured another drink, sliding it in front of father. A trail of condensation smeared across the otherwise pristine and antique bar top.

"So. You're a grown woman, now. Is that right?" Father said.

"No, sir."

"Ah. So, I'm confused, then." He sipped the freshly poured whiskey. "What is my teenage daughter doing running around with some boy in the middle of the night? And the Dubois kid, for that matter."

"He's just a friend."

"A friend, is he? Ah, okay, okay. I see. And what do you think your mother would say about you whoring around with your . . . *friend?*"

He hadn't mentioned her in over a year. Not a word.

"Honestly, Father, he's just a—"

He slid the nearly full drink across the bar and into the wall, where it shattered more violently than I could've imagined. Shadow didn't flinch at first, but then he pulled the towel from his shoulder in a nonchalant way and began cleaning the mess like he had known it was coming.

"You see," Father continued, "I didn't raise no whore, and I sure as hell didn't raise a liar."

"Yes, sir."

He leaned his head to the side. I kept my eyes cast downward. "And there's nothing worse than a liar."

All I could do was nod. Nothing else was remotely appropriate.

"If there's one thing you will learn from your father," he said, "it's how lucky you are to have been born into this family. The *Roux* family."

"Ain't that right," Shadow grumbled.

"And the last person who will tarnish this family's name is my one and only daughter."

"Yes, Father."

He let his words linger for what I presumed was dramatic effect. "There's two things in this world that any one person has to go on." He pointed the pipe my way. "The way you carry yourself, and your family name. You understand?"

"Yes, Father."

He pulled down his vest and adjusted his tie. For the thinnest of moments, if I wasn't mistaken, his softer side began to show.

"Perhaps one day, you'll understand where I'm coming from, love."

I had to remind myself that it was Father in front of me and not some other parent. Not anyone else. As harsh as his advice had seemed at times, he only meant the best for me.

He was right: I was his one and only daughter. His only *child*. Period. His way of raising me, especially after Mother died, was just a little stiff. I couldn't fault him for that. Not any man. Not after what he had been through.

Father only meant the best for me.

"Off to bed," he said.

I pushed my hair behind my ears, some of the strands clinging to my lips and face. As I stood from the barstool and turned to the door, he stopped me.

"Excuse me. Are you forgetting something?"

I turned back and gave him a peck on the cheek. The raw scent of tobacco clung to his skin like an aftershave.

"Goodnight, Father."

As I reached the door, he offered up one more piece of advice.

"Lauren."

"Yes, Father?"

"Wash that smell off of you before you get in bed. You stink."

He turned to Shadow and struck another match.

"Yes, Father."

TWENTY-THREE

August 27, 2005

A mountain of gray-brown sand casts a menacing shadow over Catch-em's shed at the boat launch.

I park my car under one of the century-old oak trees between St. Genevieve Church and the docks. Moss hangs in a torn curtain, swaying in a gentle, deceptive breeze. If not for the news, the day would be merely another serene sky, lingering over the glassy bayou—but it's anything but. The approaching storm sends out no forewarning, no messenger to announce the sinister clouds ahead. Only calm.

As I walk over to the dozen or so volunteers who are filling sandbags at a backbreaking pace, I see Catch-em standing next to his battered Chevy pickup. He's handing the bags to the volunteers, one by one, as they shovel heap after heap of sand into the bulky white sacks.

Woody hops over the piles of empty bags in the bed of the rusted truck, watching the process intently with his head following each and every sack as they exchange hands from Catch-em to the shovelers.

One of the bags slips from the vehicle and floats to the ground like one of his feathers, causing the duck to flap his one good wing and quack in a bossy rhythm. He bounces up and down on the edge of the tailgate, his eyes darting between the bag and his handler. A puppy waiting for the ball to be thrown.

"Boy, I done told you," Catch-em says. "This ain't no job for the crippled." He gestures the elderly bird farther into the bed of the pickup. Woody shakes his head and waves the man off, then pecks at the plumage of his mangled wing, which is ruffled by his let-me-do-it temper.

"Hi, Catch-em," I say. "You have enough to go around?"

"Lauren." He nods in my direction. "It's been a while. And yes, ma'am, we do. Got enough here to cover this side of the bayou, I would think."

"Well, if you don't mind, I'll take a few myself."

"You know about how many?"

"As many as my trunk will hold, I suppose."

Catch-em seals the deal with a lift of his hand, and Woody barks at me in an ostensible agreement.

I can't believe the man is still here after all these years, handing out launch tickets and scooping bait from the same live well. He's got to be pushing seventy at this point, but he doesn't look a gray hair over that summer. I turn to the bayou behind me.

The marina across the way is lifeless for the most part, the boats tied down in their slips. A few men scramble between the docks, securing whatever is lying about. I step closer to the water's edge.

I can still see us in the boat, muddling along the shore with the bucket of bait between us. It was a different time, though. And circumstances have changed us—well, they've changed me.

Surely not for the better.

"Lauren?" I hear from behind me.

I turn around. "Yes, Catch-em?"

The man hesitates, seemingly thinking more than what he's willing to say. He turns back to his shed, then again to me.

"Would you like me, or someone else, to help you out with these? Follow you home and give you a hand, maybe?"

"Thank you, but I'll be okay."

"You sure? This is a lot to handle by yourself." His focus

shifts around the gravel lot, then to his rubber boots. "I'm sorry to hear about Mr. Roux, by the way. That man did his fair share around here for sure."

Well, that's one way to segue.

"Thank you, Catch-em. I appreciate it. If I end up needing help, I think I have someone who can give me a hand."

"You holding up okay since you got back? I can only imagine how much you got going on after being away for so long."

"Yes, I'm making it work. How about yourself?" I do my best to steer the conversation elsewhere. Anywhere, other than how bad I did or didn't have it over the last several years. "You not tired of this launch yet?" I glance around. "I thought that bird of yours would be running things by now."

Catch-em huffs. "Yeah, that duck is too big for his britches. His cranky ass will outlive me at this rate." He waves me back toward him. "Come on. Let's get these bags loaded up for you."

I walk to my car, then back it up to the volunteers. They load the trunk with as much as it can handle. I glance in the side mirror as one of them slams the trunk shut, and Catch-em ambles to my window from the back of the car. He leans down, his hand on the roof.

"Thank you," I say. "And be careful. This storm's supposed to be something else."

"Of course. And you take care of that house. It's a lot to keep up with."

"Yes, sir."

As I pull out of the lot, I see Catch-em in my rearview mirror, standing in front of the pointed mountain of sand. One of the volunteers steps up beside him, and Catch-em points at me. A look of concern drips from his weathered face.

I pull into the driveway. Shadow has taken it upon himself to start boarding up the windows. The house is my responsibility, now. Catch-em was right—it is a lot to keep up with.

It's even more when you and your neighbor have a past.

"I see you got started without me," I say, walking to the front porch. Shadow sets his screw gun onto the ground with a quickness, like he was caught red-handed trying to break into the house instead of board it up.

"Yes, ma'am. I hope you don't m-m-m-mind."

It's clear that Shadow doesn't plan on going anywhere. Maybe it's something I can get used to. Perhaps having him around is something I can use to my advantage?

"Of course not. I wasn't expecting you, is all."

"I apologize." He toys with his thinning hair. "I figured I'd get started sooner rather than later with how quick this storm is rolling in."

"I see."

He looks past me, to the car. "Can I help you with anything?"

"I got some sandbags from the boat launch, but they can wait until you're done with the windows." I move to unlock the door. "Thank you for the help, Shadow."

"Yes, Miss Lauren." He steps toward me and reaches out, his dirty blue shop rag in hand. "Forgive me for asking," he says timidly, "but . . . do you think there's any way that I can s-s-s-s-s— Would it be possible for me to maybe s-s-s-stay here? In the house? Tomorrow night? This storm is supposed to be pretty bad."

He looks out past the cemetery, to his treehouse on the other side of the graves, buried beyond the wood line. Then back at me.

My mind scrambles for the appropriate response.

"I'm sorry, Miss Lauren. I shouldn't have asked." He turns back to his work, wiping his head with the rag before tucking it into his back pocket. He picks up his drill from the floor.

"Shadow, I'm sorry, but Father"—I'm not sure how to phrase it, exactly—"Father only just passed. You know?"

Hopefully, he can read between the lines. He's just as familiar with Father's rules as I am.

He pulls a screw from his pocket, twirling it in his hand, running his thumb across the threads. The metal presses into his skin until his finger pulses a snowy crimson.

"Yes, ma'am." A grin creeps its way to the surface of his crooked smile, but I can tell that it's forced. "I got it." He scratches his forehead with the head of the metal hardware. "I got it."

"Please, Shadow. I don't mean anything by it. Even though Father is gone, this is still his home."

"Ain't that right," he mutters to himself. I'm not sure I heard him clearly.

"I'm sorry?"

That faux smile shows up yet again. "I understand," he says, speaking to the board as he lifts it to the window and shoves it against the house.

I didn't ask for any of this, but I have a gut feeling that keeping Shadow around might be more tedious than I thought.

TWENTY-FOUR

August 1988

It had been days since I'd heard from Lance—and even longer since I'd seen him.

Father was sitting in his recliner, glued to the ditzy blond and her ramblings on the morning news, gnawing on his pipe like a Catahoula on a deer leg. I finished cleaning the last of the dishes from breakfast, along with the rest of the kitchen, and set the table for dinner; Father never acknowledged lunch. Lunch was more of a fend-for-yourself sort of meal. At least ever since Mother died.

"Damn weather's never right," I heard from the living room. "Not even in the same ballpark."

I felt his eyes upon me, like he was waiting for me to respond. I folded the dish towel and placed it on the counter, flush with the edge of the sink—just how he had taught me. Then I poured him a glass of sweet tea from the fridge and walked into the living room, setting his drink on the end table before sitting down in my chair next to his recliner.

Father lit his pipe and jabbed it at the television, a gesture he usually reserved for the hired help. "These forecasts, I tell you . . . it's like watching some voodoo crapshoot."

He swiveled his head in disapproval. As his glance caught me, he must have sensed something afoot.

"What's *your* problem this morning?" he asked.

I rolled back my shoulders.

Was it the glistening of my face? Surely not—I cleaned the kitchen every morning. Was it the sudden onset of fatigue he could somehow sense in my expression? Possibly. The nausea, perhaps?

"I'm okay, Father. Can I get you anything else?"

The huff and billow of smoke that followed was an apparent "no." His eyes returned to the news.

"You know," he said, "you're at that age where a sense of responsibility will do you some good."

Was he referring to what he already had me doing, or what he thought I *should* have been doing?

He shifted in his chair. "Your mother isn't around anymore to be an example of what women do. Or maybe I should say 'what a girl does to become a woman.' You do realize that you have responsibilities around here for a reason. Yes?"

That was the second time he'd mentioned her in recent weeks, up from . . . never.

"Yes, Father."

"With that said," he continued, "I think it's time you start thinking about what you're going to do about your education. I imagine that's what your mother would be telling you right about now."

Where was that coming from?

"And I think nursing might be the appropriate route," he said. "You know, follow in your mother's footsteps. Either that or become a doctor."

He sipped from the glass of tea, then turned and looked out the window behind us. "You see this? The damn sun is taunting us. And they're calling for inches of rain? Damn meteor-*whatever* doesn't have a damn clue what they're talking about."

"What if nursing isn't for me?"

He set down the glass without looking at it. "'Isn't for you'? As far as I'm concerned, lawyer, doctor, and engineer are alternative options, but being a girl and all, nursing is your best bet. Accounting, maybe, but that's only if you're good with numbers, and well, let's face it—that most certainly is not you. Not *my* daughter."

"But what if I—"

"Besides, you need to do something that will help this town. Nursing is the perfect career path. You follow in your mother's footsteps with nursing, and you follow in mine by working for the community."

"Yes, Father."

"Now, tell me. What's your deal this morning? Whatever it is, I can see it all over your face. And let me tell you, it doesn't suit you."

"Well, me and Lance have been—"

"No. No, ma'am. I don't think so." He pointed the pipe my way. "You need to stay away from that kid, you hear me? As a matter of fact, you can keep away from that side of the fence entirely. I don't want to see you with—"

"I'm only wondering if you've seen him. I haven't heard from him in a while, and I'm only worried is all."

"Little girl, the only thing you need to be worried about is you—and this family. Not them. Not some no-name boy who doesn't have two pennies to rub together. You understand?"

"Yes, Father."

"I've bent over backward to make the Roux name mean something, to build a reputation in this town. So the least you can do is appreciate it and not throw it all away by getting mixed up with some kid—some boy who will do nothing but bring you down. You understand?"

"Yes, Father."

He crossed his legs and tapped the stem of the pipe against his ivory-colored teeth. "Now, get on out of here," he said. "Go and do something useful with yourself instead of . . . hell, just keep to yourself, Lauren. Focus on you, and that's all there is to it. Boys should be the last thing on your mind, you hear me? Plain and simple."

Of course, Lance was anything but plain, and the fact that he lived next door was far from simple.

Father was right about one thing, though. Maybe I should have appreciated what he'd done for me, as a single parent.

As I stood to leave, to "go and do something useful," I was both taken aback and bewildered by his need to say more.

"Just stay out of it."

—

If Father wouldn't tell me where Lance was, Marcus Dubois would—assuming either of them knew.

Much like anything in life, theory was easier than method, promises simpler than following through. Attending mass was easier than curbing temptation.

Agreeing with Father was easier than keeping away from someone who'd had their tongue down my throat only days prior.

So, I walked straight out of the back door and around the fence. Father wouldn't follow me—not during the news hour.

Lance's father had become like a second parent to me over the summer, as brief of a time as it had been. Neither Lance nor I had our mothers around—so our fathers were it. I adored my own father to the moon and back, albeit in somewhat of a reluctant, tough love kind of way. Marcus, on the other hand, was the easy-going type. A surrogate, so to speak.

Some guilt festered inside of me on the evenings I'd spend over there and not at home with Father. But Marcus gave me what Father couldn't—the gentle side of family life.

I knocked on the back door and listened to the footsteps from inside.

"Oh. Hey, Lauren," Marcus said once he opened the door.

"Hi. Do you have a minute?"

"Sure," he said in a flat tenor. He moved onto the porch and closed the door behind him.

His dry expression caught me off guard. I'd never seen Marcus without a smile, or at least a subsurface grin lurking beneath his typical come-on-in demeanor. His expression was different.

Maybe Father was right.

"Is Lance home?"

"Lance isn't here, Lauren. You should head on home."

Head on home?

"Do you know when he'll be back? Or where he is?"

"Lance is in Texas, Lauren." His eyes were on autopilot, like he could hear me but not see me.

"Texas? Why is he in Texas?"

Marcus turned and put his hand on the door handle.

"Look, I've got a lot of work to do today. I really can't afford to do this right now."

"Can you at least tell me when he'll be back? I was hoping to catch up. I haven't seen him in a while."

He stepped toward me and buried his hands deep in his pockets, looking out over the placid bayou.

"Look, I'm not sure he *will* be back. He moved to Texas because he had to."

Moved?

Something was definitely new in his face. Something forced, perhaps.

His voice dipped into a coy register. "This might be something that's best you stay out of," he said. Only then did his eyes find mine.

"Why did he move?"

"Don't, Lauren. You should really go."

At first, it was more of a warning, a piece of advice. Then he turned to go inside.

"Please, Mr. Dubois." I figured a more formal, pleading approach might work. Whatever it was, I could sense that it wasn't him. Father steering me away from Lance made sense—that was expected. But Marcus? No. That wasn't him.

"What is it you're doing looking for Lance, anyways? I don't think your father would be too thrilled to know that y'all have gotten as close as you have, much less that you're over here right now looking for him."

"No, sir. I'm sure he wouldn't, but Father only means the best for me."

"Yeah, well, if you know what's best for you, you'll walk back home, forget that you were ever here, and don't come back. I'm sorry, Lauren, but you know as well as I do"—he glanced next door—"that that's what's best for the both of us."

He eased the door shut but stood just inside, waiting for me to turn away.

I walked to the rope swing near the water, but as I rounded the fence, Shadow was there on the other side, leaning against the line of dog ears. Once he saw that I'd spotted him, his figure melted into the looming shade cast by the oak tree that flourished where the Roux estate began.

Where the Dubois land ended.

TWENTY-FIVE

August 27, 2005

I want to leave, but I can't.

Shadow is still outside, boarding up the windows. He should be done soon. I invited him to stay for dinner after our conversation earlier. I felt bad telling him that he couldn't stay in the house for the storm, so I figure it's the least I can do; Father had him over for dinner more evenings than not.

If St. Tammany Parish is issuing a mandatory evacuation order, along with every parish south of here, this hurricane should be interesting to say the least. We need to get out of here, but when someone I love—my family, for that matter—has spent their entire life in one place, leaving is easier said than done.

And by one place, I don't mean Slidell. I mean here, in this house.

It's no fault of his own, though. I could blame it on Father, but that wouldn't be fair. Father did the best he could with the hand he was dealt. That's all anyone can do. I'd be lying if I said that my past decisions didn't have any part in it—but that's beside the point.

So, we stay, for better or for worse. Besides, being locked down for this hurricane might be the perfect opportunity to set straight certain relationships that have been taking on water for years.

The front door opens. Shadow removes his shoes in the foyer and pushes his aged hands back through his thin, silvery hair. "Miss Lauren," he says with a nod. He walks into the kitchen. "Windows are all boarded and good to go. I can get those sandbags out of the car and in place if you'd like."

"Thank you, but dinner is almost ready," I say. "Why don't you take a break. We can worry about the rest tomorrow morning."

"Yes, ma'am. Of c-c-c-course. And thank you for the dinner invitation by the way. I appreciate it."

"You're welcome, Shadow."

He grabs one of the folding trays from inside the pantry and carries it to the sofa, as he always does for dinner. It was his routine with Father. Same spot, same time. Only now, Father isn't in his recliner across from him.

"Is your place ready for this storm?" I ask. "I can only imagine how cumbersome it must be to board up something like that all by yourself."

He turns his head only enough for me to hear him. "It's getting there. I still got a lot to secure before the end of the day tomorrow, but I'll get it done. Ain't got no choice in the matter."

Lines are important in the Roux family. Father tended to blur them when it came to his hired help, whether he meant to or not. But if there's one thing he taught me well, it's that you can never be too careful when it comes to the family name. When it comes to how I carry myself.

I pull back my shoulders.

"You'll be fine," I say. "The treehouse will be fine."

A brief scurry of feet run across the floor above me.

I grabbed some groceries earlier, before my run to the docks for sandbags. Like in any hurricane, I need to stock the house with anything and everything that doesn't require electricity or gas to eat. I open the pantry and double check that what we've got will last at least a day or so. If anything, it's overkill for a party of two.

This is possibly our last decent meal before the storm, so I figured I'd make it a good one—shrimp and grits. It was Father's once-a-week, so it's ours, too. The table is already set from this morning.

"It's ready," I say.

Shadow rocks himself out of the sofa and shuffles into the kitchen.

"Smells good," he says. "As always."

Father taught me how to make it not that long ago. "Hopefully it tastes the same."

He fixes himself a plate, along with a glass of sweet tea, and turns back to the living room, where his television tray awaits at the edge of the couch.

"Have a seat," I say, gesturing to the kitchen table before Shadow has a chance to leave the room.

He looks to the living room. "But I—"

"Sit."

It appears as though the man doesn't know what to do. He stalls in the middle of the floor, taken aback perhaps. I'm not sure he's ever sat at the table with the family.

"It's okay," I say. "Sit down."

He looks at the two placemats at the far ends of the table, then takes a slow seat between them. I bypass preparing a plate just yet and sit at the head of the table. He looks at the other end, then back at me.

"I'd like to speak with you about earlier," I say.

He picks up his drink. "Really, Miss Lauren. It's fine. I totally under—"

"What you need to understand, Shadow, is that Father hired you a long time ago to help us out with our home and everything that comes along with owning this estate. But Father is no longer here."

He pauses midsip and sets down his tea on the oak table. "Are you . . . saying you don't n-n-n-n-n-need me any—"

"No. No, no, no." I move his drink onto a coaster and wipe the sweat with my sleeve. His eye begins to twitch, where it was motionless only seconds prior. "I'm saying nothing of the sort. All I mean is that you and Father were close, but this home is my responsibility, now—and I have more to worry about than just me. So, I think some boundaries are necessary for this to work."

He looks insulted, but I have to do this. This talk, or whatever it is, is unavoidable by my eye. I need Shadow, and I know for a fact that he needs me—at least, he needs to be associated with the family. Or the *name*.

Father made sure of that.

"Alright."

"When you asked about staying over for the storm, I said no because we still need you around. We need you to help us out with this house and the property—as an employee."

"I'm sorry. I don't g-g-g-get it."

"When Father was around, you two were very close. I think it's obvious that y'all had more than merely an employer-employee relationship."

He tilts his head, seemingly waiting for more.

"I think that was great," I continue, "but things have changed. What I'm trying to say, Shadow, is that I'd like to keep you working for the family, but it's really *me* you'd be working for."

I'm not sure how else to word it without coming across as overly peremptory.

Shadow huffs but in an approving sort of manner. "Well, Miss Lauren, I figured as much. But this storm"—he sips his tea—"is supposed to be—"

"As much as I like to think how similar Father and I were, I am not Father." I let that sit for a moment. "My relationship with you will be different. It *is* different."

"Okay, then."

He brushes the edge of his eye with the back of his hand in what I guess is an effort to quell the tremble of his eyelid.

"Do you think you can handle that?"

His expression sinks into the chair like one of those melting clocks in the painting.

"Of course, Miss Lauren. I appreciate the opportunity to continue working for the family."

"Good. I was hoping you'd say that."

I stand up and walk to the banister, lean over, and look up to the hallway above me. "Baby boy? Dinner is served."

"Yes, Mother."

As I walk into the kitchen to fix my plate, Shadow has already left the dining room and returned to the couch. I consider asking him to eat with us—then I laugh the thought away, out loud but to myself.

Those teenage feet bounce down the stairs and around the corner, as they do for most meals.

"There he is," Shadow calls in a teasing voice from the living room. "I had a feeling you wouldn't turn down your paw-paw's favorite."

"Not when Mother makes it," Cody says.

TWENTY-SIX

August 1988

Most people my age were slumped over a toilet after one too many hand grenades, after pregaming their way through a case of this beer or that, then sneaking their way into The Dungeon for the first time at four in the morning—only to leave Bourbon behind an hour later as the sun shattered the rooftops into luminous shards of orange and black. Not me, though. I took the road less traveled.

The bleachy odor from inside the toilet bowl seared my nose from the inside out, although it was probably better than what it could have smelled like. Father's dinner party was in full swing downstairs, so I went up to the third floor, where I could vomit in peace and quiet.

Father's get-togethers had become far too regular after Mother died unexpectedly. Now, he had them nearly every other weekend. If I had to guess, it was his way of coping with the loneliness. Anyone with a commonsensical eye for people could see that the relationships were trivial; most of the guests he had over to the house were nothing more than vague connections, people he knew in passing and to whom he rarely spoke when they showed up—so they could say they'd been over to the Roux house "for the weekend." Whatever that meant. Like our home was some sort of tourist attraction.

My stomach tightened like a fist around a water balloon, and chunks of the day's lunch splashed into the bowl yet again. Whatever it was—either the water from the toilet or the sweat from the corners of my eyes—it dripped from the tip of my nose.

The bathroom light came to life, and the tip of a boot found its way between my ribs. A shadow loomed over me as I sat on the floor, hugging the bowl.

"Get the hell up," I heard from behind me. The inflection in his voice from the dip behind his lip was unmistakable. I turned toward him, but my eyes refused to open under the blinding lights.

"Yeah. I remember my first beer, too," Shadow said.

Little did he know, I wasn't sick from drinking.

"You finally b-b-b-b-b-broke down and found your way into your father's stash, huh? Ain't that right?"

"Leave me alone, Shadow. And turn the light off on your way out."

He turned off the light, then flicked it back on. Then off. Then on again. That time, I managed to open my eyes so he could see just how miserable he was making me. Miserable and irritated.

"Come on," he said. "I won't tell if you don't."

Our history had determined that that was a lie.

Having Shadow around was a peculiar thing—like a long-lost uncle with multiple personalities. More often than not, he acted like he cared, like he was around to help me. In reality, I had to remind myself that he worked for Father. He worked for the reputation of our family. At the end of the day, he was going to do whatever made his boss happy, plain and simple—even if that meant butting into the daughter's whereabouts day and night.

"You need to get up. Your father ain't gonna ignore the fact that you aren't downstairs with everyone else. Come on. Get up."

I felt the boot in my side once more, harder this time.

"I *said*—"

The door slammed into the wall from what sounded like Shadow's whole body being thrust against it.

"That's enough," Father said coolly, a calm grit in his voice. "Lauren isn't drunk."

He yanked me up by one arm and dragged me out of the bathroom. My feet were pulled out from beneath me like a flag to the wind.

"What are you doing?" I said. "You're hurting me." But I didn't dare pull away.

Before I could say anything more, the squeezing returned deep in my gut. The vomit sprayed across the carpet and painted Father's leather shoes a pinkish brown. He stopped in the middle of the hallway and looked down at his feet, his hand still gripping the top of my arm. My pulse was heavy beneath his fingers.

He slung open my bedroom door and dropped me in the middle of the floor. The door bounced off of the wall after leaving a dent in the paint there.

Briefly, Father turned around and spoke to Shadow in the hallway, but I couldn't make out what they were saying. He removed his shoes and handed them over before shutting the door and locking it.

He turned toward me and pulled back his shoulders.

"You think I'm that naïve, do you?" he said. "You think I don't know?"

I shook my head. "No, Father. Not at all."

"Then why!" he screamed—but only those two words. He looked back at the door, seemingly recalling that he had guests downstairs, guests who were now mingling among themselves. He lowered his voice, but it remained as stiff as his grip only seconds prior. "Then why is it that I have to figure it out on my own? You can't come to me? Is that it?"

"No, Father."

"Then what?"

I had no idea what he was asking. I lifted my shoulders, then lowered them at a languid pace.

He walked to my dresser, running his hand across the top of it, rubbing his fingers together in disapproval. Feeling for the dust that I couldn't see. There was always room for improvement, no matter how petty the chore.

"Tell me," he said. "Where did I go wrong?" He looked at me and unbuttoned his suit.

"You haven't, Father."

His hand continued across the dresser and over to the small wooden box at its center, against the mirror. He flipped the latch and opened it, looking back to see how I would react to him finding the notes from Lance—the notes I could tell he had already discovered at some other time. He slammed the box shut with a force that rattled both me and the mirror beside it.

"Did we not have this conversation not long ago?" he said. "In my study?"

"Yes, Father."

"I'll ask again, then. Where did I go wrong?"

He walked toward me, his feet an inch from my hands as I sit on the floor.

"Sit up straight," he said. Then he grumbled, "Why do I even bother?"

He sat on the bed in front of me and leaned forward, clasping his hands between us. I could smell the smoke on his breath and clothing.

"So, tell me," he said. "What do we do now?" The question was obviously rhetorical. His words leeched sarcasm.

"I'm sorry, Father. I know there's nothing I can say or do

to fix what I've—"

"Oh, I don't know if I'd go that far. I'm not so sure I'd say that at all." His twisted grin worried me. "There's always something we can do to right our wrongs, for the greater good of our family. To course correct where we're headed." His smirk vanished. "Sometimes, we just need a little help."

Father sat up straight and ran his hand across the comforter. He closed his eyes and drew a bottomless breath. "Somehow," he said, "I get the feeling my daughter doesn't have the same affinity for this family's future as I do. For *your* future in particular." He lay back on the bed and rested his hands, folded, on his stomach.

"In a way," he continued, "it's my fault. At least, in part. I suppose I haven't been clear on what the future of our family means, what your mother and I have worked so hard to build— for you, more than anything."

"Father, I—"

"I'm speaking." He didn't look at me. Didn't move. "Your mother is gone, Lauren. She's been gone, and she won't be back."

I jumped at the screeching and drilling outside my bedroom door. Father didn't react to it at all. He just lay there, watching the ceiling without blinking.

"I've been dealt an impossible hand, Lauren. You may not see it now, but one day you will. You'll learn to appreciate it when you're older."

Appreciate it? Appreciate what?

The door rattled.

"You see, your mother and I were a team, as is any couple. At least, the good ones. And as a team, we had a plan for our family. A plan for you. We all go at some point," he said, "but every one of us is the product of an unbroken line of success.

Thousands and thousands of years of success." He sat up. "*Survival* is what it really comes down to."

I had never heard Father speak the way he did then. Not with anyone, much less me.

"You understand?" he said.

The drilling continued from the other side of the door. I turned to look, but Father demanded my attention.

"No, no," he said. His hand reached out and turned my chin toward him. "You're going to look at me when I speak to you. What your mother and I built, Lauren, is something special. We've done more than just survive. We've thrived as a family. And you—*you* are the one who is going to carry our success forward." He looked down at my stomach. "Now, I made a promise to your mother, and I intend to keep it. That will not be tainted by some piece of trash you decided to sneak off with and fuck on the neighbor's dingy boat."

I'm going to do what?

"You understand?"

No. Not in the least.

From the sound of it, my mother and father had a life that—even as a teenager—I wasn't privy to. They had an idea of what I should be. What I *would* be.

And that scared the shit out of me.

He pointed at my stomach. "This, Lauren. *This* is not what it means to thrive as part of the Roux family."

I heard the sound of car doors slamming, engines starting, and rocks shifting in the driveway.

I realized that somehow, someway, Father would try to fix what he deemed was wrong. I could see it in his eyes—I was no longer a plan, but a liability.

The drilling on the other side of the door stopped, followed by a one-two knock. Father stood up and buttoned his suit.

"One way or another," he said, "we'll get through this." He removed his pipe from the pocket of his coat and placed it between his teeth. He winked and pulled back his shoulders.

As he opened the door, he spoke as if what he had just told me was somehow normal. He nodded at the door to the private bathroom adjoining my bedroom. "You've got a restroom all to yourself. You'll be fine. Dinner will be up shortly."

He walked out of the room. Shadow stood behind him in the hallway, a screw gun at his side.

Father turned back. "Oh, and do yourself a favor, love. Get cleaned up, would you? That smell doesn't suit you."

He pulled the door shut. At first, it felt like a dream. I stood up and walked to the door, taking my time, hoping that it was all in my head.

I gripped the doorknob and turned it, but it was useless.

Suddenly, being a normal teenager was appealing—sneaking into some bar, Father waiting up for me when I got home drunk in the early morning hours, but that wasn't how I'd played it. Not me.

I took the road less traveled.

TWENTY-SEVEN

August 28, 2005

It's morning, and we're on the clock.

The skies have grayed for the worse. Over the years, I've grown accustomed to appreciating the darker side of the weather, but not today. Today is different.

As I step onto the back porch and look out over the bayou, the air is deceptive. The breeze is soft against the side of my face, and a cool humidity not familiar to this time of the year has me anticipating how everything's going to play out.

A brown pelican veers down over the bayou, its reflection flawless. It lands on a fallen cypress tree on the adjacent bank. Only briefly does it adjust its feet on the bark that is all but stripped from the temporary perch. The bird looks up to the darkened clouds, which roll in swooping bands. Swiftly, it turns on the log and takes flight, turning back in the direction from which it came. Back up the bayou—and along with the shifting clouds.

I hear Shadow walking up the driveway with his uneven amble. The rocks shift in a dragging pulse beneath his feet.

As I meet him out front, I can tell he's reluctant to be here. His hair is more tired than usual; maybe it's the charge in the air. Maybe it's the charge between the two of us. I can't tell. The dip behind his lower lip has evolved from the usual pinch into an oozing hillock. He stands at the head of the sidewalk near my car. It's difficult to tell, though, whether he doesn't want to be here because of our previous conversation or if he'd rather be at home, prepping the treehouse.

Employees get paid, so it's no sweat of mine.

"Miss Lauren," he says. "You ready to get those s-s-s-sandbags out of the car and in place?"

"Yes, Shadow. Yes, we can."

I unlock the car and open the trunk.

"So," I continue, "I'm assuming your place is boarded and ready to go?"

He had the entirety of yesterday evening and night to prepare his home. I assume he took full advantage of the time off from work.

"Not quite, Miss Lauren. But it'll g-g-g-get there."

"I see."

He removes the first of thirty-some-odd sandbags and turns toward me. "Back door first, I'm assuming?"

"Yes, Shadow."

He carries it to the back of the home, but as I follow him, the image from the other side of the fence catches my eye—the stark contrast between us. Our two worlds are so near, yet so far apart.

The rickety two-story house is boarded from top to bottom and left to right, every window covered, although the work is hardly square. Sandbags line the doors in a haphazard sort of way. Not the way I would've done it—the way *we* could've done it.

He probably had help, of course; his kind tend to stick together.

Once it's too late, I realize that I've been standing here at the start of the fence, looking over there, for a few moments too long. Likewise, it doesn't take anyone this long to drop a sandbag—even someone as slow as Shadow.

I pry my thoughts from the past and walk to the back of the house. Shadow is standing there, looking out over the water.

"Is there a problem?" I say.

"No, ma'am," he says with his back to me. Then he turns. "No, Miss Lauren. There's no problem."

The bag is set against the house but off to the side. Crooked. Away from the door and useless.

"I beg to differ," I say.

Before I can fix it myself, he picks up the bag and sets it straight—dropping it to the ground while looking dead at me.

"Thank you," I say.

"Yes, ma'am."

We walk back to the car.

"Divide the rest between the front and back doors," I say, "as well as the garage." I turn back to the front door. "Let me know when you're done. It shouldn't take you long."

"I thought we were unloading these together."

"Sorry, Shadow. I need to start moving things upstairs. You know, just in case."

"Yes, Miss Lauren. Of course."

If this storm is as bad as they say, not everything will be saved. I'm not naïve. I take stock of what's important and begin moving what I can to the second floor, to Father's study; putting anything on the third floor is likely overkill.

The first thing that I notice in the living room is Father's chair, next to the end table that still holds the box with his pipe. I have yet to convince myself to move it—and my chair next to his recliner, too.

I pick up the box and open it. The smell of him escapes and finds its way to my memory. To the two of us sitting here for the morning news. Father rambling about the weather.

If he could be here now, oh what he would think about this "storm" everyone is fussing about. I can still hear him: *another god-forsaken hurricane. Damn thing looks like a light breeze.*

I move to grab the pipe, but then I notice a strand of shag next to it. I can't bring myself to touch it, not when Father was the last one to do so. Not when I can make out the oil from his hands smeared across the shank.

Then I turn to the stairs. Anything of Father's needs to be—

I collide with Shadow and drop the box to the floor. And the scream that escapes my lips is met with calm by the man in front of me.

"Is everything okay, Miss Lauren?"

My hand finds my throat and drags down the center of my chest.

"Jesus. Shadow."

The sweat of his balding head is tacky on the edge of my chin. I wipe it with my shoulder.

"What are you doing inside?"

As I kneel to pick up the now-cracked box, a single drop of what I take to be dip splashes onto the grout between the marble floors. It seeps deep into the crack next to the bare, dirty feet in front of me.

"I thought you might n-n-n . . . n-n-n-need some help."

I grab the box and stand up. The man wipes the corner of his mouth with the edge of his thumb.

"Like I said, Shadow—let me know when you're done."

He reaches for the box in my hand, and now we're both holding it.

"Surely, you can't move all of this alone."

Slowly, gently, I pull the box toward me, careful not to damage what is already broken.

"It shouldn't take you long," I say.

He lets go and pulls the can of dip from his shirt pocket.

"Of course, Miss Lauren." He does his best to smile with the chew in his mouth. "How . . . silly of me."

He places another pinch behind his lip, then smears the excess down the front of his plaid shirt before taking a step back and turning to the front door.

Then I hear the feet scurry from the top of the stairs and down the hall.

I follow Shadow back out to the front of the house and set Father's box on the table outside, taking a seat in the wicker chair.

Admittedly, when Father was still around, I never saw much of the employer-employee relationship between them. It seems as though he always did what Father needed, without much coercion. I didn't anticipate having to supervise the man.

Just as my skin starts sticking to the chair, I see Lance round the fence.

Shadow drops one of the sandbags back into the trunk of the car and looks at me, then at Lance, then back at me.

I stand up and do my best to reach him in the front yard before he gets any farther.

Lance lifts his chin to Shadow, but the man walks past us with one of the bags, without so much as a nod in return. Their eyes do seem to meet, though.

"Looks like you have a lot going on," Lance says.

"Nothing we can't handle," I say. His eyes find my mouth, then my chin. These dimples tend to be my card from the bottom of the deck—even after all these years.

"I should help."

He moves toward the car, but I catch him by the arm.

"What are you doing, Lance?"

"Helping. That's what neighbors do, *Lauren.*"

I shake my head. "You don't need to do that." I walk us farther into the yard and back toward his side of the fence.

"That's not how this works," I say. "I need time."

It is how this works. A little give, a little take.

He looks around. "Really? I thought we could talk. Look . . . I know my timing is shit, but can't we . . . give this a try? At least talk? Something?"

Talking and trying are worlds apart. Like opposite sides of the same fence.

"Oh, come on," he says. "You can use the help. Hell, even with you and Shadow, it's a lot."

There come certain moments in life when it pays to keep your mouth shut. When it pays to let it all play out.

"Lance, we've got it covered. Besides, doesn't Cotton need some help? He's probably getting ready for this on his own."

"Cotton is fine, Lauren. Trust me."

Trust you?

I watch his eyes move down the front of me, until they find their way to the sliver of skin between my shirt and jeans. His breaths are labored.

"We've waited long enough to catch up. Don't you think?" he says.

I say nothing. I don't need to. I can see it on his face. He knows as well as I do: the tide has turned.

He continues. "Besides, you weren't the only one with no choice in the matter. Your father is gone, Lauren. Don't you think it's time we—"

Steps in the gravel, growing louder behind us.

"Do yourself a favor and get on back to where you c-c-c-came from," Shadow says, his voice filled with defensiveness. Of himself? Of me? Of Father? "I think you've done enough."

"Done enough?" Lance says.

I step between them and gesture to the house. "Come on, Shadow. Now isn't the time."

Only, it is—now is absolutely the time.

TWENTY-EIGHT

October 1988

Two months later, I had earned my first privilege: eating dinner at the dining room table. Supervised, of course.

I sat in the corner; Father was across from me at the head of the table. Shadow sat in his usual spot in the living room, at the couch with his television tray. Father acted as if the seating arrangements were incidental, but I knew better. I had learned a great deal over the prior eight weeks. When it came to our family, nothing was left to chance.

The house was as quiet as could be.

"So, what did you do today?" Father asked. Like the options were endless.

I shrugged one shoulder. "Completed my workouts. Then caught up on some reading."

"That's good," Father said. "You still looking through those pre-med texts I bought you? With your decision to pursue nursing, that's not a bad place for you to start."

"Yes, Father. I read them every day."

He stood up and placed his dishes in the sink, then walked to me. He leaned over and kissed me on the head. "That's my girl. If you put your mind to it, there isn't anything you can't accomplish—especially with the proper education, from home or otherwise."

"Do what you love," Shadow interjected from the other room, "and you'll never work a day in your life."

You mean, like you?

"That's right," Father added. "Work with your head and not

your hands. Work smart. There's too many ignorant people in this world peddling hard work."

Shadow huffed. "Ha. Hard work." Like he could speak from experience.

Father ran his fingers down the back of my head to the base of my skull. His thumb meandered into that dent at the top of my spine. Then he looked to Shadow as the man ambled into the kitchen, not far from Father and me in the dining room.

"We good?" Father said, nodding to the man who was scraping his plate as if it were his one and only meal for the day, the grease hanging strong at the corner of his mouth, mixing with that tacky white paste that was always in the crook of his lips.

He looked at me, for whatever reason. "Yes, sir," Shadow said, standing at the counter.

Father gave me one more pat on the head and pushed my hair back behind my ear. Then he walked off.

Shadow leaned over to watch him as he exited the room, until he was out of earshot.

"Finish up," Shadow said. "I got things to d-d-d-do."

I slid my plate forward. "I'm done."

He paused, picking at his few teeth with his thumbnail. "You know where the sink is." His just-another-day glare suggested the whole arrangement between him and Father regarding me was somehow a hindrance. His boredom shone through.

I carried my plate to the sink, rinsed it, and opened the dishwasher.

"Now, hold on," Shadow said. "Ain't nobody said anything about you handling the d-d-d-dishes." He snatched the plate from my hand and dropped it into the sink. "What is this? Daddy gives you an inch, and you just gonna take a mile? I don't think so, little girl."

He slammed the dishwasher closed with his foot and leaned against the counter, pulling a can of dip from his pants pocket.

"I'm going to bed," I said.

"Now, you wait a minute. Just cause you're down here don't mean you running around as you please." He unscrewed the can and plucked a pinch of the tobacco between his fingers, lifting it to his mouth as his tongue worked inside. "You can wait all of two seconds until I'm ready to—"

"Shadow, I'm going upstairs. To my room."

He closed the can and shoved it back into his pocket.

"What is it? Father trusts me to come down here and eat, but not to walk up the stairs?" I turn away. "It's not like you won't be right behind me. Locking the door. As always."

I took the first few steps up the stairs, then paused, sure he would be on my heels. Only, he wasn't. I continued to the top of the stairs before it sank in—that could have been my only shot.

So I waited another second, then two for good measure, before realizing I was alone—outside of my room.

There came certain moments in life when it paid to take a chance—when it paid to make a run for it.

Before I could talk myself out of it, I backtracked down the stairs and turned to the front door. The tile beneath my bare feet was ice cold and soundless. As I grabbed the lock, I looked back at the kitchen. Shadow was loading the dishes.

I turned the deadbolt. Lucky for me, the clunk that it made coincided with one of the plates hitting the rack of the dishwasher.

My hand twisted the doorknob without so much as a click. I stepped outside. The cement felt like sandpaper. My feet had only felt the softness of my bedroom carpet for weeks.

I missed the days of being a normal kid, sneaking over to the neighbor's house for dinner.

Please be home, I mouthed to myself.

The cold draft of indoor air was cut off as I eased the front door shut, and the outdoor humidity swept across my chest. But a hand slid across my mouth, and the door was flung back open. The herbaceous scent of tobacco seeped from the fingers that were shoved beneath my nose and dragging me backward.

My feet were swept out from beneath me, and before I knew it, I tripped and fell onto the frigid, rigid tile of the foyer.

He closed the door without a sound—no click, no creak. Or maybe the adrenaline erased it from my memory.

"You ungrateful little whore," Father said. "You don't learn, do you?"

Dishes shattered about the floor behind me, followed by a rush of heavy feet. I leaned back, away from Father, but several of the ceramic shards melted into the center of my palms.

"So nice of you to join us," he said.

"Mr. Roux, I was just—"

"Save it, Shadow." Father's voice climbed steadily. "Excuses don't belong in *this house*."

"Yes, sir," Shadow said.

Father's gaze weighed heavily; his eyes alone did much of his talking. "Do you realize what you've just done? What would happen to all of this"—he looked around, adjusting his vest—"if your disappointment to this family gets out? Your future would be over. Don't you get that?"

He crouched in front of me, Shadow behind me.

"You cannot afford to do this, Lauren. You have plans. You have a life to live. Don't do this to yourself, you hear me?" Father looked to Shadow, then back at me. "You deserve better than this."

"Ain't that right," Shadow said.

I was so close.

"Now, I need you to say it," Father spoke. "Tell me this will not happen again."

From behind me, Shadow grunted.

"Tell me that you're on board with what's best for you and this family, Lauren. I need to hear it."

The argument in my head had reached a full stop. The family side of me, the loyal side, knew the only option was to agree with Father if I wanted what was best for my physical self—and the baby. The logical side of me, the mental half, knew that if I wanted to come out of this in any way sane, the only option was to stick to what I had already started. To escape.

So, I said nothing.

"Lauren." Father spoke as if I were ten years younger than I was. "Lauren. Don't do this. I need you to tell me that you will not try this again. I need your assurance, love."

A single drop of welling water fell from my cheek and splashed onto the marble floor. Father looked over my shoulder at Shadow.

"Nod, Lauren. Tell me that this will not happen again."

I couldn't do it. As much as I wanted to oblige the man who was clearly struggling with life after losing his wife and raising a daughter on his own, who was mentally losing it one lonesome night at a time, I couldn't do it. He needed to know that it wasn't okay. That *I* wasn't okay. I pulled my knees to my chest—the only comfort I could garner in the moment.

"No?" Father spoke calmly, but he looked up at Shadow with a disappointed scowl. "Have it your way—but you will learn. One way or another, you will learn."

Father grabbed me by the arm and dragged me to the stairs. I held tight to the banister at first, but the pain persuaded me to let go. My skin throbbed heavily beneath his grasp.

He raised his voice, but only enough to get the point across. "You *make* me do this," Father said. "You think I enjoy this? Do you?"

I tried my best to stand on my own two feet, to walk myself up the stairs and down the hallway, but Father's pace was too great to match. He pulled me over the top of the stairs, not once but twice, all the way to the third floor. He pushed open my bedroom door and dropped me in the center of the room.

I couldn't see him, though. My hair was smeared across my face, along with the sweat. And I didn't have the courage to move it from my eyes.

Not at first.

Father called for Shadow and told him to lock the door. The man pulled the door shut, and the bolts shifted against the wooden frame, one by one.

His hand found my arm and lifted me from the floor.

"Come on," he said. "Let's get you up. Come on, Lauren."

He set me on the bed and sat beside me, his hand on my knee.

"You know"—he looked around the room, studying what I had done with the space, unfamiliar given he rarely took the time to visit—"you remind me a lot of your mother when we found out about you."

I had no idea what he was referring to, but I was fairly certain that keeping your daughter to yourself like some sort of liability wasn't genetic.

"Your mother didn't know what to do when we found out about you, either. And much like her, you'll get through this, Lauren. You're strong. Just like she was." He nudged me with his elbow. "But where the two of you differ is that your mother understood the importance of family."

I pushed the hair from my eyes. His voice didn't match the expression on his face.

"Father." I moved my hand across my stomach. "This is family."

"No. That"—he pointed—"*that* is a slap in the face, love. That is not what your mother would have wanted for the future of this home. Not for you, not for me. Not for our family."

His hand fell from my leg, and he stood and buttoned his jacket.

"Unfortunately, given our hiccup this evening, things are going to change around here."

What did Mother want?

Father knocked on the door, and Shadow answered.

"Get some rest," he said. "We have a visitor stopping by in a few days. And by the looks of it, you need the sleep."

The door closed, and there he left me. Waiting.

—

Maybe Shadow didn't get the message—or maybe Father was more worried about my well-being than he had led on. After all, he couldn't be around 24/7.

It was just before six in the morning when Shadow barged into my room.

"Wakey wakey," he said.

I sat up. "Shadow?" The sun had yet to find its way through the shades. "What are you doing?"

"Orders from the boss, little one. Orders from the boss." He stood on a chair in the corner of the room, screwing a small white camera into the ceiling.

A fine stream of dust fell from above, layering on my bed. Father appeared in the doorway.

"Like I said, it's time for a change."

"A change?"

"Yes—a change. I want to trust you, Lauren. I do. But first, I need you to trust the process. We'll get through this together, but that means doing what is necessary to thrive in our current situation." He looked to the camera. "This is only a temporary arrangement—until you and I feel a bit more comfortable. Besides, having an extra pair of eyes around here with a newborn on the way isn't necessarily a bad idea."

Shadow nodded. "Ain't that right."

"This isn't normal," I said. "You can't just erase me like I was never here. Someone will notice. *Everyone* will notice."

Shadow looked at me, then at Father.

Father shrugged it off.

"Sometimes, my love, a white lie here and there is necessary in life. Not to succeed, but to flourish." He put his hands in his pockets. "As far as anyone else is concerned, you're overseas with family."

"Family? What family do we have overseas? Where?"

He lifted his shoulders, and there they remained.

"Who knows."

And just as unexpectedly as he'd appeared, he vanished.

TWENTY-NINE

October 1988

"Lauren, this is Miss Amy," Father said.

The lady dropped her bag onto the floor and wobbled toward me with arms wide open. She leaned over and hugged me as I sat upright in bed, gripping me tight and robbing me of air.

She smelled of a musty bathroom potpourri. Her slack, leathery skin brushed my cheek, and her breasts hung against my stomach with a meandering mind of their own.

As she sat there, she pushed my hair back behind my ear as if we were reuniting after some years apart. "Oh, darling. How are you holding up?" The back of her hand caressed my stomach in a rather obvious and dramatic way.

I looked to Father and pulled the sheets farther up my legs.

"Miss Amy is an old friend of your mother, love."

"That's right," she said, gawking at my belly. Then she turned to Father as if he had failed to elaborate. "A *nursing* friend. Me and Bobby—sorry, your mother and I—go way back."

"Right," Father said. "Miss Amy is a nurse practitioner. She worked at the hospital with your mother for quite some time."

"Well, former nurse, darling. Officially, that is." She swatted the air between us. "These days, it's all about home care." She adjusted her stiff salt-and-pepper hair with an upward push of her hand. "Just a midwife helping out where I'm needed."

Her grin was sluggish and broad, spreading over her face like the muck on top of the water in a boat's wake.

"I don't understand," I said. "Why do I need—"

"Darling, let's not be silly, now," she said. "You need someone to look after you, of course. You just leave everything to Miss Amy, you hear?"

She stood up and ushered Father out of the room, swaying this way and that. She swatted the air behind him as if she were sweeping him out the door. Then she rocked flat-footed in her all-white scrubs and sole-supporting tennis shoes—getting her bearings in the space, it seemed.

I made one last attempt to put a cinch in whatever was happening. "Father . . ."

He didn't speak, though—only stood in the hallway, lighting his pipe, as she eased the door shut with that clownish grin.

"Now that *you know who* is out of the way, we can focus on what's important, darling. Now, tell me." She sat on the bed yet again, the edge of the mattress groaning and sinking to the floor. "How far along are we?"

She must have seen something in my expression, because her demeanor shifted from all business to reassurance in no time at all. "And don't you worry about our little talks now, darling. Whatever is said between these four walls stays between you and me, you hear?" She patted me on the leg. "Consider me your anything and everything."

My what?

She lifted the bottom of my shirt like she was sneaking a peek at a freshly baked snack. "Well, by the looks of it, you ain't no more than a couple of months. If that." And there it was again—that broad twist of her lips. "That sound about right?" She pulled my shirt back down and patted the fabric over my navel.

Perhaps it needs to bake a while longer.

"I'm confused."

"What is it, darling?"

"What are you doing here?"

The lady leaned over and unzipped the large black medical bag at the foot of the bed. She pulled out a stethoscope and blood pressure cuff.

I looked behind her to the door—the door that I knew was locked from the other side.

She pulled my arm toward her and wrapped the cuff around my bicep, then pumped the ball while looking at her thin golden watch.

"I'm looking after you, of course." The glint in her eye had the opposite effect of what I suspected it would have if we were on the outside, not confined to that slowly shrinking room.

She tore the cuff from my arm. "Blood pressure is good. Now, let's get a listen to that little one, shall we."

The second lift of my shirt was what did it. I pushed her hand from my stomach and pulled the covers closer.

"What is it, darling?"

"What is it? I don't know you. And why are you going along with this instead of getting me out of here? This is crazy."

"Oh, I'm a former nurse and friend of Miss Bobb—of your mother, like I said. Just a midwife helping out where I'm needed."

"Yes, I got that."

She pulled the stethoscope from her ears and put her hand on mine.

"Look, darling. I know all of this is a lot to take in. And that's completely normal for someone in your position." Her eyes wandered down me once again. "But we will get through this together."

She squeezed my hand.

I had no desire to "get through this." I wanted out.

Immediately. Her whole back-and-forth was backward. From what I could gather, she was attempting to make me comfortable, when all I wanted was out of the room. Out of that house. Out of the entire situation. The problem was that I was unsure of how to phrase it. What were my options, really?

My silence was mistaken. "Good," she said, placing the earpieces back into her hairy ears. "I'm glad we're on the same page."

The stranger lifted my shirt and pressed the cold, hard metal of the stethoscope against my stomach. Head down, eyes closed, she began nodding in agreement with whatever she was thinking.

The cold worked its way higher, the top of her hand resting against my left breast. More nodding. Smiling.

Then it slid up to my chest. Her palm lay flat against me with the stethoscope beneath it.

Sometimes, it paid to take a chance. "He's keeping me here against my will."

The chuckle that followed was nothing shy of unnerving. It grew and grew until her rose-purple skin screamed for air, and the bed shook to its core.

"Oh, darling. I can already see we're gonna get along together just fine. Oh, my." She swatted the air. "Much like myself—so I've been told—you have one wicked sense of humor." Her hand patted her chest. "Oh, my."

The lady stood up and placed the instruments back into the bag. She dabbed the sweat from her forehead with a towel.

I tucked the sheets around my waist and beneath my arms. "I'm serious," I said, lifting my chin to the camera in the corner of the room. "I know you've seen the locks. I can't leave. I'm stuck here."

She paused with her double chin tucked, her eyes peering up at me from her downward gaze. The sags of skin below her chin flapped from side to side as she shook her head.

Then she lifted her hand between us and, like a disapproving metronome, rocked her finger from side to side.

"No." Her tongue clicked against the roof of her mouth in a repetitive tsk. "We're not going to entertain that kind of thinking, darling."

She walked to me, but this time, she grabbed the chair from my desk and pulled it next to the bed. She sat down, and the wood moaned beneath her.

"Now, I know you're all grown up, and you've lived with the man for some time now. But let me tell you something about Edward Roux."

Lived with him? He was my father—not some friend of a friend like he was to her. The woman's banter was growing awkward and confusing, frustrating even, the more she spoke about Father as if I'd never met him. The more she talked, the more I realized that her concern was entirely misplaced, focused on whatever Father must have told her and not the obvious fact that I was unable to get up and walk out of there.

"That man"—she wagged her finger at the door—"that man is as caring as they come, darling. And you? Well, you should consider yourself one lucky girl."

"Lucky? I'm trying to tell you that I need help. Can't you see what's going on? Don't you see what's happening?"

The legs of the chair creaked along with her laugh.

"Oh, my. You know, your father warned me about you." She leaned forward. "He said, 'Amy, you stay on your toes, now. That girl don't know up from down with all those hormones coursing through her system.' And now I see it. Oh, can I see it."

"Please," I said quietly. "I don't have anyone else."

She leaned in farther, her eyes narrow, her mouth flat. I

could see it: she wanted to say something. The words were right there.

Her eyes drifted past me, her mind seemingly wandering—considering what she was being asked to do, perhaps.

One last time, I whispered it. "Please."

Her focus drifted over me, until our eyes met in the middle.

This lady was my way out. If she really did know Mother, this wouldn't last. She leaned closer, her hand propped on her knee.

Her mouth inched open, but all that followed was an empty grin.

She popped me on the leg and jolted from the chair. "Oh, my!" She chuckled as she wobbled to the foot of the bed and lifted her bag. For a moment, she turned back, her sagging chest bouncing with laughter. Then she cocked her head to the side and frowned. "Now, what is it, darling?"

No matter how hard I tried, I couldn't stop the hurt that raced down the edge of my nose, leaving a barren trail in its wake, until the emptiness fell to the sheets.

"Why are you doing this?" I asked.

She rocked from side to side as she moseyed to the door. Her shadow cast about the floor and over the edge of my bed, within a hair of my toes.

"Because, darling." The door opened. "I'm a friend of Miss—a friend of your mother, of course."

THIRTY

August 28, 2005

"You're back!" Brody shouts from the driveway as she thrashes one arm overhead, practically pushing Shadow to the side as he stammers with a sandbag in each hand.

Back in the day, Brody was always the smothering type; if she wasn't touching you in the middle of conversation like a strung-out Italian, or blowing this or that out of proportion, something was wrong. Now, the fact that she looks and, so far, acts no differently than she did seventeen years ago—head-turning and brash—is beyond annoying.

"Hey, B," I say.

She wastes no time. She squeezes me, then holds me by the shoulders, looking me up and down like I should be damaged from my "travels."

"You good?" she says. "It's been so long. What's it been? Fifteen years?"

"Something like that."

"I wasn't sure you'd ever come back. I just wish it was under better circumstances. Sorry about your dad. Mom is all tore up about it."

"Thank you," I say.

She jabs me in the arm. "We should catch up." She holds out her hands, palms up, like she's feeling for the incoming rain. "Again, perhaps under better circumstances."

Shadow walks past us, ambling from side to side with a bag swinging from each hand.

"I brought a few more," she says.

"I'm sorry?"

"Sandbags." She points to her car. "I brought a few extra. Y'all have a lot more to seal up than we do, so I thought you could use a few extra."

"Oh. Thank you. You didn't have to do that."

"That's what family's for. Besides, you just got back. You can use the help."

Brody inches closer and leans in while looking next door. Her perfect vanilla hair is vaguely rustled by the charge in the air. Her skin glows a buttery tan.

"So, tell me," she says. Her elbow finds its way into my side. "You and Lance." Her eyebrows jump. "Y'all reconnect yet?"

I push back with my own elbow. "Oh, please. That was a long time ago, B. A very long time ago."

"I know, I know. I'm just sayin'. Ain't nothing wrong with a little *catching up*."

Shadow returns from behind the house and walks back to the car.

"Hey," Brody says, "I can give y'all a hand. Y'all have way too much to prep with a place this big. Let me help." She turns back to her car, but I catch her by the arm.

"No. Shadow can handle it."

She gives me that pestering oh-please look that I remember all too well.

"Really, Lauren?" Her voice is low, only for the two of us to hear. "You're gonna make that man carry all those by himself?"

Brody turns back to her car, but I grab her again. This time, she looks down at my hand like I'm the crazy cousin and not her.

"Hey, Shadow," I say. "You mind grabbing the extra bags from Brody's car when you're done? I'm sure you can find somewhere we can use them."

She jerks her head back and tucks her chin, eyes wide.

Shadow leans into the trunk of my car. "Yes, M-M-Miss Lauren."

I turn toward him. "I'm sorry?"

"Ma'am?"

"It's Miss Roux, Shadow."

For a second, it looks like he has more to say. His eyes find Brody. She says nothing.

I move forward until I'm a step away from him and place my hand on his shoulder. "You understand, don't you, Shadow? Father is gone. 'Lauren' just isn't the same."

Again, his eyes move past me. I feel her hand on the small of my back.

"Hey, Lauren. Let's take a walk. Catch up, yeah?"

Shadow looks down at my hand on his shoulder. "Yes, Miss Roux." The smile that follows is forced, as always. "Of course."

Brody tugs the bottom of my blouse, pulling me back.

"Come on," she says. "Let's head next door."

As we turn away, Brody takes my hand in hers. She guides me up the driveway to the head of the cemetery. "What was that all about?" she says.

"What?"

"*That*. With Shadow." She glances back. "I don't remember things being so . . . tense with him. That something new?"

Finally, she lets go of my hand.

"It's all new, B. It's only been a few weeks since Father passed, so I'm still trying to get my bearings. Mother obviously isn't around, so everything falls on me, now—the property, the house, *Shadow* apparently."

"Jeez. Sounds like you lost a father and gained a kid." She jabs me in the arm.

We pass the cemetery and walk through Cotton's yard, then make our way out back to the bayou. Helping out the neighborhood from his sailboat has always been Cotton's thing, distributing canned goods and other supplies from that boat that's more storage than anything else.

The moment we reach the dock, I realize just how little time we have. Rolling waves of gray and pale-white flow above us in a fast-moving stream, driven forward by on-and-off gusts of hastening winds.

A wall of black crawls closer in the distance.

Cotton appears, carrying a case of water from the boat's cabin. "Well ain't that a sight," he says. "Two ladies I ain't seen together since they were little girls." He looks at me. "Welcome back."

"Thank you, Cotton."

He steps out of the boat and places the waters onto the dock. "Sorry about ya dad, Lauren. I only heard the news recently."

"It's only been recently."

"Well"—he turns to the boat—"feel free to grab whatever y'all need. I'll give it about another hour, then I'm closing up shop." He looks to the sky. "Time's a ticking."

The boat is exactly how I remember it: pristine natural wood, white and gray sails, not a tinge of imperfection from bow to stern.

And then there's that—the cabin that changed everything.

"You okay?" Brody says, her hand on my back.

"What?"

"Are you okay?"

"Yes. Why wouldn't I be?"

"It's last minute," Cotton says. "So there ain't much left— aside from some bottled water and a few perishables."

As I step onto the dock, the cool air sends a shiver down the front of my neck. The cabin door of the boat is open, and the edge of the sofa taunts me from within. Suddenly, somehow, the skies appear darker. My skin sweats in the moist air.

Brody steps down into the boat.

"Here, let me give you a hand," Cotton says. He follows her.

I stand at the edge of the dock, looking down at the chopping water as it breaks against the hull of the sailboat—nothing at all like the calm of that night. Instead of a yellow moonlight, the oily cotton above is reflected, ripped and twisted, in the water around us.

His voice echoes in my memory. *I promise. It's fine.*

I close my eyes. The hull of the boat talks in the bayou in front of me.

"Lauren?"

A wet breeze caresses my face, and the first roll of thunder shakes the weathered boards beneath my feet.

The touch of his hands down my back.

"Lauren. Lauren?"

I open my eyes to find Cotton reaching out, helping me into the boat.

"Why don't we go ahead and grab what ya need," he says, glancing up. "By the looks of it, we ain't gonna be out here much longer."

"Okay."

I step into the boat, but all I can see is him, walking me to the cabin under that moony night. The boat rocks, and I catch myself against the cabin door. Cases of water are stacked on the makeshift sofa.

"Here—you step out, and I'll hand them to ya," Cotton says to Brody.

After that, I hear nothing but the memory of his body against mine. The boat is caught by a stronger gust of wind, and it rocks some more. The bayou moans in a hollow voice beneath me. And the tremor of the waves moves through my feet and up—between my legs.

I lean over to grab one of the cases of water from the seat, and that's when I feel it: the hand on the small of my back. The cousin who knows no boundaries. I pick up the waters and turn, but they fall from my hands, and they hit the floor of the boat without a sound.

"Can I give you a hand?" he says.

I look up, but all I see is a shadow—*his* shadow—framed in the doorway of the cabin, rocking from side to side.

THIRTY-ONE

April 1989

Sitting up was out of the question.

I glanced down at my feet, but all I saw were my swollen toes protruding from the other side of my stomach like cypress knees from the swamp—a jagged line of unpainted nails blocking my view of the bedroom door.

My room had become my whole world, every experience of every day, every night, and the fraction of seconds between. After the first few months, being stuck in the room had grown easier, once I had abandoned the expectation that I would be able to leave—at least in the near future. And having someone around on a regular basis helped, even if she wasn't quite my cup of tea. Miss Amy was all that I had from the outside.

Simply put, she grew on me. Miss Amy was there for me, there for us, at a moment's notice. Not only was she around when I needed her, but she listened. And not just to hear me, but to understand me. She lent an ear to all of my concerns no matter how trivial, including my worries when it came to being a mother, my thoughts on Father and what family life would entail once the baby was born. She never could've replaced Mother—but she was damn near approaching some semblance of a parent figure when I needed it most.

And for that, I was grateful.

I counted in a way I had grown accustomed to in recent weeks. "One." I rolled my belly to the side of the bed and back. "Two." And turned my head as well, rocking again. "Three." Then I swung myself over the edge of the mattress. The springs cried out. Even walking to the restroom had become a chore.

As I stood up, it seemed as though I was too late.

The warmth fell down the inside of my legs and soaked into the carpet between my feet, then around and beneath them. I bent over as the pain ran deeper inside me. It didn't stop, though, and it was far too great—too new and unfamiliar. As it turned out, making it to the restroom in time wasn't the problem.

My water had broken—a sound I had never known existed, not to mention the heaviness of the feeling.

I called out. "Miss Amy?"

My feet squished beneath me, and I fell to the edge of the bed.

I spoke louder. "Miss Amy!"

Her weighty steps traveled down the hall and into my room.

"Now, now, darling. I'm here. I'm here." She reached down and helped me onto the bed. "Oh, my," she said. "I suppose now is a good a time as any." She turned to the bedroom door. "Mr. Roux?" Her voice climbed and cracked, but no answer followed. "Mr. Roux!"

"What are you doing?" I said.

"Helping you lie down, now." Her feet shrieked in the liquid below. "Oh, my. Mr. Roux, darling!"

"I thought you were prepared for this. Why are you calling for Father? He doesn't need to be—"

The pain deepened from the inside out.

"Here." She rested her hand behind me and helped me back and onto the pillows there. "Let's get you comfortable until I can get the bath going."

Father strolled into the room at a slothful pace, his pipe belching one cloud of smoke after another.

"What's all the ruckus?"

Miss Amy sprang upright and braced her hips. "Well, sir. It looks like someone is well on their way to being a new pawpaw." She slapped him on the shoulder. "That's what."

Father looked down at his shoulder and brushed it clean.

"Well if there isn't anything you need from me, I'll be in my study." He turned away.

The agony spread further. "Father, please. I can't," I said. "Not here. I need a hospital. What if something happens?"

Miss Amy paused halfway to the restroom and gave Father a look as if to say, "This is all you."

"No." Father spoke in a flat tone before struggling to relight his pipe, fighting with a miniscule matchbox. "A Roux sticks to the plan—and I didn't raise no quitter."

Miss Amy swatted the air. "Oh, this one here ain't no such thing. Ain't that right, darling?" She stared at me as she walked backward to the restroom. "Let's draw this bath and get you situated." She disappeared behind the door but then popped her head out. "You wait on Miss Amy, you hear. Don't you go pushing all by yourself, now." She giggled. "Oh, my."

Faintly, I heard a voice from the hallway. "Ain't that right." But it may have been in my head.

"Anything else?" Father said.

"Please."

He waved out a second match and tossed it onto the dresser. The grayish plumes whirled like two indoor tornados, merging into one under the slow fan.

"Keep me posted," he said over his shoulder as he left the room. The two figures projected onto the wall grew smaller and smaller yet, until they vanished altogether down the hallway.

The faucet squeaked from the other room, and I could hear the water as it broke against the porcelain tub.

Miss Amy had said I was fortunate. Apparently, a two-hour labor was a good thing.

I pushed myself up in the bed, and she handed me the bundle of blue-and-pink-striped blankets. The previous months melted into a paltry afterthought at the sight of his rosy cheeks—and his full head of twisted blond hair. And the cry. That gentle weep stole away whatever hurt remained on the inside of me.

I no longer felt like the same person, and the fact that I could see a change in myself was all that I needed in the moment. Unless I was fooling myself, I had changed for the better—as people rarely do. My world was no longer mine; it was ours.

Miss Amy sat in the chair next to my bed.

"So . . . what's his name?"

Some-odd nine months, and I hadn't given it a second thought. How such an important detail managed to escape me, I wasn't sure. But it didn't take me long to figure it out.

"Bobby," I said. He looked like a Bobby.

Miss Amy caught her chest with an open hand. "After your mother? Oh, darling. She would be so proud of you. Bless your heart."

"No." Father appeared in the doorway. "Pick something else."

I looked to Miss Amy. Perhaps she didn't hear him? I wasn't sure why, but I half expected her to answer for me. Maybe it was the way she had lifted me up in recent months, or the way she stood between me and Father in our disagreements. Whatever it was, I found her silence unfavorable.

"What?" I said.

"Pick something else," he repeated.

Miss Amy grinned and ran a finger down one of the baby's

plump cheeks. "I'm sure anything you come up with will be perfect, darling," she said in a reassuring tone.

That wasn't quite the defense I was looking for.

"His name is Bobby," I said. "There is no other name."

"No. It is not. That name is taken," Father said. "It's been taken for quite some time." He walked into the room and stood next to my bed, peering down at the two of us from what seemed like a mile above. He adjusted his vest. "What else you got?"

I took the question as a rhetorical one.

"Perfect," he said with a half grin. "Cody it is." Then he abandoned the pipe at his lips and reached out.

I only held my everything that much tighter.

"Come on." Father leaned over and pulled him from my arms. He cradled him in one hand and adjusted his pipe with the other. "Cody, huh? You look like a Cody."

"Have you heard from them?" I asked.

Father stopped the awkward rocking motion and turned his eyes to Miss Amy. She stood up and pushed the chair under the desk.

"If you need me—"

Father's eyes cut her off midsentence. She wobbled out of the room without looking back.

"He has a right to know," I said. "His *family* has a right to know."

Father leaned over and placed him back into my arms. A few embers fell from his pipe and landed on the white blankets before dying out for good. He walked to the window.

"Regardless of what you think of him . . . of them . . . it's the right thing to do," I said. "It's the decent thing to—"

"He abandoned you, Lauren." He spoke to the glass and not to his daughter. "Don't you get that? He left." Only then did he turn toward me. "Or did you forget that?"

"I haven't forgotten anything. But family is family. Is it not?"

He turned his head and mumbled inaudibly to himself. Father pulled out the desk chair and swiveled it on one of its four legs toward the bed. He unbuttoned his coat and draped it over the back of the chair, then sat down and leaned forward, smiling at his grandson.

"You tell me, Lauren. What is family?"

I should have known better than to act like I had the answer, much less deliver it the way that I did.

But I looked down, and I spoke. "Him."

Father placed his pipe on the desk, then turned back toward me, clasping his hands between us.

"Lauren, I can see where you're coming from. I can. But what you need to understand—what you don't have the benefit of knowing at this point in your life—is that . . . no one cares."

"No one cares? Cares about what?"

"Here." He gestured for the baby. "Let's just say," he continued, "for the sake of argument, that little Cody, here, grows up with the Dubois name. You and Lance get married, our families unite, and we all live happily ever after."

Father began rocking his arms yet again—something that, I suspected, I never would get used to.

"Okay. And?"

"And one day, Mr. Lance does what their kind does best."

I gave Father a look that conveyed just how tired I was of the conversation. "And that is . . ."

He forced a smile. "He leaves. Again. Just like his father— and his father before him."

"Before him?"

"You see? You don't have the benefit of knowing what family entails. And that"—he handed him back—"as your father, is my job." He grabbed his pipe. "There's a reason for everything, my love." He pulled the matchbox from his vest pocket. "You may not see it now, but one day, you will. And it's my job to make sure that you do."

Father stood up and pushed the chair back under the desk before pulling a match from the box. He struck it and held the flame to the bowl of his pipe.

"No one is overly concerned that you have a child," Father said. He tossed the third match onto the dresser, and the smoke was pulled into a whirlwind across the middle of the room. "What does matter is that you had this child with Lance Dubois. Now that—*that* is something that would only lead to heartbreak, once he leaves you again and you're alone."

"I can handle myself," I said.

Father moved toward the open bedroom door. He took a drag and held it, speaking in a breathless and drone voice. "I know, love. But there are certain moments in life when it pays to be certain." The smoke bled from his nose. "Family names are not the time to roll the dice. If another man is going to be responsible for the safety and wellbeing of my only daughter and grandchild, he needs to fit the bill. And Lance Dubois ain't it."

When he put it like that, Father's feelings about Lance began to make sense. Perhaps I was too caught up in the idea of Lance—instead of paying attention to what he had done by leaving the way that he did.

A lone shadow stole from the doorway and down the hall.

THIRTY-TWO

August 28, 2005

He's actually here. The clouds roll in pale waves behind him.

I stand motionless in the cabin of the boat with the case of water at my feet. Brody calls out from the dock. "Hey, I'm gonna run some of this back to my car, okay? I'll be right back."

"Sure," I say, his figure still between us.

Lance bends over to pick up the waters. "Here, let me help."

It's the perfect opportunity. I lean over at the same time, grabbing as he does. Our hands collide.

It's only been seventeen years.

"Sorry," he says.

"Don't be."

I step back and let him help.

He carries the case of water out of the boat and sets it onto the dock. Cotton is fiddling with some cleat at the end of the pier. Lance turns back and meets me at the cabin.

"Thanks for letting me help," he says. "Change of heart?"

"I wouldn't go that far."

"Ah." He leans against the cabin door. Then, he has the nerve to say more. "But you were willing to go pretty far once before."

I push my way past him, but he grabs me by the arm.

"What are you doing?" I say.

"Oh, come on. I can't joke about being kids?"

"Joke, huh?"

He shrugs it off. "Look, I'm sorry." A flash of light reaches us from a distance, followed seconds later by an ominous grumble. The boat rocks. Lance reaches out to catch me, but perhaps as a gut reaction, I swat at the gesture. He throws up his hands, looking genuinely shocked.

"What happened?" I say, possibly with a bit too much of a bite. The words flow out of me like a sickness. I fold my arms, and my shoulders stiffen. "You just up and leave people? No explanation? No goodbye? Nothing?"

He looks out at the bayou, then up to the clouds. They eddy in muted tones, closer to black than white, now.

"Where's this coming from?" he says. "You really gonna hold a grudge over some teenage summer?"

I look back at the cabin—back to that makeshift sofa.

"You left without a word, Lance. Even your father wouldn't give me an explanation. At least, not a proper one."

"I had no choice in the matter, Lauren. Look, I'm sorry about your dad, I really am. But all those years should've been plenty of time for you to get your story straight."

He moves past me and grabs the piling to pull himself out of the boat—but I grab him by the arm and yank him back down.

"What the hell?" he says.

"You care to elaborate on that? Or you just going to walk away—again?"

"It doesn't matter." He forces a saddened smile. "I left, and that's all you'll ever see."

He reaches for the post yet again, and I pull him back.

"Fine," he says, "you wanna know why I left? Do you?"

"Yes, *Lance*. I do."

He turns away and shifts his focus to the water, his back in my face.

"My Uncle Holden owns a hunting ranch in Texas, and just before I left, we found out that he was sick. He had cancer."

"Yes, Lance, I know that. Your father told—"

His eyes find mine and don't let go. "Would you let me finish? You want the explanation or not?"

I say nothing.

"Their family needed someone to help run the ranch while—while my aunt took care of him. Until he passed. My dad thought that I was the only person who could help, and I was. They had no one else. No other family besides us. Dad needed to stay here and work so we wouldn't lose the house. So, he encouraged me to go. And I did."

"Yes. I know that," I say. "But that still doesn't explain—"

His look returns.

"But Dad was never the type to convince me to do anything, much less encourage me to do something so big. Something that was so . . . life-changing. Even if it was family. So, I had my suspicions from day one."

"Suspicions? About helping out a dying family member?"

He goes on as if I haven't said a word.

"I was supposed to be starting college soon." He turns to me again. "I had *you* here, Dad, Rowan. It didn't seem like him. Part of me didn't buy it—that it was him alone who was pushing me to leave here—whether it was family or not."

"What are you saying, Lance? Your father turned out to be something different than you thought?" I can't help the sarcasm that leaches deep into my words. "Is that really the excuse that you're—"

Another flash crawls over the sky, closer and all too bright—and the sound that follows shakes the boat beneath our feet. We flinch at the sound.

"I'm sorry, Lauren. I am. But—"

"Hey, Lance," Brody says. "How's it going?"

"Say what you want." I move closer to him. No matter the excuse, no matter what reasoning he's worked out in his head over the years, it will never be enough to make up for it. Any of it. "Invent whatever stories you can to make yourself feel better at night, Lance."

Brody turns away and meanders to Cotton at the other side of the dock.

"But don't pretend to care now," I say. "I waited for you to come back. Only to be—"

I step closer to him, until there is no wind. No mist falling from the gray. No flashes of light over the bayou.

"No," I say. "It's too late. There's too much to undo. Too much that you don't know."

He reaches out, but I turn away.

"Too much that you'll never know."

At first, I hear nothing. We just stand there in silence. Then I feel the boat rock as he steps out and onto the dock.

THIRTY-THREE

August 28, 2005

We can use the help, but the truth of the matter is that Shadow saw what I saw earlier, while Lance was offering to lend us a hand: those beady eyes peering at us from above, flickering between the slender white curtains on the third floor of our home. Perhaps it's time we have the talk. Again.

Ostensibly, Lance is unaware. Fences are meant to keep people out—neighbors included. But the fence didn't do much to keep him away back then—nor did it keep me away from him.

Just as I close the front door, I hear the feet scurrying above me. I look up to see Cody hanging over the banister. It feels like only yesterday when that bedroom was all we knew.

"Mother?"

"I'm on my way up, love."

Nearly seventeen years later, and today is one of the few times the little guy has nearly given me a heart attack. And for good reason. Life would be easier if we could leave—for this storm and, perhaps, permanently—but I don't see that happening anytime soon. He's the same now as when Father was around.

Was that only weeks ago?

Cody has yet to leave, and I suspect he couldn't part ways with this house if he wanted to. It isn't Father's fault, though. He's gone now, and yet, here we are. I can't say that I'm surprised.

I look back to the front door. It took me years to work up the nerve to leave this house.

Temporarily, of course—once I had earned it.

"Mother?"

"On my way, love."

As I walk up the stairs and round the corner, walking to what I once considered *my* room, I can still feel my skin burning beneath Father's grasp. My blood pumping at a tiresome pace.

But I'm thankful for it. Without Father, there would be no fence. Who knows what would've come of such an inappropriate union?

Cody is sitting cross-legged in the middle of the floor, reading, working his way through my old biology and pre-med texts. I tell him endlessly that he can be whatever he like, but he always finds his way back to medicine. "Nursing, probably," he says.

I wonder who he gets it from.

I lie back on the bed. The memory of tobacco wafts over me. He closes one of the textbooks with a thud. The sound rattles me, but I imagine Father wouldn't have flinched.

"Mother?"

"Yes, love?"

"How come—Why doesn't he visit?"

It's a good thing that Cody broached the subject and not me, because I'm not entirely sure how to go about it. It's different, now that Father is dead.

"Who?" I say, giving myself time to think.

"Lance."

This isn't the first time it's come up, but it is the first time that Cody has mentioned him since Father has passed. Father always explained it best. Me, not so much.

"Well"—I fold my hands on my stomach and close my eyes—"do you remember what paw-paw taught you? About your place in life as a Roux, my love?"

"Yes, Mother."

"And?"

"Something about my name and standing up?"

Something about? No. No, no.

I sit up and lean forward, clasping my hands between us.

"You listen good, son. Your grandparents are the only reason you're here. You understand?"

"Yes, ma'am."

"And whether they're gone or not, you *will* respect that."

"Yes, Mother."

"Now, what did paw-paw teach you? I know you remember."

He inches his chest up, pulling back his shoulders. "To carry myself like a Roux," he says.

"That's right, son. That's exactly right. There's two things that you need to hold on tight to in this world. And that's—"

"My family name and the way I carry myself."

His back straightens a breath more.

"Of course, my love."

"But shouldn't I be a Dubois? Shouldn't my father have the right to—"

"Hush."

"If Lance is my father, I should—"

"Quiet, son. If you know what's good for you, you'll stop while you're ahead. We've had this conversation before—too often, in fact."

And we have. But Father always knew how to put an end to it before it ever got started.

"Yes, Mother."

I sit back and run my hand across the comforter. The plush, cool air crawls over the hairs on my arm.

"Your grandfather may not be around any longer, but the

future of our family is you. You understand?"

No response.

"All of this"—I look around at the room—"this will one day be yours."

"This? What's this?"

I lean forward and run my hand through his knotted hair. "That's okay, son. You don't get it. It's okay. But one day, you will. One day, you'll understand the importance of your name."

He looks away, out the window. Oh, how Father would've fixed me if my attention was so lax.

I reach out and turn his chin toward me. "You *will* look at me when I'm speaking to you. You understand?"

"Yes, Mother."

"Now, you know why Lance doesn't come over here. Don't you?"

"Yes, Mother."

"After what that man has done to this family, he doesn't deserve you. The Dubois people don't deserve either of us."

"Did he really do that?" he says.

"What's that, love?"

"Lance—did he really leave when you were about to have me? When you were pregnant?"

"Yes, son. He did."

"And what if he hadn't?"

"Hadn't what?"

"Left. What if he hadn't left when you were pregnant? Would things be different?"

All this time, and that was something I hadn't considered. Maybe things would be different; maybe they wouldn't. But that's beside the point.

"No, son. That wouldn't have changed a thing."

"Then why can't I see him?"

"And what purpose would that serve? Do you really want to be associated with someone who walked out on you? Who walked out on *us*?"

"No, ma'am."

I stand up and roll back my shoulders; the conversation is painful in more ways than one.

"I didn't think so."

As I turn to the door, he catches me flat-footed once more.

"Mother?"

"Yes, son?"

"I'm sorry."

"For what?"

"Staying."

And that's when a small piece of me withers. As a mother—but more importantly, as a Roux—it's on me to fix what that man has done.

It's on me, now, to embrace the role of Father.

I walk to the corner of the room and reach up, pushing the small white camera so that it points up to the ceiling. I pull the thin cord from the back of it.

"Don't worry, my love. Sometimes, we just need a little help."

I wink and walk out of the room.

THIRTY-FOUR

November 1989

For all intents and purposes, I wasn't there.

It was Thanksgiving, and Father was throwing one of his get-togethers, political acquaintances who had nothing better to do on a national holiday than to stand around with a drink in one hand and a cigar in the other, trading stories about who had devised the most obnoxious red tape. As far as anyone knew, I was out of the country with family. Indefinitely. In truth, I was there in my bedroom on the third floor.

I wondered how many of his know-you-in-passing connections were even aware that he had a daughter—much less a grandchild.

Miss Amy had moved into the only other bedroom, the one next to mine, a few months back so she could help with Cody. At least, that was Father's reasoning. The third floor was ours— a second home, so to speak. I wasn't blind, though. She was there to keep tabs on me as well.

Sure, I thought about it: screaming at the top of my lungs, making a scene, yelling loud enough and long enough that someone, anyone, in the house would grow suspicious. It seemed simple enough, but what I had to consider were the numbers stacked against me. Miss Amy rarely left the house from what I could tell; Shadow was anywhere and everywhere, day and night, looking for any opportunity to better his standing with Father. And Father . . . I looked to the camera in the corner of the room. Father was always around.

It was unsettling how a reputation changed people two-fold: once so they could acquire it, and once so they could keep it.

My crazed story about what I'd been through over the last year, put against whatever reasoning the three of them could devise in a hurry, wouldn't have stood a chance. No way. Drumming up some obnoxious scene wasn't worth the risk of the consequences after.

If I was going to get out, my best shot was to do it while Father was preoccupied and while no one would know I was gone—until it was too late.

I'd gone back and forth in my head a thousand times about whether I should make a go for it, or just sit back and take whatever Father had in store. But at the end of the day, every night as I put my head on the pillow, it all came back to what was best for Cody. It was no longer just about me. Sure, Miss Amy helped, and I appreciated it dearly. But Cody deserved so much more than what I could give him sitting in that house. In that room.

The thud of car doors and echo of voices filled the air below me. Miss Amy walked into my bedroom.

"It's about that time, darling," she said. She leaned over the all-white bassinet next to my bed and smiled as she pushed a curl of hair from his forehead. "You know the drill," she mumbled.

And I did. I wasn't allowed beyond my room and the adjoining restroom anyway, but on days like this, I was to cease to exist—and that meant Cody, too. Both of us were to remain tucked away like some CD with too many scratches—not good enough to be of real use, but too valuable to toss out of the car window.

The music began to play from down on the first floor. I had come to know the song as more of a forewarning than a form of entertainment. Father would play "She's Like the Wind" when he noticed guests were arriving. It was the unspoken sign for me to stay put—like I had anywhere else to be.

The song took on a special meaning for me, though. There was something timely about the idea of wanting someone I knew I couldn't have. The song itself was only about two years old, but I felt as if I had known it for far longer.

Even sitting in bed with my son at my side and Miss Amy hovering over us, I could feel his breath on my neck, the warmth as it poured down my chest and between my breasts. His body pressed against mine with that look in his eyes, like he was wondering how he had come to be inside me.

Perhaps I was a fool for thinking it had been anything other than a head-on collision between our worlds.

I coughed.

The hardest part about my last-minute plan was leaving Cody behind. If I was going to make it count, I had to go it alone. I'd come back for him.

I exaggerated the sound and held my throat, really dragging out the raspiness of my breaths.

"Oh, my," Miss Amy said. "Are you okay, darling? Can I get you something?"

I coughed harder and with a bit of a wheeze—something I had learned to do long ago, when I wanted to stay home from school and convince Mother that I was sick.

"Yes, please."

"I'll be right back. I have some water in my room." She swatted the air. "No need to ask twice, now."

The one good thing about Miss Amy's room being next to mine was that it had made her lazy over the past several months. At first, she was Shadow reinvented, locking every bolt and checking it twice. But after a while, because she spent most of her time between our two bedrooms, she unknowingly began to let down her guard. Even if she was only a few feet away, it was down all the same.

I couldn't blame her, though. Who would have taken the time to lock all four locks on the bedroom door when they would only be gone for a few seconds—in the next room, no less?

Her complacency was my one and only opportunity.

She left the room but kept the bedroom door cracked. A sliver of light found its way past the row of shining locks.

The moment she turned down the hallway, I sprang from my bed and darted out of the room. My way out was clear as day, and the silence of the carpet beneath my feet only aided my escape.

I didn't need to bring anything with me; it would've slowed me down. My plan was to climb over the banister about halfway down the last set of stairs. That way, anyone in the kitchen and living room wouldn't be the wiser. Then I could take the hallway behind the kitchen to the door that led to the back porch.

There was no other way. I only hoped that Father had kept his guests inside. Once I was gone, it didn't matter where I went. My only goal was to find someone. Anyone.

I tiptoed down the first set of stairs to the second floor and past Father's study, which was open but dark. The voices on the first floor grew louder, echoing throughout the house.

I looked behind me, back up to the top of the empty staircase—and the seconds grew shorter.

Then I crept to the bottom set of stairs and poked my head over the banister, looking down to the dining room and edge of the kitchen. From what I could tell, everyone was either in the kitchen or the living room.

Only for a split second did I glance back.

"Oh, my," I heard from up above, followed by the coggle

of heavy feet.

I cleared the top four steps in a single bound, then threw myself over the railing. My bare feet hit the marble floors without a sound. As I stood up and took the first step toward the hallway that ran behind the kitchen, I noticed it: the small red light flashing in the corner of the ceiling.

There were more.

How I noticed it, I had no idea. The camera was tucked away like a motion sensor for an alarm. Seemingly harmless, which made sense.

"Mr. Roux, darling? Oh, Mr. Roux!"

"Shit." I darted down the hallway, but as I moved past the French doors to the kitchen, I was cut off—by an old lady and her cane. I fell back against the wall and ducked out of view of the swinging double doors.

"Oh, I'm sorry dear," the lady said. "I didn't mean to startle you."

Her hazy, washed-out, empty eyes wandered from side to side, and the mangled wooden cane shook in her hand as she shuffled closer to me.

"I wasn't aware that Edward Roux had personal help around the house. How lovely."

I looked down at my bare feet, sure that my gig was up.

The woman inched closer.

"I must say, you did a fantastic job on the roast, my dear. Now, tell me"—she lifted the shaking cane and pointed at the French doors, and what I guessed was on the other side—"how did you manage to craft something so tender?"

She rested the cane in the crook of her arm and pulled a wadded tissue from her pants pocket.

I took a step closer to the back door.

Feet hurried above me, waddling from one end of the hall

to the other. "Oh, my. Mr. Roux!"

The old lady looked down at my naked feet.

I opened my mouth, but the words didn't come.

"Well, come out with it, love. Hired help doesn't need to be so shy, my dear." She stepped toward me and wiped the tissue across her nose with a trembling, papery hand.

The floor at the top of the stairs creaked and moaned as the haze in the old lady's eyes floated over me. She smiled a toothless grin.

"I'm so sorry," I said. "Please excuse me."

I opened the back door and stepped out with a single foot, sure that I could—

"Ain't that r-r-r-right."

The door slammed shut, and the adrenaline flooded my veins. Father and Shadow were there, waiting for me on the back porch with not another soul in sight.

"Going somewhere, love?" Father said. Then he spoke to Shadow. "Get her upstairs. Quietly."

The man reached for my arm, but I pulled it away. "Don't. Touch me." I wanted to make sure that Father saw the disappointment in my eyes.

"If you know what's good for you . . ." Father said. But he had no intention of elaborating on the threat. He pulled his pipe from his coat pocket and placed it between his teeth.

Shadow peered through the glass door.

"What about old lady Reeves?" he said.

Father smiled and walked toward the main entrance, off of the living room. "Miss Reeves, darling." The lady ambled back through the French doors inside and toward his voice.

Shadow opened the door and attempted, yet again, to guide me by the arm. As I pulled away, Miss Amy appeared in the hall, panting and damp with sweat.

If plan A wouldn't work, it was time for plan B. So, I screamed. "Somebody help m—" But Shadow's hand covered my mouth and pulled me backward before I could get it out.

"Oh, darling," she said. "You gave me a fright there for a moment." She leaned back against the wall and patted her forehead with the back of her hand.

Shadow turned to Miss Amy and stabbed his finger at her with his free hand. "You," Shadow said. His stiff finger wagged in her face.

To my surprise, that was all he could come up with.

Miss Amy slapped his finger and chuckled. Her sagging breasts swung dangerously this way and that. "Oh, my. He *is* a character," she said to me. His hand was still covering my mouth, my back pressed against the front of him.

I grinned and spoke between his fingers in a muffled voice. "Ain't that right."

And her laugh only grew more wholesome.

THIRTY-FIVE

August 29, 2005

I 've had a change of heart, but I take it to be a good thing. People rarely change.

I told Shadow he can stay in the house for the storm. If something were to happen to him, my conscience would never let it go. Not to mention, Father would haunt me to the end of my days. I'm not completely heartless. Besides, some things need tending to around here.

The surge has already topped the sandbags, and darkness floods the house. The only home I've known shrinks to endless corners of a single void.

I sit at the top of the stairs with a candle on the floor beside me. The flame waltzes on the wall, but it pales in comparison to the lightning, which brings the house to life for the briefest of moments before plunging us into the emptiness over and over again, like bobbing for apples in the copper tub at one of Brody's childhood birthday parties. It's calming and chilling all the same.

The shadow speaks from the hallway as he leans over the banister. "Thank you, Miss Roux." The flashes catch him in profile, as he looks down at the flooding below us.

"Of course, Shadow. Don't mention it."

Water seeps beneath the front door and washes over the marble. I watch in broken frames as it turns the pristine floors into the bottom of the bayou. The house shakes, lightning crawls, and I can hear wood snapping out back of the house, one tree after another.

The smooth and woodsy fragrance of the sandalwood

candle is snuffed out by the soured rot of mud-stained water as it inundates the dining room.

"So, what made you change your m-m-m-m-m-mind?"

Nothing *made* me do anything.

"Nothing in particular," I say. "If Father were here, I find it hard to believe that he wouldn't take you in for the time being." I look at the man as he leans farther over the railing. "Things are changing, Shadow."

He cranes his neck out past the banister and produces a slow rope of spittle. I move to say something more, to stop him, but I instantly realize that it doesn't matter. The flashes of white ignite the line of dip as it falls like a glowing rope to the water below us. The spit is lost to the tide, washing into the kitchen.

"Whether we like it or not," I continue, "everything is changing."

Splashes of water echo throughout the foyer, like waves beneath a dock.

"Yeah, well"—Shadow looks out of the black windows, in the direction of his treehouse—"change comes easier for some of us than it does for others." He looks back at me. "Ain't that right?"

I consider my options and what Father would have done in this situation. As far as I can tell, there's no reason both of us can't benefit from the current circumstances.

The brown sludge reaches the bottom tread of the stairs.

"What if it doesn't have to?" I say.

"D-d-d-do what?"

"What if dealing with this storm, and everything that follows, doesn't have to come easier for only one of us?"

He pulls a can of dip from his shirt pocket and begins smacking it against his hand. Then he unscrews it. "What do you mean?"

It's all too surreal—having a simple conversation with someone as the house, everything Father ever worked for, is flooding around us.

And all we can do is watch.

I look out the windows, which reveal nothing but black rain beating the house in bands, backlit by the disjointed flashes.

"Your treehouse is fucked."

In the next round of lightning, I can see that Shadow has stopped what he's doing and is standing motionless against the balcony.

"Yeah," he says. "It ain't stood a chance in a storm like this." He places a pinch of dip behind his lip.

It slips out. "Father considered you nothing more than hired help."

The man grumbles and slips the can back into his shirt pocket, then nods. "Yeah, well. Technically, that's w-w-w-what I am, Miss Roux."

"No, Shadow. I think it's safe to say that's what you were. Father is no longer here, I'm no longer a child, and, well, you've become a bit more than hired help."

The candle burns down until the flashes of light show me the dead stream of smoke swimming across the room.

"Like I said, things are changing. And maybe that means your place around here can change, too."

"You gonna talk in circles or come out with it already?"

I smile, but the darkness doesn't show it.

"Eating in the living room . . . meager pay . . . the grunt work . . . *living in a treehouse?*"

"Your father helped me out with that house. Ain't no reason to be talking bad about—"

"No," I say. "I'm doing no such thing, Shadow. I loved Father. He was the type of man that I only hope Cody can grow up to be, someday. Father was everything to me, Shadow. He *is* everything."

I can't get a read on what Shadow is thinking. Not in this shadowy void.

"What I'm saying," I continue, "is that this is the perfect opportunity for a fresh start. Like I said before, we still need you around, but—"

"You made it very clear that you're my boss, Miss Roux. And I told you that that's fine by m-m-m-me."

"And I am your boss. That doesn't need to change, Shadow. But this storm is making me realize what it is that's really important."

"And that is?"

He grunts yet again. We look down as the water drowns the second tread at the base of the stairs.

"Family."

The shattering of glass outside mixes with the whistle of the wind, followed by what I guess is a muffled scream. But whose?

Lightning flashes, and Shadow appears a few steps closer.

"I'm listening," he says.

I pick up the candle and light it yet again, then set it on the floor between us.

"You're a member of this family, Shadow. You have been for a long time."

"Uh-huh."

"But I think it's time you start being treated like one."

"You knew your daddy b-b-b-better than anyone, and you know what the man preached. Two things, Miss Roux."

"Yes, Shadow. I do."

We speak at the same time. "Family and posture."

"I'll never carry the Roux name," he says. "The Roux blood ain't in me. And there ain't nothing I can do about that."

"No. But aren't you tired of getting the short end of the stick?"

He huffs, like I'm only reiterating what he already knows.

"I mean, take a step back and really think about it, Shadow."

His expression melts through the teases of light.

"Cotton got the house, the inheritance, more of the property than you, and you're stuck here with what? A sliver of land and a makeshift house—thanks to someone who *isn't* your brother? Yes. It sounds like the blunt end of the deal to me."

Lightning flashes. He's several steps closer.

"I do like the sound of a fresh start," he says. "What do you have in mind?"

"Simple: our home is your home."

"Hm," he says. "And the treehouse? My land? It ain't m-m-m-much, but it is mine."

"Of course, Shadow. That doesn't need to change. I'm not trying to talk you into doing anything. I'm simply offering you more. Life is too short. Family is . . . family."

The flame flickers, and Shadow appears next to me. He sits down on the step and leans back against the railing.

"Things are changing, huh?" he says. "Is that for the better?"

The water splashes against the third step, and the dining room chairs topple over below us, lost to the incoming tide.

"Well, that depends," I say.

"On?"

"You, mostly."

Shadow lifts his chin and spits some of the dip between his jagged teeth. It clears the stairs and lands amid the flashes of water. He nods in the candlelight.

"Okay," he says. "What about me?"

I grab the candle and stand up. "I need to check on Cody."

"Yes, ma'am."

A small part of me feels guilty for leaving him in the dark. "Being a part of this family, Shadow, is more than a responsibility." I pull back my shoulders. "It's a duty."

Shadow lifts his chin.

"You up for it?"

"Yes, ma'am. Anything for Mr. Roux."

THIRTY-SIX

November 1989

I regretted nothing.

"And where did you think you were gonna go, now, darling?" Miss Amy said with a thick Southern swat of her hand. "And barefoot nonetheless." She waddled to the basinet and scooped up Cody in one fell swoop, then carried him to the bed.

"To be honest? Anywhere but here."

She loomed over me while she rocked him in her arms, brushing aside his stray curls and swaying as if he were her own. Then she leaned over and placed him in my arms with a delicate touch.

"You know, personally, I think you could've made it—if it weren't for a touch of bad luck." She pulled my desk chair to the bedside and sat down. The wood groaned. "But one thing you should keep in mind, darling"—her hand adjusted the baby-blue binky in his mouth—"is that you have two people to look after, now."

The most intriguing thing about Miss Amy wasn't her background in nursing or her oversized sense of self-confidence. It wasn't the too-clean sneakers and white scrubs she wore day in and day out, like she was stranded in some monotone insane asylum for the critically OCD. No. It was the fact that regardless of what happened, no matter how horrible the circumstances, her reaction was all the same: an uncanny, nonchalant calm— like she was on autopilot, just going through the motions.

"Besides," she continued, "right here at home is the best place for a young lady like yourself. Your father has only the utmost love for his family, you know." She patted my leg. "Now *that*, I can respect. But that Shadow fella . . ." She inched closer and tilted her head down until her chins formed a never-ending, rolling valley. Her top lip curled into a disapproving sneer. "That man is about as hungry as they come, darling."

"Hungry?"

She rolled her eyes and wagged her chins. Her whiskers trembled. "Blind obedience, darling." The morning's black chicory lingered on her breath like an invisible stain. "Men of his kind will do anything to—"

Father spoke from the doorway. "Sometimes, we confuse obedience with devotion."

Miss Amy didn't look at him, just smiled and continued to stroke Cody's cheek.

"Of course, Mr. Roux." She stood up and straightened her top, which had begun to lose control of her bust. "I myself am about as devoted as they come." She walked to Father and rested her hand on his shoulder as she brushed past him. "It's just a matter of what we're devoted to." Her eyes fluttered as she looked back.

Miss Amy walked out of the room and shut the door behind her. Each lock slid and clicked from the top down. She wasn't going to make the same mistake twice.

To my surprise, Father had no scowl on his face, only a businesslike look about him. He sat down next to my bed and leaned back and crossed his legs. His teeth chattered on the stem of his unlit pipe. The whiskery corner of his mouth crept upward.

"What?" I said.

He closed his eyes and shook his head. "Nothing, love. Nothing at all."

I debated whether I should bring up my failed run for it. If

Father wasn't going to address it, maybe it was simply best to let it go.

Maybe not.

"Are you mad?" I asked.

His leg tapped without pause, and his smirk broadened.

"No, love. I'm not mad. Nor am I surprised."

How could that be possible?

"What I am . . . is curious," he said.

"About?"

"Why. I want to know why it is that you thought you'd be better off"—he looked to the side and shrugged—"*anywhere, really*, other than here at home. With your family, where you belong."

"Is that a serious question?"

"Yes. Yes, it is, Lauren."

I had always heard the horror stories of single mothers: the sleepless nights, post-partum depression, never-ending days stringing into tiresome cries and midnight feedings, working during the day only to come home and slave around the house, the doctor's visits . . . resentment. Did I mention the sleepless nights? But what did I have to complain about, really?

Not many mothers had their own midwife.

Father leaned forward. He opened his mouth, but I could tell he was struggling to find whatever words had escaped him. He tapped the pipe on his knee, then opened his suit jacket and removed a disheveled envelope.

"Here." He held out the faded paper with his eyes on the floor.

"What's this?"

He pushed it closer. "A letter."

"From?"

He only gestured with it, as his eyes found my own.

I propped up Cody in front of me with his head in my lap, then grabbed the blank envelope and opened it. At first, my anger was directed toward Father for keeping it from me.

Dear Lauren,

I hope this letter finds you well. I am sure you have more questions than answers, and for that I am sorry. First of all, I would like to apologize for leaving so abruptly.

Keeping my head down, I flashed my eyes up at him.
"It was in the mailbox a few weeks after he left," he said.

I wanted to stop and explain why I left town, but everything happened so quickly that I was gone without really having the time to think about it. My uncle Holden is sick, and I am in Texas caring for him until my aunt can figure out what to do with their business. They need the help, and they have no one else.

I ran the tip of my finger over the thumbprint of ink at the top corner of the page. Remnants of a dying ink ribbon were written into the faded letters.

As much as I feel that I owe you an explanation, I do not think it is a good idea to see each other again if and when I come back. The more I think about it, the more I realize that you deserve better. You deserve someone better than a Dubois, and I know you will find him. Although you may not see it now, one day you will.

Sincerely,
Lance

My anger folded inward. How had I been so naïve to think that he'd come back for me? So trusting?

Father's hand reached out and found my own. It'd been some time since he had shown any sort of affection toward me or Cody. I wondered if it was because Miss Amy and Shadow were around just as much as he was. A man like Father didn't stumble across a reputation like his by accident—so it made sense that he had developed a wall around even those who were closest to the family.

"I'm sorry, love," he said. "Hopefully, now, you can see why I did my best to steer you away from the boy for so long."

"No, I don't. Why now? If you were so dead set against the two of us seeing each other, then why would you keep this from me?"

Father crossed his legs and fidgeted with a whole lot of nothing.

"You had enough on your plate as it was. I figured something like that"—he pointed to the letter—"would've only added to your stress at such a difficult time. I knew it would only upset you even more."

"And if I found a way to write him? What would you have done then? I knew where he was, Father. Marcus Dubois told me that he was in Texas. But the rest of that letter would've been useful."

He leaned forward. "I know, love. I know. And I'm sorry, but don't you see? This is precisely what I've been trying to avoid. This is what I've been trying to protect you from. The heartbreak. Don't you see?"

I dropped the letter to the floor and reached for Cody.

"I gave you that against my better judgment," Father said. "So, you're welcome."

"I didn't say anything."

He reached down and picked up the letter, then placed it on my nightstand. "You know, things can change around here, love. This situation in which we find ourselves doesn't need to be forever. It *isn't* forever."

Father stood and buttoned his coat.

"Today was nothing more than a bump in the road," he said. "I have faith in you—in this name that we carry."

His eyes caught the sunlight through the curtains as he straightened his back and nodded only once. "Play your cards right, and have some faith in the man who *does* love you." He winked.

He rapped on the door, and Shadow opened it.

"You know that I love you, yes?"

I had always known that Father loved me. Just like anyone else, he had his own unique way of showing it.

"Yes, Father. I do."

I looked down at Cody. "And I love you."

Maybe it was time to be grateful for how good I had it when it came to being a single parent. A teenage parent. And that letter? What else was I blind to?

THIRTY-SEVEN

August 30, 2005

A booming thud shakes the sodden home to its frame.

"What was that?" Cody says. He looks down at the floor beneath us.

"I have no idea." In reality, I do have somewhat of an inkling.

The water has largely receded, but the smell is only getting worse. I can taste it in the back of my mouth now, sticking to that thing at the back of my throat. It reminds me of one evening during that summer when Lance and I got back from one of our fishing trips, when I tied off his boat at the Bayou Liberty boat launch. More often than not, even in the winter, the bayou has a distinct smell about it, a familiarity—like a mix of brackish water and white oak dissolved in a dense, lingering fog. Like a wooded saltiness. But not that day.

I remember the way we looked at each other when the smell hit us as we stepped out of the boat. Someone who was crabbing off of the docks had left their scraps of gutted trout in the water. The wakes of passing boats had pushed the black-speckled remnants on shore right next to the last dock where we parked, where the flies, buzzards, and their shadows swarmed in shifting clouds over the glassy water.

Katrina's standing mud and flooding smells a bit like that: the rot of abandoned bodies, left to the devices of a churning tide.

Glass shatters at the front door.

"Come on," I say. "Follow me."

"What? No. If someone is looking for us, we should—"

"I'm not arguing, son." I turn down the hallway. "Let's go. Now."

Just as I make it to the end of the hall, I hear his voice—and Cotton's, too. "After you, my boy."

I urge Cody to move faster. "Come. *On.*"

He scurries toward me with his eyes on the foyer below us. "What about Shadow?" His flashlight darts across the ceiling, and I cringe in response.

"I'm not worried about Shadow. He can handle himself."

As we reach the mirror, I look to the wild boar mounted on the wall beside it. Father loved telling the story of how he had taken the trophy when he was a wee teen.

His uncle Jonathan owned a fair amount of land in southwest Alabama, and my grandfather used to take him hunting there every other weekend in the late fall and early winter. "The property wasn't anything special," Father used to say. "But one hunt in particular stands out."

He was thirteen when he and his father were sitting on one of the four makeshift wooden ladder stands on the overgrown trail that ran down the center of the property. Father rarely saw anything other than a few squirrels and rabbits here and there. He would sit on a sheet of plywood with his father behind him on a shell bucket. One day, no more than ten minutes into an evening hunt, the most mammoth pig he'd ever seen trotted right beneath them.

All it took was for his father to lightly tap him on the shoulder as the pig crossed the ditch in front of them and stepped out onto the roadway. He lifted his twelve-gauge and shot the creature in the head, flipping it onto its back. He shot twice more, and the boar ran off with a deafening squeal.

He told me they looked for it all night but found nothing—

not a single drop of blood. Nothing. The only evidence of the pig being there at all were the tracks in the mud that led to a long rut, where the animal had run away without being able to lift its head from the ground.

It wasn't until the next morning, when they returned with his uncle's retriever, that they found the pig several hundred yards away in a tangled, bloody thicket.

"Wild pigs are tanks," he used to tell me. "And that's the last time I hunted wild boar with a shotgun." He would point to the rifle over the fireplace in his office.

I reach over and pull down on the boar's tusk. The mirror pops open, and I step into the hot and humid safe room. It's blacker than black can be, and the floor transitions from soaked carpet to a clean and bare foundation. A lack of electricity has turned the house into a sauna that makes me feel as if I'm drowning in a soup of dense air, one gasp of wet oxygen at a time.

"Come on," I say to Cody.

He steps inside, and I slide the mirror back into place. From inside the room, I can faintly make out the hallway and stairs leading down to the first floor, as if there's nothing between us and the other side. Of course, no one can see into the safe room.

Cody shines his flashlight in my eyes.

"I thought you said that I was never allowed in here," he says. "What's going on? Why are we here?"

The room is somewhat new to me as well, although not as new as it is to Cody. Father only showed it to me last year, once I asked far too many times about the cameras and how they worked. He was willing to explain his reasoning behind the surveillance once I had proven myself to be a Roux—and not merely the daughter of one.

"Things are changing, my love."

Neither of us can hear anything from inside the soundproof room, but we can see the faintest of shadows shifting on the walls at the other end of the hallway. Lance and Cotton are inside of our home.

I sit down on one of the two black cases on the floor. "Sit," I say, with a gesture of my light.

Cody looks out through the mirror. I can see the gears turning in his head. He sits on the other case of dried goods and supplies, but his eyes remain there.

He whispers. "What are we doing?" His effort to be quiet isn't necessary. Not in here.

"Son . . . this storm is your opportunity. This is what you've been waiting for."

Finally, his attention shifts from the mirror to myself. "What opportunity?"

"For a fresh start, my love. All these years, you've been waiting for a chance to walk out of here. For a chance to get out of this house—and speak to your father."

I look through the glass. My eyes strain to see the end of the hallway and the dim shadows floating up the stairs.

Cody looks unsure of himself—just as I did at his age. "I— I'm not so sure. Why now? Where is this coming from?"

Because it may be the only chance we have.

"Because we deserve better. Because *you* deserve better, Cody. Don't you want answers? Don't you want to know why your father left you?"

"I thought you wanted nothing to do with them? I thought—" He looks out of the mirror.

"This isn't about me, son. This is about you, and this family as a whole. It's about thriving instead of being stuck inside of this house."

We could leave, now that Father is no longer with us. But

for someone like Cody, who has known nothing other than the inside of this house, "can" and "want to" are different narratives altogether.

An anxious mind is more convincing than the closest of family. It keeps you content to stay put—even in the most miserable of positions.

The two figures appear at the top of the stairs. I turn off my light and grab Cody's, pointing it down at the floor. "Turn it off," I whisper.

"They can't hear us."

Old habits are hard to break.

"No, son. They can't."

My nerves begin to settle. I watch Lance as he turns down the hallway toward Father's study.

"It's time you have some answers," I say. "Don't you want answers?"

"I think I'm past the point of needing—"

"Don't shortchange yourself, son. You hear me?"

"I don't get it. Just two days ago, you were telling me how he doesn't deserve me and that we don't need to be associated with someone like him. What are you—"

"Oh please, son. If you're anything like me, you'll never let it go. Look at me: I've been trying to forget about it for all these years. And where has it gotten me? Neither of us should give him the time of day after what he's done to our family. To our name." I edge closer and grab his hand for effect. "But you know as well as I do—we can't let that go."

Cody drops his head. "Yes, ma'am. Of course."

"Now, if you want this—if you finally want to speak with your father and get the answers you deserve—there's only one way to go about it, and that's not on his terms. Not after what he's done to this family. What he's done to you."

"Yes, Mother."

"Do you remember what paw-paw said about the things we need to do sometimes, in order to flourish in life? The sacrifices we need to make in order to succeed as a family?"

"Yes, ma'am."

"And that is?"

"The white lie."

"What about it?"

He looks at the mirror, then back at me. "Sometimes, a white lie is necessary to flourish in life."

"Not to succeed—"

"But to flourish."

"That's right." I place my hand on his cheek. "That's right."

"Just tell me what to do," he says. "All I want is to talk to him. Just once."

"I know, son. I know."

Suddenly, Shadow appears in the hallway, steps away from the mirror. He looks to the pig on the wall beside it, then behind him, where the two men have disappeared, then back at the pig. His hand reaches up to the animal.

"No," I say to myself. "Shadow, no."

Just as his hand reaches the tusk, Lance and Cotton appear from around the corner, and Shadow scurries away. They step into the hallway, and their light points straight at us. One slow step at a time, they move toward the mirror.

"You'll get your chance to speak with your father," I say. "Both of us will. But we need that to be at the right time—when he can no longer abandon you."

His affection never ceases to amaze me.

"Or you," he says.

"That's right. He'll never hurt you again. He'll never hurt either of us."

"What can I do, Mother?"

Lance and Cotton approach the mirror, and without a word spoken, as if neither of us is certain the mirror works as well as we believe, Cody and I scoot back farther into the room. We put as much distance between the four of us as possible—even if it's a matter of inches.

I turn back to Cody. "Don't be fooled, son." We look at Lance on the other side of the glass. "He looks like someone who cares. Trust me, I know."

Our boy inches forward to the mirror. Their light moves over our footprints on the other side.

Cody stands in front of them, one breath away, and reaches his hand to the glass.

"How could he not?" Cody says.

"What?"

"Care. How are you so sure of him, when he has no clue about who I am?"

I stand up next to him and pull his hand down from the mirror, then turn his chin toward me. "Because. He was once sure of me, too."

His attention is broken, and he turns back to the trunk on the floor. He sits and watches as the men turn away and walk down the hallway yet again.

"Okay," Cody says. "I just want to speak to him. What do I need to do? Just tell me what to do."

"That's easy, son." I sit down, too. "He has no idea who you are."

"You want me to lie about who I am?"

"This is about you, my love. This is about your family and getting the answers you deserve."

"That's a bit more than a white lie, Mother." He shakes his head in the smallest of ways. "I don't know. I'm not sure that I can—"

"Maybe it is. Maybe it isn't. But what I know it to be is a decision you have to make for yourself. Just know that the consequence of doing nothing is far greater than the pain of wondering 'what if.' You're a Roux, son—and a Roux is no quitter."

THIRTY-EIGHT

January 1990

I hadn't thought about what he'd do if he caught me.

Even with Cody gone at night, I would wake up and check the crib out of habit. Some mornings were a soft landing, and I'd wake up on my own and roll over to see him gone. Other times, I'd lurch myself awake out of fear of what I thought had happened to him. But the worst nights? A cold sweat would drown me as I'd wake up from the nightmare time and time again—like a murderer who thrived on watching his victims pass out as he strangled them, only to lessen the grip around their neck at the last second so he could do it all again.

Then, as I'd look over at the crib, I'd realize it wasn't a nightmare at all—just life.

Miss Amy did her best to soften the blow, even though I could see that she was stuck in the middle between my shortcomings and Father's headstrong ways. She always had a good way of explaining Father's approach to the whole arrangement with her and Cody, and his rather backward way of helping me through a pregnancy I never would have been able to manage on my own.

I rolled over and stared at the crib, empty other than the blond Cabbage Patch doll with a blue jumper—Father's gift to his grandson, although I suspected it was more to keep me company at night. Minutes turned into an hour, an hour turned to three. Cody's grumbling cry would tell me when Miss Amy was on her way, coming down the hall with my little boy.

The orchestra of locks turned one at a time at the door's

edge.

"There she is," Miss Amy said as she closed the door behind her. I sat up, and she placed Cody in my arms. "Sorry for the late entrance, darling, but the little guy was a touch ornery this morning."

If the time was morning, the morning was like Christmas morning. And all I wanted was him.

Father knew it, too. He had unfettered access to my one and only heart string that he could tug on, day or night. But he cared about his grandson—*that* I was sure of.

Just not his daughter's life choices. Of course, that was no one's fault but my own.

"Oh, that's okay," I said. "I wouldn't have him any other way." I pushed his binky into his mouth.

Miss Amy cradled her cheek in her hand. "I suppose I'd be a touch off my rocker, too, if I was separated from such a cute thing each and every night."

Just then, Cody reached out, ran my hair through his hand, and smiled. A tear broke free from the corner of my eye and raced down my face before I ever knew it was there.

"Oh, darling." Miss Amy placed her hand on my knee. "There's no need to get all twisted up, now. All of life is temporary, my dear. And this too shall pass."

But more of the tears followed, and Cody smiled harder. Miss Amy looked over her shoulder at the bedroom door, then back at the two of us.

"I hate to ask," I said, "but do you think that—" I looked to the door as well.

"What, darling? What is it, now?"

Cody grabbed my finger and refused to let go.

"Do you think that maybe, just for tonight, Cody could—"

"Now, Miss Lauren"—she gave me that you-know-better

look of hers that she'd perfected over the last few months—
"you know that Miss Amy can't do that, don't you? We both
know good and well what your father would say and, quite
frankly, what he would do if I were to let that happen."

My ears rang with the silence between us. All I needed was
one night. Just one night with my baby boy. One night to get me
through this slump that I'd brought on myself. But maybe I
deserved it after what I'd done to lessen Father's trust.

"Please," I said. "Father never comes up here at night. Not
with you here. He doesn't need to know. Just this once. Please?
He'll never know. Besides, even if he does find out, it can be a
chance to show him that what happened before was a mistake.
Please, Miss Amy."

She batted her eyes and grinned from her hairy chin.

"Well, sometimes, you gotta take a chance in life. And this
little guy"—she pinched Cody's plush cheek—"is worth it, if you
ask me."

She must have sensed a change in my expression.

"What?" she said. "You gonna deny this cute thing?"

"No. That saying, is all."

"What's that?"

"That was Mother's advice to me, no matter what I was
going through. 'Sometimes, it pays to take a chance in life,' she'd
say. It was her two cents no matter my worry."

Miss Amy stood up and straightened her bust. "Well, who
do you think she got it from, now?"

She walked to the door. "Don't worry, darling. I'll make
sure that Cody stays with you for at least one night. You let Miss
Amy handle Ed Roux, now, you hear?"

———

"I'll be back first thing in the morning, darling," Miss Amy said as she checked on Cody next to me in the bed. "I'll have him out of here before you're up."

I clutched her hand as she turned away.

"Thank you, Miss Amy. It's good to know that I have someone around here to—"

"You just get some quality time in tonight with the little one, you hear?" She leaned over and tucked him in tight between me and the body pillow at the edge of the bed. "Sleep tight, now." She spoke in a quiet tone, yet her voice was somehow large.

I did my best to stay awake with him, to hold him, to watch him, to feel his tiny and wrinkled hands in mine, to smell his bubbly baby hair, but he was out after five minutes at the most.

Like on most nights, I tossed and turned. I dreaded the morning, when he'd be taken from me once again—even if he wasn't really taken so to speak, only sleeping in Miss Amy's room at Father's insistence. Hours passed, and eventually, all too slowly, I fell asleep for good.

Before I knew it, the cascade of locks at the door woke me up, and Miss Amy was back as if she'd never left. That was the worst thing about sleeping in the same room that I spent every day in—I would wake up feeling well rested, only I never got to experience the rest. The days came and went quicker than a misting summer rain.

Miss Amy whispered as she sat on the edge of the bed, and a wiry creak crept up from the springs below us. "Where's my little guy, now?" She pulled back the covers, and as I sat upright, she covered her mouth with a gasp—and a bloodcurdling scream followed. "Oh, no. No!" she yelled. "Oh, no. Mr. Roux, darling. Oh, no. Mr. Roux!"

I looked down and saw Cody's pale and lifeless body

beneath me, suffocated and stiff.

"Cody?" I grabbed his face and turned it toward me. I shook his little body, but he wouldn't move—not on his own. His limbs flailed, rigid, with the rest of him. "Cody! Wake up!"

"Oh, my." Miss Amy stepped away from the bed as Father appeared in the doorway. "Oh, no."

Cody's glassy, glossed-over eyes were wide with hurt, but he wasn't there. Not really. His lips had adopted the hue of carved plums.

"What's going on?" Father said. "What is this?"

He walked toward me and leaned over Cody's body. Then he lit his pipe and looked down at us with a casual displeasure. "I told you," he said. "I told you you'd learn. One way or anoth—"

And the wet chill drowned me awake.

I looked down at Cody between me and the pillow. My hand slid across his chest. His little heart fluttered beneath my fingers, his breaths shallow and drawn out.

"Jesus Christ." My arms collapsed beneath me, and I fell back to the bed.

A scurry crawled in the hallway just outside of the bedroom. I sat up, just as a shadow stirred beneath the door.

"Miss Amy?"

Cody drew a deep breath, then let it out as a whimper.

I looked over at my alarm clock. It was one minute past 5 a.m.

The walls quivered, and a labored scream filled the hallway. The locks flew open, and Miss Amy was shoved into the room— by Shadow.

"Now you sit r-r-r-right there," he said with a spurt of short breaths.

"How dare you," she said. "How dare you put your greasy

hands on me. Who do you think you're—"

Cody cried out in a string of gasps.

Father appeared in the doorway in his gray-and-white striped pajama pants and a wifebeater. His chest hair curled under the yellow glow of the hall light. "What's going on?" he said. "What is this?"

Shadow pointed. "It's her. She's the p-p-p-p-p-problem."

"You can leave now," Miss Amy said to Shadow. "Your boss can take it from here." She looked to Father.

Shadow lurched toward her—but Father stepped between them. He said nothing, and Shadow turned away and retreated from the room.

"I'll ask once again: *What* is going on?"

Miss Amy grabbed the edge of the bed and pulled herself up to one knee. "Don't go looking to her, now." She pointed at me. "This is all me." The lady raised her right hand. "I'm to blame, now."

Father's eyes found Cody lying on the bed. "What is this?"

Shadow chimed in from the hallway. "It's her." He pointed at Miss Amy yet again. "She's sneaking around here in the middle of the n-n-n-night. She's got Cody in here when he ain't supposed to be. That's what." Shadow inched his way back into the room, and his right eye twitched violently.

Father looked anything but surprised. "That true?" He spoke to Miss Amy.

She pushed herself up until she was standing, her breasts knocking this way and that. "Yes. Yes, it is, Mr. Roux." Then she gestured my way. "This girl—this young *lady*—needs that boy. And that boy needs her."

Shadow rushed farther into the room, but Father grabbed him by the collar and held him to the wall. "That ain't what Mr. Roux asked you, lady."

Father snapped back. "And I don't recall asking *you* anything."

"Lauren needs her son," Miss Amy continued. "I take full responsibility for letting him stay with Lauren last night. I'm the one who talked her into it. It was all me."

She gave me a reassuring look and a nod. From that point forward, I saw the lady in a new light—one that burned for the sake of me and my everything. There was something more to Miss Amy than a mere helping hand. I could see it—albeit faintly, in a dense smog.

Shadow pushed forward, but Father shoved him back against the wall.

"Ain't nothing but excuses," Shadow said.

"And I don't think anyone was talking to you."

We all looked to one another in a round-robin. That moment was the one and only time I'd ever seen Father be anything but cool-headed with Shadow. The whole room felt it.

Father looked at me, then at Miss Amy.

"You brought me here for a reason," she said. "Remember?"

I grabbed Cody and spoke up. "I'm sorry, Father. It's all my—" But Miss Amy's eyes cut straight through me. I couldn't say what it was, but she had Father under the tip of her thumb.

"I've got Lauren," Miss Amy said. "You know that."

"Oh, give me a b-b-b-break. What crazy you talking, 'brought here for a reason'?"

She looked to Father. "Family, yeah?"

"You?" Shadow said. "Family?" His laugh bellowed. "What do you know about family? About *this* family?"

Miss Amy fought back a smile.

"Knock it off," Father said. "Both of you. Shadow—out." He gestured to the hall.

"But M-M-M—"

"Out."

Shadow had nothing good to say. Nothing at all, for that matter. He backed out of the room with his eyes darting between us.

"Okay," Father said. "You got her. Just keep in mind . . ."

"Yeah, yeah," she said. "Him, too." She waved behind him as she ushered him out of the room. Father turned back only briefly, and she eased the door shut.

"What was that?" I said.

"What, darling?"

I lifted my chin to the door. "*That.*"

"Oh, him?" Miss Amy swatted the air between us. She spoke gently, with a touch of satire, a bit of sardonicism. Her breath had not a worry in the world. "Edward Roux is a family man."

I couldn't help but laugh. "Okay. And?"

"And . . ."

She leaned over and kissed Cody on the forehead as she brushed my cheek with her hand.

"Who do you think got this family started, now, darling?" She winked under the dim light of the room. "Like I said before: your mother and I go way back. Back before Edward Roux ever knew what it meant to start a family."

Suddenly, Miss Amy no longer felt like the stranger I had presumed she was. She was wedged somewhere between family and a best friend, although I wasn't all too sure of the difference between the two.

"And as far as I'm concerned," she said, "the Roux family is my family." She pushed my hair back behind my ear and tapped my chin with the tip of her finger.

Then she stood and walked to the door. The look on my

face must have said more than I intended.

She swatted the air between us. "Oh, darling. I love you, too."

THIRTY-NINE

August 30, 2005

This storm is no disaster at all. It's a break in the present so the wrongs of our past can be righted.

"I'm not sure that I can lie to him," Cody says. "What if something bad happens?"

Sometimes, it's hard to believe that he's mine—with his twisted sense of consideration for those who have already hurt him in the most desolate of ways. I'm not sure where he gets it from, but it's definitely not from me.

Cotton and Lance seem to have left, so I crack open the glass door to the safe room and let in some fresh air, but I forgot about the smell. The wet odor drafts into the room, and I quickly appreciate a normal and blistering Louisiana summer.

"You can't think like that, son. The bad has already come and stayed. The bad is what you've been living through for the longest time, now. The bad . . . is all that you know—thanks to a certain someone. Don't you want to fix that? Don't you want to leave this house?"

"I do, but—"

"There is no 'but.' Either you do, or you do not. You're a Roux, son. Not a coward."

At first, he says nothing, but I can see his mind working from the outside in. He fidgets with his flashlight, flicking it on then off, holding it tight against his palm and looking at it from the other side. The peachish-red of his flesh glows like a burning, internal scar.

Sweat drips from his chin and disappears into the dark

between us.

"What happened to me?" he says, almost inaudibly, seemingly all to himself.

It catches me off guard. But the sad part? Without having to think about it, without hesitation or doubt, I know precisely what he's talking about.

So, I act as if I don't—in the hopes that he'll let it go.

"What are you asking me?"

"You know what I'm asking you."

"Excuse me?"

He taps the light more forcefully against his palm. It flickers.

Just before the storm, I had a gut feeling that we were overdue for one of these—one of Cody's spells of questions and doubts and pushback that sent Father up the wall and 'round the corner. Me? I've just accepted it as a quirk of my quirky son. After all, I wasn't without my own eccentricities in my teenage years.

Who isn't?

"What happened to me? It's been weeks since we've lost paw-paw, and—"

"We didn't *lose* paw-paw, son. He didn't pass away to anywhere, he isn't gone—he's dead." I look in the direction of the cemetery that's surely unrecognizable by now. "And we know exactly where he's at."

"Why can't I leave here? This isn't normal. This can't be normal."

Father didn't stand for the episodes. He loved his grandson just as much as I do, but no one dared question the way he ran his family.

I learned that the hard way. But I'm better for it, of course.

"You can leave here, son. You just haven't tried. Like you

said, it's only been a few weeks. Take a look around—what's stopping you? Now is the time. Now is as good a time as any to walk out of here." I chuckle and do my best to make light of the situation. "Not for good, I hope. But now is the perfect chance for a fresh start. Don't you think?"

He shrugs and flicks his light on, then off again. "I don't know. Maybe. Just the idea of it makes me sick."

"There's nothing wrong with you. You're a Roux—and Rouxs flourish. *You* will flourish. You hear me?"

This time, he nods with no verbal response. His breathing shallows and quickens to a string of drowning gasps. His hands quiver, and his light falls to the floor.

"What's happen-ing," he mutters.

I move next to him and pull his head in close to my chest. His hands wrap around my waist, and I feel the cool of his tears run between my breasts.

"Shhh," I say tenderly. "Mother is here. You're okay, you're okay. Mother has you, now."

His breath moves across my chest and ruffles my hair.

"Aren't you weary of this, son? Aren't you tired of feeling this burning inside? This need to have answers and move on from being held back by some man you hardly know?"

"Yes, ma'am."

"Good. That's a good boy." I caress his hair, and his breathing slows. "That's my boy."

"Please. Make it stop. How do I make it stop?"

"It's time, son. Now is the time for a change. Now is *our* time."

He draws a deep breath and lets it go at my neck. "Yes, ma'am."

"Shhh." I pull him closer. "Mother has you."

"Please. Just—just tell me what to do. Please. How do I

stop it?"

I start to rock, and his shaking stops. His hands ease up, and his head burrows deeper into the crook of my neck. "Please." He sighs.

"Of course, my love. Mother is here. Mother is here."

"What do I need to do?"

I hold him tighter. "Well, that depends, darling."

He lifts his head from my chest and wipes the tear from his cheek with the back of his hand. I run my thumb under his eye and dry what's left of the crying.

"Depends on what?" he asks.

"Us."

"Us?"

"Our family. It's just you and me, my love. Just you and me."

"Yes, Mother. Of course."

I reach my hand to the back of his head and pull him back down to my chest. His heart races against my own.

"Tell me." I rock back and forth, feeling my everything against me, my one and only. The last of me. "Who are you?"

All I need is a straight answer. Some sort of reassurance that we're on the same page.

He sits up straight and runs his wrist under his nose. He pulls back his shoulders—and gives the moment one last sniffle.

Then he nods. "I'm a Roux, Mother."

"Yes." I can't help but smile like the proud parent I am. "Me too, son." I lean over and pick up his light off of the floor. He reaches out, and I hand it over. "Me too."

FORTY

October 1995

Father was right: one day, I got it.

And it changed me for the better.

People rarely changed; I was fortunate in that way. The two most important men in my life brought more meaning to my small corner of the world than I thought was possible. Six years ago, a third man had changed me, too. He wasn't for the better, though. Or maybe he was—depending on your bent and backward perception.

Maybe "man" was too strong of a word?

I found it interesting how some people worsened you, while others bettered you. And you ended up as some disheveled average of the two. It turned out to be true—you *are* the product of your environment.

People included.

Miss Amy was showing Father how to cook something in the kitchen—something to do with seafood and grits. It was a strange combination, to say the least. Father thought so, too. But Miss Amy insisted she had yet to run across someone who didn't like her signature . . . grits and something or another.

It felt good being together as a family. It felt like home again. Like the warmth of a sofa and covers, coffee and a good book on Thanksgiving morning. It felt the way it had before Mother died. All it had taken was for me to get out of my selfish ways and realize what was important in life. As it turned out, all I needed was a heavy dose of tough love.

And Father knew it, of course.

In the end, what brought us together wasn't time. It wasn't Slidell or a sense of community; it wasn't Father's gatherings or his pull around town. Not at all. It was nothing of the sort. What brought us together was one thing and one thing only—*family*.

Cody.

"Mother, what's for dinner?" Cody fanned out his UNO cards in a dirty, haphazard manner. They covered his face. I held tight to the only cards I had left—both wild, one a draw four.

"Oh, you know, love." I looked over my shoulder, to the kitchen. "One of Miss Amy's Cajun concoctions."

"I heard that, darling!"

I leaned over the table and closer to Cody on the other side. "Looks like we're in trouble," I said in a fake mordant tone.

A dish towel landed between us. Cody's chuckle bled throughout the room as he looked into the kitchen with a mischievous grin. Then he sat up straight and fought back the smirk that edged its way to the surface of his expression.

"I'm not sure y'all deserve it, now," Miss Amy said as she walked into the dining room, "but dinner is served."

I heard Father announce dinner to Shadow from the kitchen, to where the man sat in his spot in the living room. The background voices on the television mingled faintly between the rooms.

"Cards off the table," I said to Cody. He kept his hand as straight as he could and placed them on the floor.

"Here we are," Miss Amy said. She set our plates in front of me and Cody. "Miss Amy's signature shrimp and grits. And I suspect"—she looked back at Father as he walked into the room—"your father's new favorite. At least, that's based on the sheer number of taste tests I had to veto in the kitchen."

Father sat at the head of the table, Miss Amy at the other end.

The wholesome and hardy scent of butter and green onion filled the room, accentuated by the blackened spice of the orangish jumbo shrimp. I had my suspicions as I looked down at my plate and the oily grits—what I considered more of a breakfast food—floating in a shining, orange-yellow butter.

"Well," said Miss Amy. "Have at it, my dears."

Father wasted not a moment. By the time we finished our first bites, a quarter of his plate had gone missing.

Miss Amy winked at me, tilting her head toward Father. "At least we know it's a hit with someone."

Cody giggled. Father continued his demolition of the dish.

"They can eat or not eat," he said through the briefest pauses between bites. "No matter to me."

Cody took a bite, and his eyes doubled in size.

Father nodded to his grandson. "I'll be having seconds either way."

I took a bite myself and was pleasantly surprised. It worked. Who would've thought? Shrimp for breakfast—at dinner.

"See." Miss Amy must have sensed my approval. "Miss Amy knows her way around the kitchen, now." She swatted the air with her napkin, then leaned forward and spoke to me while looking at Father. "Don't let your father tell you any different, you hear?"

Cody dropped his fork and buried his hands in his lap. One of his boyish, dejected faces washed over him, turning his plump cheeks a washed-out pink. "That's no fair," he said dramatically.

Miss Amy and I looked at one another, appreciating how cute his little fits had become.

I said, "What's that, love?"

"It's not fair." He crossed his arms tight. His frown hardened. "How come you have a father, and I don't?" he said.

Father froze midbite, his head down, eyes up, the buttered

grease dripping from his fork, his gaze darting between his grandson and me, taking in the standoff.

"You have paw-paw. Who do I have?" Cody said.

Father dropped the fork to his plate and wiped his mouth with the towel—but his posture remained bent over the table, his elbows firm at the edge, as his eyes waited for me to end whatever his grandson was stirring up.

Never had such a large room felt so full.

I set down my fork. "Come again?" I said.

"What about *my* father?" Cody said. "I have no father."

Father straightened his back, pulled back his shoulders, and tilted his head—until his neck popped. At first, I wasn't sure what to say, but I could sense that I needed to devise something quick. Father drew a deep breath and gave me a shallow nod.

I turned to my son.

"That's enough," I said. "There's a time and place for those kind of discussions, son. But this isn't—"

"What about me?" he continued. "What about—"

I slammed my fist onto the table without really thinking about it. The plates were sent into a frenzy as they rattled and turned in the smallest of ways.

"Oh, my," Miss Amy whispered to herself. She covered her mouth with her napkin.

"I said, that's enough."

Father nodded at me once more.

"Can I meet him, then?" Cody said. "When can I—"

I snatched up my plate from the bottom and hurled it against the wall. Ceramic shards flew back at us and littered the table; and the yellowish grits dripped from the blue-green wallpaper like sweat in the Bayou Liberty sun.

"That's my girl."

Miss Amy pushed back her chair and dropped her napkin

on the table. It drifted to the tabletop in what seemed like slow motion. "I do believe I've forgotten the bread." She turned to the kitchen.

I leaned over the table, an inch from Cody's face—his cheeks were stuffed with the shrimp and grits, and his bottom lip shook violently. He gripped the seat of his chair with both hands as the dimples in his chin deepened.

Father sipped his water.

"When I say enough," I said as calmly as I could, "what I mean is, that's enough. You understand?"

"Mm-hm," Father said, followed by a gulp. He rattled the ice in his glass.

Cody nodded. His cheeks bulged.

I grabbed the fork from his hand and placed it on his plate. "Now, I need you to say it," I said. "Tell me. Tell me that you understand what I'm saying, son."

He swallowed a portion of the food and nodded again.

"Yes."

"Yes?"

"Yes, ma'am."

His manners were more than rusty. I picked up his towel and wiped a touch of grease from the corner of his mouth, then placed it on his lap. Folded.

"Good. That's good," I said.

Miss Amy returned with a tray of garlic bread and another plate of the shrimp and grits. "Here we are," she said. "Fresh out the oven."

I sat down and placed my napkin back into my lap. Miss Amy put the fresh plate in front of me.

"Careful, darling. It's still hot to the touch, now."

"Yes, ma'am," I said.

I swiped a few of the shards from in front of me and

adjusted my plate.

Family drama didn't belong at the table—not the Roux table. Especially when it involved *him*. Dinner time was family time.

Period.

"So," Miss Amy said, looking to Cody, "how is it?"

He shrugged and returned to chewing what had been marinating in his mouth. "It's okay," he mumbled through the food.

We all looked around at each other, all except for him.

"It's really good," Cody said. "Very."

Miss Amy swatted the air. "Oh, please. Ain't nothing but an old recipe from an old book." She giggled cheerfully.

"A book?" I said. "How old are we talking?"

"Older than you," she said.

"That's pretty damn old." Cody spoke with a straight face.

"Son—"

Father weighed in that time. "That's enough, now."

"Well," she continued, "I'm surprised you don't have any recollection of that dish from your younger years." Miss Amy looked at Father.

"Let's not go stirring the pot, now," he said. "Talks of would-be fathers at the dinner table are enough for one night. No need to go dragging mothers into it as well."

Miss Amy raised her hand. "My apologies, darling. There will be no such thing."

"Besides." Father slapped the tabletop next to Cody. "Who needs a daddy when you have a perfectly good mother right in front of you?" Our eyes met in agreement. Father nodded.

"Ain't that right." The words mingled with the evening news from the other room, at a near-grumble, as if they were spoken to himself.

And some of the grits slid down the wall and onto the pristine marble floors.

"Oh, my."

FORTY-ONE

October 1996

I t was nearly one year since Father's trust in me had taken a turn for the better. Every day, and every night for that matter, was a chance to prove myself a bit further. More than anything, it was a chance to prove myself to the Roux family, as *part* of the Roux family and not merely some product of it—to show that I was more than the sum of my mistakes.

Being restricted to dinner at the dining room table had come and gone like a blurred dream, and both Cody and I were free to move about the house unhindered. Such freedom was surprisingly difficult for Cody, though. He remained in our bedroom more days than not, only going downstairs for food and water.

Baby steps, I supposed.

I passed the time by reading and studying, or helping Miss Amy with Father's to-dos around the house. Father made sure that I had any and all resources available to keep up with my schooling. Thanks to him, I was able to avoid the lesser part of college altogether: the people.

"The crowd is for nothing more than building your own flavor and brand," he'd say. "Figure out what you want to do first, and the people will follow."

He was right, of course. If not for that house, and Father's support, the "college experience" would've only been a distraction.

Whenever it was time for me to branch out, when Father could see that I was ready, I'd flourish as something more than merely a cog in the Roux wheel—that, I was sure of.

"Oh, darling," Miss Amy said. She leaned in. "Take it from me, now. You're gonna be a wonderful nurse someday." She tapped my knee. "You just wait and see."

We sat in the living room as she folded laundry. Miss Amy sat in Shadow's spot on the couch—she took full advantage of getting jabs in on the man whenever she could, even if he wasn't around. Over the last year especially, they'd devolved into oil and water, one sour interaction at a time.

I sat next to her with my towering, sloshing bowl of Cocoa Puffs; my hand was always a bit heavy on the Puff. Miss Amy kept me in full supply, a habit I'd developed when I was pregnant with Cody.

"Maybe," I said. "My only worry is that I won't be able to take advantage of the one benefit that comes from attending college. Nursing requires a degree, and I'm not getting a degree sitting here at home."

I almost said, "between these four walls," but what made it worse was the fact that I had an endless number of walls and halls to keep me bored.

She gasped and playfully slapped my leg with one of the dish towels. "Oh, that's no way to talk about your future, now, darling. That's what Miss Amy calls none other than the devil's thinking."

I spoke through a mouthful of chocolate as the milk found the one opening at the corner of my lips. "Well it's true."

"You can't think like that, darling." She stopped folding. "Look how far you've come, now. And I know, deep down"— she placed the tip of her index finger at the top of my chest— "deep down, you can see just how much this home is setting you up for success. Just how much your *father*, of all people, cares about your success. Just give it time, now. You'll see. You'll thrive like never before."

"You really think so?"

"Oh, yes, darling." She resumed folding and looked around the room, raising a towel in her hand. "Can you name a Roux who hasn't?"

Miss Amy always had a way of explaining the muddy—of clearing up the uncertainty that invariably found its way into my mind. In recent years, worry had become an old friend, like a moon to the setting sun. Sometimes, it was there in the background when I'd least expect it, sitting against a blue backdrop when life was otherwise bright.

Ever since Mother died, a massive hole had torn through my life and devoured everything good in my new and banal existence. I liked to think I was good at hiding it, but her departure had crushed every joy and hope down to the smallest of points, including what little light I had salvaged in the mundane.

But Miss Amy softened the hardship. For the first time, someone had begun to fill that void. Although, I would have been lying if I said that I didn't feel a touch guilty about it.

Her sudden appearance in my life, at one of the most trying of times, was a gift that I'd grown into. If I dared say, she resembled the closest thing to a mother I had seen in recent years.

"What is it, darling? You look parched. Something on your mind?"

I wavered on whether I should ask. Perhaps it was crossing some line. "No. I'm fine."

"Oh, don't you try and fool Miss Amy, now." She tossed one of the folded bath towels onto the coffee table in front of us. "I know you better than you think."

"Can I ask you something? Something a bit . . . personal,

maybe?"

The milk in my bowl had tanned to a shade of pinkish-brown.

She swatted away at the air, batting at the tension between us. "Miss Amy is an open book. Even you know that by now. Don't you?"

"Yes, ma'am."

"Okay. Out with it, then."

"Why—why is it that you stick around here? You're an accomplished nurse. Why me? Why are you dead set on being here? And for so long, now?"

At first, she said nothing, only went back to folding towels. Her eyes were thinking. Her foot tapped the tile, her head rocking from side to side as she stacked the laundry with excessive precision.

Then, her gaze found mine as if I should've already had the answer.

"Well," she said, "what do you think?"

I thought she was stalling. "No clue," I said.

She adjusted her posture and straightened the top to her cotton-colored scrubs, then folded her hands in her lap. "I wish that called for a simple answer."

I said it as mildly as possible. "I'm not going anywhere."

"Ah. Well, let's just say . . . you weren't the only one who lost someone when your mother died, darling."

I sat back, farther into the couch, sinking until I could sink no more, and crossed my legs.

"You see, Miss Bobby was a few years older than me, so I was lucky enough to learn from your mother as she blossomed from a young lady in nursing school into a smart and beautiful woman—and mother to a gorgeous little girl, at that." She nudged my leg.

"That's it? You watched her grow up? You're here because of her?"

"Oh, it's so much more than that." She looked out the window, to the blankets of green-gray moss hanging from the oak trees out back, blowing in the evening sun and drowning in a tree line of bayou shore. "Your mother taught me what it was to be more than a nurse. What she taught me was how to be a worthwhile human being. She taught me how to be decent, darling."

She looked at me with cinched lips. "Your mother educated me on what it means to be devoted to someone. To some-*thing*."

For a moment, she appeared lost in thought. I could sense the memories playing in her mind like an endless projection, black and gray, flashing on the big screen with all of its skips and scratches. All of its flaws and imperfections in the dust of a seedy theater.

"But then," she continued, "it was all gone. In the blink of an eye." She rolled up one of the towels like Mother and I used to do when I was little, and she popped the edge of the coffee table. A snap cracked the air. "And just like that, I lost my best friend. But as it turns out"—she stood up and tugged at the bottom of her top—"a little piece of Bobby was left behind."

Miss Amy winked as she leaned over and picked up one of the stacks of laundry.

Part of me couldn't help but feel for the woman. There I was, wrapped up in some trivial back-and-forth with Father, arguing over boys and privileges, while Miss Amy seemingly had no one. In that moment, I realized just how selfish I could be.

But her response raised more questions than I had answers.

I reached out and grabbed her wrist. "Wait."

She looked down at my hand, as if her niceness did, in fact, have some semblance of a boundary.

"That can't be it."

"I'm sorry, darling?"

"That can't be the only reason you're here. For all this time? My mother?"

Without looking away, she placed the stack of towels on the end table as if they were sheets of glass that had begun to crack. Slow. Deliberate.

I set my bowl of by then chocolate milk onto the arm of the couch and pulled my legs beneath me.

The woman put one hand on her hip, her elbow jutting out to the side, as she leaned in close. The raw fragrance of dripped chicory wafted from her breath.

"Darling." She spoke with a heavy shade of advice. "If it meant bringing your mother back"—without looking, she pointed behind her, out the window, to the rope swing at the end of the dock—"I'd hang myself over that bayou. In a split second."

It was one of those sentences that yearned for silence.

She dropped her hand. "She may be gone," Miss Amy said, "but Edward Roux is not." Her finger wagged an inch from my nose, as her expression faded to a somber emptiness. "You keep that in mind, now."

FORTY-TWO

August 31, 2005

Convincing him to go out there and lie to his father was hard enough. He did great for his first time beyond these walls, though, whether he drowned in a sea of panic or not. I'm proud. But stepping outside of this house was only the beginning. Now is the time for what really matters. Now is the time for his father to step up and play his part—in the tragedy that is our family.

I pull a spare metal flashlight from one of the emergency cases, flip it backward in my hand, and shove the butt end of it into one of the CCTV monitors. The glass screen crumbles to the floor in the tiniest of tiny pieces.

Cody shields his eyes with his forearm, then peers out from behind his outward-facing hand. "What . . . what the hell are you doing?" His voice crackles and pops.

I spread out the shards with my foot, scattering them farther across the cement floor. The thousands of pieces crunch beneath my shoes as my flashlight ignites the glass into an endless array of fiery fragments.

"If we're doing this, we're going to do it right," I say.

Cody backs himself against the wall as if an invisible someone is pushing him, and his light darts over the floor. His eyes glow in the half light of the humid and boiling room. Blue and white rays scatter from the glass like we're at some teenage ballroom dance.

I shatter another of the screens.

"Mother . . ."

It's now or never.

"What, son?"

"I . . . I don't know if—"

"Are you going to help me or not?"

I turn toward him. His focus shifts around the room, bleeding with confusion.

"What, son? What is it? You want this, don't you? You want your answers, yes?"

He lets out a heavy breath. "Yes, ma'am. I do."

"Good." I shove the flashlight into his chest. He holds it to himself with one hand. I can see that he needs a bit of motivation. "Then do something about it." I lift my chin to the glass door—to the mirror that separates us from the living hell on the other side.

He looks at it, then back at me.

Do I really need to say it?

"*Do* something about it," I say.

Cody looks down at the flashlight. Even in the dim of the room, I can see the red and white of his knuckles flash from his hand as he grips the metal in thought.

He looks at me once more.

"Do. Something." My voice is calmer now.

He looks back to the one-way mirror, then steps toward it. For a moment, he looks up and down at his faint and ghostly reflection, as if he's seeing himself for the first time. It's there, but his image is only a clear shadow. It seems as though he's caught off guard by what he sees. His eyes get lost in *his* eyes, and his finger finds his own, running down from his chin to his chest, his gaze growing larger.

His attention appears lost. His eyes face the other side of the glass, but he isn't all there. Cody is wandering, gone, in his own head—unsure, timid and frightened.

He steps back, then hurls the flashlight through the mirror. I thought he'd react to the falling glass in some way, but he doesn't. He doesn't flinch, only stands there.

"That's my boy," I say. "That's it."

His breathing races, and his hands begin to tremble as he fidgets with his hair. "Now what?"

"Now, it's time to step up. Now is the time for you to do what a Roux does best. Now . . . is *your* time."

I walk toward the shattered mirror and pick up one of the larger shards of glass. Then I turn back toward him and grab his hand, turning it palm up between us—and place the glass in his grasp.

"Now, son, is time for you to do what you have to."

"Have to?"

"Yes. To *thrive*. You understand?"

I hold out my wrist.

His hand closes around the shard. Slowly. Carefully.

I shut my eyes and wait, imagining what it will feel like to close this chapter of my life that I've dreamed of ending for so long now. To right the wrong that's changed me for the better and for the worse, to right the mistake that has given me my everything, who stands in front of me—the wrong that has weighed me down for years.

The idea of walking out of here flows through me, the idea of—

"I can't."

For a second, I hope that my ears have failed me.

I ease open my eyes. "Do what?"

"I . . . can't."

I step forward, until we're face-to-face.

"Yes, son. You can—and you will. You understand?" I grab his arm and move the glass to my wrist. "You understand?"

I ease my eyes shut and feel the past begin to slough from my conscience as the edge of the triangular shard of mirror slides into my skin. At first, I feel nothing. Then an oily warmth embraces my palm and flows into the crevasses that separate my fingers.

My hand opens, and I hear the glass hit the floor.

"Our time is now, son."

I lean my head back and raise my hand above me. The bloodied warmth drips down the front of my throat and runs between my breasts, a warmth all too similar to his breath that summer night. I squeeze my hand. The flow quickens.

Cody stands in front of me. Silent.

"I'm injured, son. Your mother is hurt, and you're under duress. I need help—you understand?"

"Yes, ma'am."

I lie on the floor and invite the glass to stick against my tacky skin.

"You have no idea what's happened." I squeeze my hand harder—and wipe the stray hair that sticks against the side of my face. "You're frightened. You need help."

"Yes, ma'am."

I stretch out my arm and lay my head against it, my legs across the bed of broken glass. My eyes fade as I draw a deep breath, then let it out gently.

"Now, son. Your time is now."

———

"Hey! Get over here!" I hear Cody call out on the balcony. "It's Lauren."

As I lie here with my eyes closed, I can see him, I can feel him, in the boat on that wet summer night. His tacky body sits beneath me, his breath pouring across my chest and neck, deep inside me as I move over him—inch by slow inch.

"Hurry! Up here!"

I squeeze my hand a bit more, and the warmth bathes my palm and the glass beneath it.

"Lance!"

I hear footsteps climbing the stairs. They pause at the end of the hallway.

"Over here."

They race toward the room. Toward me.

"What do . . . what—what do we do?"

The glass crunches beneath his feet as he steps into the room. I can feel him as he kneels beside me.

And it's all too perfect.

Now, Lauren. Your time is now.

So, I prop myself up and onto my forearm.

"It's about time you showed up."

I expected the look on his face to be so much more. Maybe guilt. Or fear? But it's nothing of the sort.

All I see in his eyes is emptiness. A fatherless, teenage lifetime.

That's when our son appears behind him—and the bat finds the side of Lance's head.

FORTY-THREE

October 2004

It was like losing a mother all over again.

Miss Amy ambled down the stairs, her luggage gnawing at her heels, and placed the all-white bags in the center of the foyer. Shadow was a few steps behind her, carrying one of her larger suitcases in both arms. He tossed the bag against the front door and walked away—as if he had something better to do.

"Oh, thank you, *darling*," Miss Amy said sardonically as the man turned away. "Always the loving sort, you are."

The man waved at the air and mumbled something or another about family as he walked to the kitchen. Miss Amy gave me an ain't-it-typical sort of look. To my surprise, Shadow stopped at the entryway to the kitchen, turned back, and leaned against the wall, popping a can of dip in his hand. Observing. Gawking. Enjoying the circumstances, perhaps?

"Ain't no one gonna ruin our goodbye, now, darling." She spoke to me as she held her arms wide open and forced a smile that I could tell was marinated in a few days of pain. "Give Miss Amy one of those signature hugs, now."

She may not have been able to wrap her arms around me entirely, but I hadn't felt that supported, that held, that embraced by someone since . . . well, I wasn't sure.

Just when I could no longer breathe under the weight of her chest, and she released me, Cody came rushing down the stairs; Miss Amy was the only female figure he'd ever known, other than me.

She turned toward him and held out her arms. Cody jumped

from the fourth step, then jogged toward her. "You better get over here, now," she said. And they collided head-on.

Even as a teenager, Cody still had that round, boyish quality about his face.

Shadow huffed from the edge of the room as he tucked a pinch of dip behind his lower lip. "Talk about dramatic," he grumbled under his breath.

Miss Amy only glanced his way. The fact that she said nothing was evidence enough to support her statement that she wasn't going to let someone like Shadow stand in the way of her goodbyes. I knew that biting her lip was beyond difficult when it came to him.

Her attention shifted from a passive-aggressive scowl to a saddened smile as she addressed Cody. "You be good, now, you hear?"

"Yes, ma'am."

She pinched his plump cheek.

Father appeared out of nowhere at the top of the stairs, then walked down to the foyer with one hand on his pipe, the other hanging by a thumb from his vest pocket.

"Not so fast, there," he said between a string of rapid puffs, a train barreling down a track of treads. "You're going to need some help getting all of that out to the car."

He paused on the bottom stair and looked to Shadow, who was spitting some of the dip into an empty beer bottle. The liquid swashed and bubbled behind the dark amber glass.

Shadow pointed a thumb at his own chest. "Who? Me?"

Father only nodded. Shadow huffed.

"Come on," Father said, tilting his head toward us at the front door. He seemed to be making the best of an unideal situation. "You and Amy are the only ones going out."

Father stepped down from the bottom stair and made his

way over to the window, next to the front door. He eased back the curtain with the stem of his pipe, looking left. He released a thick cloud of smoke. Then looked right.

"Good, good," he moaned to himself.

Shadow walked over to us at an indolent pace. He stood there, seemingly waiting for further instructions.

"Oh, before I forget," Father said to Miss Amy. And he removed a slender white envelope from the inside pocket of his plaid sportscoat. It appeared to have nothing in it—save for a single rectangular piece of paper. He held it out in front of her, but she looked bewildered. "Take it," he said. "You take your time finding something else, yes? I don't want you worrying about pay before then." He pushed it out farther, until she grabbed it as if it could bite her. "You understand?"

"I . . . I don't know what to—"

"No need to say anything," Father said, waving a hand between them. "Just want you to know how much I appreciate what you've done here. How much *we* appreciate it." He looked to me and Cody. "Isn't that right?"

"Absolutely," I said with a smile. I meant it, more than I could say in the moment.

Cody slung his arms around her once again, and Miss Amy stared at the envelope with growing eyes, knowing exactly what was in it. No need to glance inside.

Father always took care of Miss Amy—one way or another.

She looked at him. "Thank you." She spoke slowly and with a deep gratitude for what the last several years had meant. I could tell. "I appreciate it, Ed. Really."

I didn't want to see her go, but the truth was that Father had brought her into our home to do a job—ostensibly, a paid job. Now that Cody was older, Father didn't need her. At least, not in the same way that he had before. And not in the way that

I needed her still.

Miss Amy's departure was going to be tough on Cody as well, but I had no idea to what extent.

"We'll keep in touch, darling. You hear?" Miss Amy said to me. "You have my word. No matter what."

Shadow let out an obnoxious sound—it came off as a calculated interruption of the moment—and spit loudly into his bottle.

"I'll write," Miss Amy said. She pulled me in close and kissed me on the head. "Soon."

The woman turned to open the door.

"One moment," Father said. He moved to the window yet again, peering out of the floor-to-ceiling curtains as the ghostly smoke from his pipe vanished into the fabric. He looked at Miss Amy and nodded. "Okay."

But as she opened the door, our heartfelt goodbyes were quickly snuffed out by Cody's reaction to what we all knew would be an ongoing issue for years to come, although unspoken between any of us. The impact of our upbringing was always addressed with our eyes, not our words.

I stepped aside and leaned against the wall, watching as Miss Amy moved into the doorway.

But Cody . . . Cody paced backward and tripped over his own two feet. His gaze was held captive by what I, too, sensed there, in the open foyer of our home: the thick St. Augustine grass, cut to perfection in an obsessive crossing pattern in the front yard; the feel of the Louisiana dew, damp on our skin, deep in our lungs; the sunlight as it approached our feet without being scattered over a set of dusty wooden blinds—the world, seen by our own eyes and not filtered through some pane of condensation-riddled glass.

It wasn't the first time, of course. Cody had developed an

aversion to the outdoors over the years, as seen here and there through an open door or cracked window. But for some reason, with Cody, it was *every* time. All the time. He reacted to the outside like it was a sickness, some twenty-first-century pandemic.

His hands turned backward as he felt for some sort of support behind him. He stumbled, but nothing was there—only the wet, outdoor atmosphere as it crashed with the frigid indoor air. Then his hand found his throat in a frantic way, and his breathing grew labored one raspy inhale at a time.

"Cody?" Miss Amy said as she turned back. "Are you okay, darling? You look positively sick."

"Ain't that right."

"Cody?" I said, moving toward him.

His eyes were fixated on a world that moved without him, on the other side of the door. His back hit the dining room wall, and he slid to the floor, grabbing for air.

"Cody!" I rushed to his aid.

"Ain't nothing some rest and good ole-fashion talking won't cure," Father said.

Shadow picked up the oversized suitcase and turned to the door. "Ain't that right."

"You're fine, love." I spoke to Cody as I pushed my hand back through his golden curls—a calming trick that had yet to lose its touch. I sat there and held him.

Miss Amy began to sob in broken gasps in the doorway. She dropped her bags and walked back into the home. She stood in front of us there, looking down as a single tear dropped from the roll in her chin and splashed against the floor, soaking into the grout as if it had never been.

She didn't speak; she made no sound, no hasty gesture, only tilted her head to the side.

I let him go and stood up, as Miss Amy dropped to one knee and braced herself on the tile, then sat down. She pulled him close and leaned his head against her pillow of a chest.

"Miss Amy's got you, darling. Miss Amy's got you."

Shadow spoke from the door. "I'll be out front."

Father walked out behind him.

Cody's episodes had become part of our daily affairs. Since Miss Amy would be gone from then on, I wasn't sure how those moments were going to play out, exactly. He responded to the two of us in different ways. As much as Father loved him, he couldn't be around it. He didn't have the patience for it, although he did his best to play it off as if he did.

Cody's whole body shook and tensed in Miss Amy's arms.

It wasn't that one of us was better than the other with Cody during his moments. We each had our own thoughts on what caused his fits, and how we should go about handling them.

Miss Amy closed her eyes. Cody let out a slow groan as his trembling grew more intense.

Then, as if she had found the off switch, she whispered something in his ear. Her lips appeared to move in the slowest way possible, like she knew exactly what to say. And just like that, Cody's body fell limp in her arms.

His eyes found mine as his lips formed the deepest of grins.

FORTY-FOUR

July 2005

The heavy steel door creaked and groaned as I eased it open—and reached my hand inside of the dark and damp space. A web entangled my hand, so I moved as quickly as I could.

Miss Amy had kept her word, just like I knew she would.

I snatched the bulging envelope from the mailbox, along with a few pieces of random mail that were still damp from the dawn's humidity: a coupon for soft-shell crabs at Kenney Seafood, the latest issue of Louisiana Sportsman with some kid on the cover struggling to hold his record-breaking redfish as a piece of beef jerky dangles from his mouth, and an ad for TaeKwonDo classes off Gause Boulevard and the corner of Front Street.

Miss Amy's letters were noticeable from afar, as they were always inside of a black envelope and stamped with a crème wax seal. As I walked back to the house, I tore open the mail.

My darling Lauren,

How are you holding up? I'm sure your father is still fresh on your mind and in your heart. I know that is the case for me.

Miss Amy had rarely visited after she moved out. Not that she wasn't able to—it was just that both of us enjoyed the letters. We reveled in the nostalgia of it. A form of voluntary distancing, so to speak.

There was just something about keeping in touch through writing, and neither of us wanted to spoil that with unnecessary face-to-face meetings.

Father's heart attack had created a void in the house. First Miss Amy, then him. The last few weeks were like being thrust into an ice bath without warning, after an all-day affair in the July Slidell heat.

I paused, looking up at the flower of a rising sun as it bloomed behind the canopy of hardwoods on the other side of the bayou. I still wasn't accustomed to how good it felt on my skin.

I was finally able to make some headway on the job front. Interviews seem to be a rare commodity these days, but I have a good feeling about this one. If I don't keep myself busy, I'm sure to go crazy. Can you imagine that? Miss Amy, ending up more crazy than I already am? Ha!

As I walked inside, I held the letter to my nose and breathed it in. Then I shut the door behind me.

"Ah, Miss Lauren," Shadow said. "There you are. Just in time. Breakfast is on the counter."

"Coffee?"

"All d-d-d-done. A full pot."

Shadow carried his plate to the living room and sat behind his television tray. The myriad of colors from the screen flashed across the kitchen walls as if we were on the outskirts of a murder scene.

I pulled a coffee mug from the cabinet and poured a fresh cup. One scoop of Splenda. A dash of half-and-half. Before it hit my lips, I could already smell it.

"Shadow?"

He called from the other room. "Yes, ma'am?"

"What kind of coffee is this?"

"The coffee?" He stood up and walked toward me. "I thought it'd be a nice change of pace. I p-p-p-p-picked it up from—"

The nerve.

"No," I said. "You should know by now what—"

"I'm so sorry, Miss Lauren." He shuffled into the kitchen and removed the filter from the coffee pot, dropping it into the trash and then jamming another one into the pot. "Just give me one second, Miss Lauren. I'll f-f-f-fix this. I'll fix it, Miss Lauren."

He scooped the coffee grounds out of the jar next to the pot—the one he was supposed to have used in the first place.

I sat at the counter and turned my attention back to the letter.

How is Cody? Any progress? I can only imagine what he's going through. First the antisocial teenage angst, and now his grandfather is gone, too. How I do miss him.

"There we are," Shadow said. "I'm sorry, Miss Lauren. Should be ready in no time at all."

The smell of roasted chicory wafted from the letter in front of me, mixed with the scent of freshly cut paper—like that first step inside of a seasoned bookstore.

"Is there anything else I can get you, Miss Lauren? Anything at all? You know me. I don't mind one bit."

"No, Shadow." I waved him into the other room. Breakfast was one of those meals meant to be savored alone—now that Father was gone.

Cody walked into the kitchen just as Shadow turned back

to the living room. The man paused.

"Ah, Mr. Cody," Shadow said. "Can I make you a plate? Coffee is on the drip."

"Coffee, Shadow. Plenty of coffee."

"Yes, sir. Coming r-r-r-right up."

Cody sat down next to me. "What are you reading?"

"Another one of Miss Amy's letters. Looks like she might have finally found something."

"That's good news, then."

Shadow slid a cup in front of me. "There we go—nice and fresh. Coming right up, Mr. Cody." He shuffled back to the coffee pot.

"You're killing me, Shadow," Cody said. Poor boy dropped his head in his hands. A late night on the N64, I presumed.

The rhythmic clank of a spoon against the inside of a mug clacked from across the way. Then Shadow turned toward us.

"Here we are," he said. "Can I get you anyth—"

"No, Shadow. All I needed was the coffee."

Cody grabbed the issue of *Louisiana Sportsman* and pulled it to him.

"That's one big-ass fish," Cody said. He flipped to the inside cover. "Looks like it was caught out in—"

"Oh, yeah. That's one big-ass fish." Shadow appeared between us. He lifted his chin to the magazine. "Probably caught—"

"So much for a quiet breakfast," Cody said, before sipping his coffee and turning the page.

Shadow lifted his hands in an ostensible apology. "Of course, Mr. Cody. My apologies. Of course." He turned back to the living room.

Cody turned the page to the centerfold, lifting the issue with one hand and turning it on end. He balanced the cup in his other hand as he tilted his head to the side and looked intently at the drop-tine buck hanging from a gambrel across the creased pages. "Isn't breakfast meant to be a solitary endeavor?" He spoke to himself in a slumbering voice.

Then he drew another slurping sip as he closed his eyes. His arm still dangled in front of him.

Maybe I can hear from the little guy in your next letter? He needs someone. He really needs someone. Just say the word, and Miss Amy is there, darling.

—

I had to get out of there.

Shadow had become borderline too much since Father died. I didn't think it was possible, but he'd started hanging around more than he ever had before. It was interesting how people's demeanor changed after the death of someone near. I had a gut feeling that Shadow was different, though. If I had to guess, he wasn't sticking around for me or Cody. No.

Humans were a strange bunch. Most of them never bothered to change; they were terrified of it. That was what I thought Shadow was: terrified. No more Father, no more ordinary. He was clinging to what shred of normalcy he could scrape together.

For me, for us and the Roux family, it was a good thing, though.

Fear catered to the dependent.

I grabbed the trashcan and rolled it out front and down the driveway, to the head of the cemetery. As I stopped and set the can at the start of the cul-de-sac, I saw someone jogging toward me. As they got closer, he raised his hand.

"Oh. Hey, Lauren. Long time, no see," he said. "How you holding up?"

No . . . "Rowan? Is that you?"

"Yessiree. In the flesh."

The boy had done more than grow. He had left boyhood in the dust.

"I'm hanging in there," I said. "I'm here."

"Sorry about your old man. I've been meaning to stop by."

"No problem at all. I haven't been back for that long."

He jogged in place and looked out past the cemetery, to the house. He pointed. "You've been out of state. Right?"

Rowan could've come to me when his best friend up and left town without so much as a word, but he didn't. He could've reached out in any way, at any time, through any*one*—but he didn't. He could've been there. But he chose not to.

All of life was a choice. Everything. Including what we chose not to do.

But one person was there, through it all. Father was there for me, even when I couldn't see it.

"Yes. Well . . . out of the country."

"Oh?" He jogged in a tight circle in the middle of the road, breathing heavily. "Yeah. I think I heard something like that. It's been a while, though, hasn't it? Years." He froze at the other side of the road, with his hands at his side. "Holy shit, we're getting old." He looked at me and huffed, shaking his head. "Time flies, don't it?"

"Yes. And you? You been good?"

His jogging returned.

"Oh, yeah. You know me." He ended up back in front of me. Ninety percent of his light gray shirt was darkened with sweat and suctioned to his trim body. His pace continued. "Can't sit still."

"You don't say."

"Ha. Well, it was good talking." He turned his back to me and began jogging away. Then he stopped on Dubois Road, not far from where I stood.

"Speaking of talking"—he turned, running in place, looking over the graves yet again, seemingly lost in thought—"I ain't gonna speak for him." He lifted his chin to Lance's house. "But there's someone else who might like to see you."

Father was dead. I just "got back." And it was already about *him*.

"Enjoy your jog, Rowan."

He turned away and followed his shadow along the blacktop.

FORTY-FIVE

August 31, 2005

I've waited the entirety of our son's lifetime to see that look in his father's eyes.

"Feels good, doesn't it?" I can't help it as the sarcasm taints my words. I can tell that his bearings on the situation are muddled at best—but Lance is terrified more than anything, as he should be.

"Yes, I was never one for surprises, either," I say, stooping down in front of him. "But what can you do?" I wipe away the bead of sweat that meanders its way down his temple.

Lance's attention darts around the room, first to Cody, then to the door below us on the first floor, then back to me. I tied his hands behind his back while he was out, to the banister in the hall just outside of the safe room.

A thin wine-red stream flows from his ear and drips from his jaw. The carpet soaks it up in a haphazard pool that absorbs him and refuses to let go.

Cody steps toward us. "It's nice to finally meet you."

But Lance doesn't look at him, just lifts his shoulders, and his brow hardens. "What is this?" he says. "What the hell?"

Cody moves toward him. His hands fidget with the stray hair curling over his forehead and falling in front of his eyes. "I said it's nice to meet you."

Finally, Lance looks at him. "What the hell are you talking about? We've already—"

"Ah," I say, and I stand up. "Again—surprises, my love. Not the best when you're on the receiving end. Yes?"

"What is this, Lauren?"

Cody chimes in once more. "I *said*, it's nice to—"

"Just shut up," I say with a steady voice. I can't help it. And just like that, Cody's expression wanes to a sense of frustration. But this isn't about him. Not really.

"I thought it was time to get the family together," I say.

Cody steps back and speaks to himself. "A fresh start."

Lance wriggles his arms and thrashes against the railing.

"You're not going anywhere," I say. "Trust me."

"Trust you? What the *hell* is—"

"I'd like you to meet your son, Lance. Your little boy. His name is Cody." Neither Lance nor I dare look away from one another. I need to see his reaction, and I'm guessing he's waiting for me to say this is all some joke.

He only shakes his head and squints. His mouth grows tense, and the blood flows even heavier down the side of his face, clinging to the edge of his jaw in a straight line. It drips in a steady pulse. "What?" he says.

Cody steps an inch closer. "Like I said . . . it's nice to meet you." His voice is stern now.

"Sure," I say. "But let's not get ahead of ourselves. The circumstances could be far nicer."

"Why'd you leave?" Cody speaks with a straight face, but his tone is broken and yearning. A voice that, I suspect, he genuinely believes will win over his father. "What happened?"

"What? Why did I leave? Leave when? Leave what? What is this, Lauren? What the hell are—"

"Cut the shit," I say.

I'm curious to see how he responds to me. If there's any muscle memory left in him—so I nudge his leg with my foot. As predicted, he pulls away and gives me a crazed look.

"What's the matter? I thought you liked it. No? Not up for

'giving it a try'?" I wink. It feels good.

"I'm yours," Cody says.

"You left," I add. "Remember? Without a word . . . a giant fuck you . . . dare I say, to your girlfriend?"

"Really?" Lance says, a slight hint of sarcasm and superiority suddenly appearing in his voice. "That's what this is? Are you shitting me?" He looks around and huffs, pushing more blood from his ear, seemingly unsure of where this whole situation is headed. What he's doing here. Where it's all coming from. "Sorry, I'm a little mixed up, here. Maybe you should explain."

Cody acts like this is all somehow about him. "And maybe you should explain to me why—"

"What did I say, son?" My patience is fraying—one taut nerve at a time. "Quiet."

He steps back. "Yes, Mother."

I turn back to Lance. "That summer? You and me? I think you can connect the dots, Lance Dubois; or maybe you have me mixed up with some other broad you screwed in the neighbor's boat, then ditched without so much as a 'fuck off.'"

"Really?" He lets out an awkward, masochistic laugh. "That?" He squirms and shifts under the layers of rope. "Maybe you should've done some asking around first, Lauren. Maybe you should've asked someone—hell, *anyone*—why it is that I left here. Like I had a choice in the matter."

"Oh, don't even," I say. "We're not playing that game. Trust me, now is not the time for excuses, Lance. Now is the time for you to own up."

His body calms, and slowly, with a bit of a curious gleam and a glint in his eye, he tilts his head to the side. "You don't know. Do you?"

"Excuse me?"

"You don't have a clue." He looks to his son, then back at me. "Ironic, considering family seems to be y'all's whole world."

Lance smiles. The blood flows into the crook of his mouth where the corner of his lips meet his cheek.

"Don't talk to me about family, Lance. You're in no position to—"

Lance continues, "At least it all makes sense, now." His attention floats off to the corner of the room. "No wonder you're all twisted up. Turns out even the Roux family has its secrets."

I kick his leg again, harder this time. He huffs and grins wider.

"Fuck you," I say.

"No."

"Go ahead, then. Spill it."

He squirms. "What? You think I left here on my own? Because I wanted to? You're the victim, and I'm the asshole? That it?"

"Yes, I already know, Lance. It was your uncle. I get it. I've heard the excuses—from more than one person, believe it or not."

"No," Lance says. He shakes his head, gently, deliberately, as time seems to grow slower. His grin broadens.

My stomach sinks a little.

"Sure. My uncle was sick. There's no doubt about that."

He sits up straight. Adjusts his posture.

Then he leans forward.

"But I didn't make the decision to leave here on my own— as I was trying to explain a few days ago . . ."

"No shit," I say. "Your father—"

"No," he says. He scoots forward, rocking from side to side. His hands pull against the banister behind him. His tongue finds the edge of his lip. Lance leans in farther, looking up at me. He speaks as if the house has no business hearing him. "*Your* father."

What's the expression? Digging yourself a hole?

"My father what, Lance? There something you need to say about my *late* father? Go ahead. But I promise you're in no position to—"

"You know just as well as everyone else does in this town: your father had more pull around here than he was willing to admit. Your father, Lauren, hid behind anyone and everyone who was willing to do his dirty work for him." He pauses and nods right at me. "The true mark of a Roux."

"What are you saying, Lance? Father *forced* you to screw me over? Give me a break."

"It's interesting what people will do in the name of some reputation that'll be gone the second they're in the ground. Like blackmailing a measly bridge operator with their job so they send their kid off to, I don't know . . . Texas? As it turns out, *ex*-mayors never really leave office. Do they?"

"Sure," I say. "Blame it on Edward Roux. That's convenient, isn't it?"

"Your dad convinced my dad to send me away. I'm guessing no one would've been good enough for Edward Roux's daughter." He sits back and shrugs. "Believe it, don't believe it. Ain't nothing I can prove at this point. Both of them are gone." He finds my attention and holds it. "Ain't so easy when Daddy ain't around to give you the answers. Is it?"

We both look at Cody as he stands in the corner, rocking, dropping his head against the wall with his eyes closed.

"So," Lance continues, "forgive me if I don't buy your bullshit about some kid you're throwing in my face after what your father did to my family. And after all this time? You expect me to believe that?" He looks away. "I do have one question, though: was it a way of getting back at the teenage kid who refused to worship the ground he walked on? Or was it a classic case of a Roux doing what was best for the family name?"

"No, Father was always upfront with his family. Edward Roux wasn't the type to lie—to me, of all people."

"Sure," Lance says. "Because Ed Roux"—he adjusts his posture—"was *so fond* of his neighbors. I thought you were different."

I turn away.

"Come on, Lauren. Think about it. Think for yourself, for once?"

"No." I turn back. "No, you said it yourself. In your letter. You wanted nothing to do with me or my—"

Lance bursts into a fit of laughter. "A letter? Really, Lauren? You shitting me? Let me guess: something about a mistake and our families not meshing? That sound about right?"

No.

"Yeah," he says. "Yeah, that does sound about right. Sounds like Ed Roux is what it sounds like."

No.

"Shut up," I say.

Cody steps forward. "What, you don't believe us? You think—"

I grab his arm and pull him back. "Make me say it one more time. I dare you."

"You two are a kick."

Cody turns away, and his darkened laugh fills the hallway.

"Yeah, I did leave," Lance says. "But I was young and naïve, just like you. Both of us knew nothing more than what our fathers told us. My dad talked me into leaving because that's what he thought was best, even if I was teenager. Besides"—he lifts his chin—"what about you? You couldn't reach out to me? It's all on Lance? Is that it?"

"You have no idea what I've been through. Don't even act like you know what I've had to deal with since you left. Day in and day out, I sat in this house, in that room, and—"

"What? What are you talking about 'sat in this house'? You left town just like I did."

"Is that what you think, Lance? Father sent me away? He just got rid of me like some troubled teen?"

"I'm sure you were here, Lauren. I'm sure you were." He leans in again. "Because Ed Roux was *such* a family man. This isn't you. This isn't what I remember at all."

I walk toward him, crouch down and push the hair from my face, so I can see his own more clearly. It's dark. But as I lean in, the memory of that night comes flooding back. What it felt like to be pressed against him.

"Tell me," I say. "What is family, Lance? What is it, *really*?"

He doesn't speak, only shakes his head. Slow and rhythmic. His breath washes over me.

I lean in and taste the blood from the edge of his lips, in the same way that he licked the sweat from my neck—on that night that changed it all. It's only fair that I remind him what he left behind.

He pulls back, but not as much as I thought he would.

"Blood," I say. "That's family, Lance." I stand up. "Blood."

I turn back to the shattered mirror and grab the bat that's leaning against the wall. Then I walk back to him.

"Which is why *I* could never hurt you."

Cody is pacing up and down the hall, mumbling to himself as his hands go this way and that. "Answers," I hear him say. "I deserve answers." He pulls at his hair and paces in longer strides.

I point the bat at Cody while looking to his father. "See?

You fucked him up way worse than anyone else could have."

"Fuck you."

"Yeah. No. We've already done that. And look at where it's got us."

I lean back against the wall and balance the bat on the ground in front of me, with my hands stacked on the knob. "Hey, Shadow."

The look on his face sends a special type of satisfaction coursing through me. Lance's eyes dart left to right, right to left, searching for what could possibly happen next.

Shadow steps out of Father's office. "Yes, Miss Roux." He looks at Lance as he speaks. "How can I help you?"

Cody freezes with his hand still tangled up in his hair, his eyes growing in size.

I stand up straight and pull back my shoulders. Then I flip the bat around and hold it out in front of Shadow. He grabs it tentatively. "Consider this your last job," I say. "At least, the last one you'll ever need."

I turn away, then pause and say to Shadow, "Consider it a family affair."

"Really?" Lance says. "First, family is blood, and now Shadow is your family? Y'all really are something else."

Shadow looks at Cody, then back at me. He hesitates. I turn my ear toward him. "What? Is there a problem, here?"

The man stumbles over his own words more than usual, and his twitching eye goes haywire. "I . . . Miss Roux, I'm not so sure I c-c-c-c—"

"Are you serious right now?"

"What is this?" Lance says. "Some sort of revenge? Really? For what, exactly?"

Shadow fidgets with the bat, lifting it in concert with his shoulders, his look wavering between his family and Lance.

I lean in so that only Shadow can hear me. "Is this going to be an issue?" I wait, but the man has no response. "Because"— I look over the railing, down to the war-zone of a house, inundated with debris and ransacked by the receding water— "the bayou has a way of making things disappear in the wake of a storm, *Shadow*."

Still, no response.

After all our family has done for the man, it's a slap in the face. I nod, consider my options, then think about what Father would have done.

"Okay," I say. "Just remember this moment."

I turn to Lance and pull the nickel-plated revolver from the small of my back.

part three

Cotton

FORTY-SIX

August 31, 2005

I 'm on the back porch, doing my best to savor one of my last cigarettes, wondering where the fuck my boat is at—or better yet, where my dock went.

Layers of mud form a suction around my boots as the smoke escapes my mouth and wanders next door, across what was once an immaculate back yard. It disappears into the wet air—the one thing that appears unchanged around here.

How in the world can it be this quiet after something so . . . ruthless?

That's when I hear it—the voice, cracking as it screams.

"Hey! Get over here!" a rattled someone calls out from the direction of the Roux house. Then I hear something about Lauren.

I take one more drag, then flick the butt out into the mud, where it smolders in an endless chaos. As I turn and walk toward Lance's back yard, I see him going down the stairs and heading next door as well. He's talking with the person on the balcony of the Roux house, although I can't make out who it is or what they're saying.

As I climb over the maze of downed trees and endless piles of debris, I look up—and see a figure entering the Roux house through the back door, just as Lance walks to the front of the home.

I move faster.

After I make it past Lance's place, I work my way through the tree that took out the fence on their property line. From there, I make it through the thick of the aftermath, one heavy and muddied foot at a time.

I pause in the Rouxs' back yard and look behind me at where I just came from. With the fence gone, the trees uprooted and broken like the weather's playthings, the receding bayou covering the ground every which way I look, out across a flat and sodden landscape—it puts life into perspective. It makes me wonder what boundaries, if any, really exist in this world of a cul-de-sac.

Before I realize it, I've stood there several moments too long, lost in what hit us out of nowhere. Taking in what no one expected. Not to this extent.

Then I look up to the balcony where the person was standing, but they're gone now. The sky is a clean shade of blue, but somehow, in front of a treeless backdrop, a darkness is cast over the Roux home.

I find my way through the mounds of debris and to the back door, which is buckled and twisted and slightly ajar. A pile of marsh grass is wedged in the middle of the doorframe. I push open the door a bit farther. As I do, I hear a string of distant whispers above me. I don't close the door but instead ease it back to how I found it.

The ceiling is beginning to sag and peel away from the joists over the living room, and the top layer of mud on the floor is beginning to stiffen—like some gumbo's roux abandoned on the stovetop.

I walk to the stairs just off of the dining room. The voices have gone quiet, now. I look up but see no one.

So I start up the stairs, hearing some shuffling and movement above me. No hint of conversation, though. But as my foot reaches the top tread of the staircase, the wall next to me explodes into a mist of fine dust; the crack that splits the air and commands the room seems to come after the fact. The chalky haze falls around me, and over me, in what feels like one frame at a time.

I turn back to the stairs, but before I get far, Lauren's voice stops me in my tracks.

"Oh, no," she says in a calm way. "Where do you think you're going?"

Only then do I look up to see the pistol aimed at my head—the glint of what little light is shining through the dirty windows reflects off of the brass rounds in the cylinder of the revolver. They glow like a pack of eyes at the exit of a menacing tunnel.

Gradually, I raise my hands. "What are you doing, Lauren?"

She curiously cocks her head. "Come on," she says. And she nudges the gun in her direction. "Why don't you join us?"

That's when I see Lance tied to the railing and Shadow standing in front of him—with a bat?

Someone paces behind them.

"Okay," I say with a heavy reluctance. "Okay."

I turn and walk into the hallway.

Being held at gunpoint is—for lack of a better phrase—an experience. Forget the storm. Having the barrel of a pistol between your eyes puts *everything* into perspective—except the reason for why a pistol is aimed at my head.

I walk toward them, and Lauren backs up, turning the gun on Lance.

"We were just discussing the idea of family, Cotton." She looks at Shadow, then back at me. "Maybe you can help us out?"

I take it as a rhetorical question.

"Or maybe not," she continues. "From what I've gathered over the years, your brother hasn't exactly been the familial type. Not with you, at least. Has he, Cotton?"

She turns the gun on Shadow, who cowers against the wall

with his arms in front of his head. The bat covers his face. "But then again, he isn't really proving himself over here, either."

"What are you doing?" I say. I feel the need to say something, anything to keep the inevitable at bay.

"Oh," she says, sounding excited and a bit too dramatic, "that's right." Her laugh is that of a wild dog, thirsty grin and all. "Tell me what you think—" She waves the gun in a messy twirl above her head. "Boy seduces girl, girl falls for boy, boy fucks girl, girl gets preggo, boy disappears off the face of the earth. What do you think, Cotton? Fair?" She looks to Lance and turns the gun on him once again.

He doesn't flinch. Instead, we lock eyes. He doesn't speak, so I assume it can only be true. I'm not sure if saying anything is my best move at the moment.

"Yes," Lauren says, "that's what I thought. So"—she pulls back the hammer on the pistol, and it clicks twice—"where does that leave us, exactly?"

"Ain't that right."

"Shut the hell up," she says.

In that comment to my brother, I sense an opportunity, although I'm not sure what it is.

Lauren continues speaking to Shadow. She shakes her head. "And I thought you were the grateful type. Guess I was wrong on that front."

Shadow's expression falls, and he looks at me with an embarrassed frown and sinking eyes.

"I don't get it," I say.

"Yeah," Lance adds, "welcome to the club."

Shadow begins to chuckle, but Lauren's glare cuts him off. She grows outwardly furious, fidgeting, adjusting her hair with the barrel of the gun. "Let me break it down for you, then." She jabs the gun at Lance. "Boy." Then points the barrel beneath her chin. "Girl." And at the kid. "Kid." I see the glare of the brass once more. "Get it?"

"So, Lance got you pregnant, and you just left town and didn't say anything?" I say. "And that's his fault?"

The woman's hyena-ish laugh returns. "Come on, Cotton. Really?" Her voices quiets. "Is that what you think? I left?" She smiles while maintaining a serious look. "No, dear. You and everyone else around here were just too blind to see what was under your nose. But I guess that isn't entirely your fault, now. Is it?"

No. There's no way. There's *no way* she kept an entire pregnancy quiet. And my boy Lance would've never been so careless.

"Like hell it isn't," the kid says.

"So . . . what? What is this, then?"

"A clean slate," she says, turning back to Lance. "Revenge. An eye for an eye. Getting what you deserve—whatever bullshit line you want to call it. I don't care."

"Well," I say, "if all of what you just said is true, is that really what you wanna do to that boy? Kill his father? And what's with the timeline, here? I don't get it, Lauren."

No part of me believes it's all true, but given the situation, I'm rolling with it. All of it.

Shadow huffs.

The kid paces in the background. "Family is blood, family is blood. Family is *blood.*"

"Lauren," I say, "we can get you the help you need. Both of you." I lower my hands. Carefully. "Now, I don't know what's really going on here, but this isn't going to help the situation. Not for anyone." I look to the kid. "Him included."

"Oh?" she says. "Was it you who was kept in this house for seventeen years? Father meant well. He did. But don't act like you have any idea about him or why he did what he did. He kept us here, me and Cody, until the day he died. And whether or not you believe me, or any of what I have to say, you'll never understand what it did to me. What it did to us."

"No, I don't. But whatever your father—"

She scowls and grips the pistol harder.

"Whatever *anyone*, sorry, did to you, was out of Lance's control, from what I can tell—if he didn't know. Yeah?"

She doesn't respond right away, but I can see that she already has the answer. She's had the answer for too long, now, and it's boiling over. Even if that means taking it out on the wrong person.

"Father was left to clean up the mess. He kept us here to salvage what was left of our family." She shakes her head.

What's happening is beyond me. From what I can tell, she's talking out of her head.

I step toward her.

"Give me the gun, Lauren. We can all walk out of here, get past this hurricane bullshit, and we'll figure it out. Just give me the gun."

She turns the pistol on me. I stop.

"It's that easy, huh?" she says. "Just let it go, forget it, act like it never happened." She closes her eyes and nods.

"I'm not saying that."

The kid pauses in the corner, talking to the wall, his hands flailing. "Family is blood." He pulls back his shoulders. "Family and how you carry yourself. Family is blood." He turns back to the hallway, pacing with longer strides.

"No one," Lauren says, "and I mean *no one*, is going to come into this house and tell me what I've been through. What I need to do. No. This is my house. *This*"—she jerks the pistol back and forth—"this is the Roux house. My father may have been extreme, he may have done what no one else would have, but he loved me. Which is more than I can say for most."

Shadow's eyes dart from me to her, then back to me. He lowers the bat. His focus shifts around the room in a frenzied confusion.

"Lance is family, no?" I say. Then I look to the kid. "He's blood, now. Yeah?"

I can see it in her eyes that she's got the answer to that one, too. "Oh?" she says. "It's that simple, is it?" She looks between me and my brother. "Is it *really*, though?"

Lauren adjusts her grip and speaks to Lance. "You—"

Shadow squeezes the neck of the bat, and the wood squeaks against his palms.

"You," she continues, "poisoned this family's—"

"No," I say, stepping toward her.

The longer I wait, the deeper we'll get. The worse it gets. The greater the chance that we're all fucked.

She turns the gun on me, but as the barrel finds my head, the bat finds hers. The wood rings out against the side of her skull. Lauren collapses where she stands, and the gun falls to the floor behind her.

At the boy's feet.

He picks it up and backs himself against the wall. His eyes dart around the room to every one of us. Then he shoves the barrel under his chin—and squeezes the trigger.

But nothing happens.

His eyes double in size, and he pulls it harder. And harder. Still, the gun doesn't fire.

I run toward him and pin him against the wall, shoving his hand above his head, slamming it against the wall. We struggle for control of the gun, but he's just as weak as he looks. I take control of the pistol. As he turns to run, I grab him by the collar and slam the butt end of the gun against his head. Slowly, he slides down the wall, to the floor, and sits there. He's conscious but dazed. I turn to Lance.

"You wanna get me out of this shit?" he says.

I move toward him, but as I do, Lauren somehow gets to her feet. Wobbling. Stumbling. She grabs the banister and leans against it for support, looking down at the first floor. Then she turns around and feels the side of her head.

She pulls away her hand and holds it in front of her face. It's caked in blood.

Her eyes jerk from side to side on their own, and her complexion pales. She opens her mouth to speak, but she says nothing. Instead, her lips form a perverse grin, and her red teeth glisten in the low light of the room.

She turns to Lance. Her smirk broadens. "You done fucked up—"

But Shadow rushes her, shoving the bat against her neck and pushing her over the railing. Her body hits the floor below us—and the snap of her neck is loud and hollow as she meets the dirt with a flat thud.

Shadow turns around, and the three of us look at one another, waiting tentatively to gauge what he'll do. His hands tighten around the neck of the bat. His jaw hardens.

I flick the safety off on the pistol.

He looks at the boy, then throws the bat to the ground between them.

"That ain't right," Shadow says. "That—ain't right."

FORTY-SEVEN

August 2008

T he house turned out nice—like an antebellum period piece.

I'd be lying if I said it doesn't make me feel some sort of way from time to time, especially in the early-morning hours when it's dead silent and the sheer size looms over me. It can be a bit much in that way, when I'm alone but feel as though I'm not.

It's important to Lance, though. So it's important to me.

Besides, I started my trawling company from scratch back in the day, so the boy could use someone in his ear until this place can stand on its own. Starting a business ain't no walk in the park.

I'm in the kitchen, going over the produce list for the grand opening tomorrow morning.

"How's it looking?" Lance says as he walks into the room with a clipboard in hand.

"Couldn't be better. Everything's stocked and ready to go, except for the crab. Jonny should be here later this evening with a few dozen number-ones."

"Yeah, the dock is all clear. So he shouldn't have any problem pulling in."

The good thing about running a B&B out here on the water is the access to fresh seafood—and Jonny is our guy. Like I've told Lance since day one, it's important to get established with a local supplier early on in the game. Out-of-towners fall over the food as if it's a Red Cross in the wake of tragedy.

"What you got going on over here?" Lance says as he leans over the stove and takes a whiff of the garlic and blackened shrimp, simmering in the cast iron skillet on one of the front burners. Butter grits sit on one of the back flames, next to a few of the green onions I've rinsed and diced on the cutting-board counter.

"Like I said—it's gonna be our signature dish. Ya just wait and see."

"It better be," he says, sounding harsh but still joking. "Ain't nothing going on that menu unless it passes the taste test." Lance jabs me in the arm. "You keep that in mind."

"Well, ain't no point in waiting around, then." I grab a spoon and combine just enough of the ingredients for a single bite, then place it into a black ceramic saucer.

Lance lifts it to his nose, swirling it, closing his eyes, and drawing a deep breath in a dramatic, meant-to-be-annoying manner. He opens one eye, and a chuckle slips out.

"Taste the damn food already."

The two of us cut up.

He takes the bite and turns the spoon upside down in his mouth, drawing it out slowly. His eyes angle down and wrinkle the bridge of his nose. "Hm. Shrimp and grits, huh?"

I throw the towel over my shoulder. "Ya just gonna stand there? Or admit that it's the best you've ever had?"

He nods and tries for another bite—but there was only enough in the dish for one test. He walks to the stove and reaches for the pan of shrimp. I slap his hand.

"Nope," I say. "I don't think so."

"But how am I gonna know if it's good enough with only one bite? I'd hardly call that an adequate sample size."

I snatch the saucer from his hand. "You'll manage. Besides, you're not the only one with an opinion around here."

"Say," Lance says, "you got a minute?"

"Always do."

He turns to walk out of the kitchen. "Come and take a look at the reception area. I need your thoughts on something."

I was surprised when Lance asked me to be equal partners—the place is his, after all.

As it turns out, if you're found to be mentally unfit by the state after trying to kill yourself, you're at risk of losing your inheritance. Who knew? Not that Cody was old enough to own the house on his own, anyway. But legally, my boy Lance is the kid's father—and closest living relative.

The whole situation is a bit miserable, really, but Cody is getting the help that he needs, as far as we know. Visitation isn't exactly a straightforward process when the person you're trying to see not only doesn't want to see you but doesn't speak. Lance could only try for so long before he felt that it was in everyone's best interest to pull back. And for that, I don't blame him.

We walk into the foyer, which has been converted into the reception area, along with the old dining room. The previous living room is where we plan to serve our meals, given its larger size and view of the bayou.

Lance lifts his hands and does a slow, walking spin. "So . . . what do you think?" He walks to where the dining room once was. "I added another chair and table to the reading nook, and the coffee bar is stocked, now, too—this way the guests have more space to kick back and relax if they're not in the new dining hall or upstairs in their room. Yeah?"

"I like it." It's perfect. "I can even bake some scones and other breakfast stuff for over there." I point to the coffee station in the corner.

It's precisely the Southern feel we were going for: PJ's Coffee in the corner, accented by some New Orleans street art from the Quarter; a sitting area with a rolling ladder and floor-to-ceiling bookshelf, containing information on Slidell and the local cuisine; and the reception desk made of live oak and driftwood, crafted by yours truly. Most importantly, it's one of a kind. All of it.

It's only when I take a step back and absorb the room as a whole that I notice the custom, backlit tin sign hanging on the front of the desk: *B&B on the Bayou.*

"Like . . . really," I say. "I like it a lot, my boy."

Lance slaps me on the arm. "Thanks to you."

"Nah. You know what you're doing. Ya pops would be proud. Ya know that?"

Family has become a regular part of our talks since Katrina. Both of us know how lucky we are to have made it out of that storm the way that we did.

Not only did we make it out, but the storm brought with it a new beginning in more ways than one. As it turns out, hurricanes can churn the waters of our muddied pasts. And Katrina churned the bottom of Lake Catherine, washing a bare and weathered skull ashore in the north Rigolets. Lucky for us—lucky for my boy and his family—authorities were able to identify Marcus through dental records.

I suspect that we'll never know the complete truth, but if I knew Marcus at all, it's a safe bet to assume that he passed away while helping someone, somehow, during Josephine. At least, that's the story I tell myself.

Hurricanes aren't all bad. Sometimes, they show us who we really are. And sometimes, they provide us with answers to questions we've long abandoned.

After an endless string of deep discussions following the hurricane, and his insistence that I help, we decided to make the best of the situation. We thought long and hard about how the

Roux estate could be of use—not only for Lance, but the community as well.

"Thanks, Cotton. That means a lot."

It's difficult for him to say it outright, I suspect, but I think Lance has the best intentions for his son. In so many words, he's expressed his want for Cody to make it out into the real world— and not waste away because of circumstances that were ultimately out of his control, because he wasn't allowed to be a kid. Because of his *family*, ironically enough.

The chime of stainless steel rings out from the kitchen. Lance and I look to one another.

"I didn't think we had any help today," I say. We turn back and move quietly toward the sound.

"I don't think that we do."

A dark figure shifts beneath the white-washed French doors that separate the rooms, followed by a deep moaning and shuffling. Feet scurry across the tile floor.

I can hear the metal of a pan gliding across the steel burners of the stovetop.

Then more guttural sounds.

I step forward and push open one of the swinging doors with a single finger.

"Hell, I didn't know culinary reviews were part of the grounds work," Lance says from behind me.

The man pauses with his fingers in his mouth as he stands over the pan of shrimp, floating there like a gator caught in the spotlight.

"Well," I say, "the least ya can do is give it an honest review, then."

He grabs another shrimp as if we can't see him—and slips it into his mouth, closes his eyes, and nods in a brief thought.

"If I'm being honest . . ." He scoops a spoonful of the grits, the grease dripping onto the edge of the stove and floor. Then he drops a few of the green onions on top of the food. "It tastes like a f-f-f-f-f-fresh start to me."

part four
Miss Amy

FORTY-EIGHT

August 2008

W hat does it really mean to be retired, anyway? What a stupid turn of phrase.

You're either a nurse or you're not. There is no "in between" or "used to be" when it comes to this career. I had to renew my license and get up to date with my continuing education, of course. But that's nothing more than bureaucratic red tape—the trivial "this is how we've always done it" of medicine.

It's simpler than that: you either know how to nurse, or you do not. Call it whatever you want—nursing, caregiving, midwifing, attending, sitting, watching—you've either got it or you don't. Ain't no time away from the bedside gonna make it fade.

I grab my clipboard from the hook behind the nurse's station and look out to the twelve patients on the other side of the protective glass. I double check the attendance and my patient activity notes.

A single, sharp ray of white light cuts across the room in an unbroken plane of floating dust, striking the faded green tennis table in the corner. It's the only color in the otherwise bleach-colored common area—as it should be.

Too much of the outside gives them a false sense of hope.

Technically, I'm still the new kid in town. I've only been on the schedule for three and a half weeks. And this morning is the first day they've cut me loose. Well, not entirely; we're never really as free as we think. Not in a place like this.

I've got Marybeth out there making her rounds, holding down the front lines, sifting through the a.m. drudgery and complaints about tasteless breakfast and too-tight restraints. She's only forty-five, but she doesn't look a blond-and-braided hair over thirty. Everyone calls her the nurse's assistant, but I know better. She practically runs the place under the table.

Then there's Big Ed in the next room, sitting behind thick glass and a slew of security monitors, watching for anything that seems out of place. He's the muscle, with the exact opposite effect as Marybeth—he looks to be in his mid-seventies, but from what I've gathered, he's in his early fifties. An ogre of sorts, with a thinning, dagger-like mustache and windshields for glasses. He's a towering brick of a man, but he's the nicest thing you'll ever meet.

There's others in the back, too, going about their mundane morning tasks and filling out the usual legal paperwork. But the three of us, we're the backbone of the place. The first to call as the sun rises. Seven days a week, at that.

I still have a number of details to pin down in this new position as the unit's behavioral health monitor, but if there's one thing I'm certain of, it's that I'm in good company. This staff is really something—particularly with the younger ones.

I step out from behind my station and lock the door behind me. Big Ed gives me a nod from behind his '70s frames. I lift my papers in response.

My position is new to the unit, but basically I'm responsible for making sure that the depressed walk and the angry talk. Other than that, it'd just be great if no one dies. At least, not while I'm on the clock.

From what I can see, Marybeth has the floor under control. Lucky for her, the tennis table and TVs do most of the chaperoning. The screens themselves are like pills, keeping the banalities of everyday life at bay. Only briefly do their empty eyes break away from the pixelated worlds that hang in the corners like wormholes to another dimension. If the patients are really adventurous, they'll stand at the tennis table and hit the ball back and forth with a complete lack of purpose.

With their hands, of course. I'm new—not ignorant.

"All good?" I say to Marybeth.

She's helping Miss Bee across the room, from one of the sitting areas to the magazine shelf and back, as part of her daily exercise. The woman is without a doubt the most interesting patient we have here.

Marybeth balances the woman with both hands beneath her elbows, ensuring she doesn't catch one of her spells and find the floor with her head.

Miss Bee lifts a shaking hand to the window. "That cocksucker ain't moved all morning." Her voice struggles. "If my dusty ass can go for a walk, then so can he."

Marybeth gives her a scalding look. "Now, Miss Bee," the nurse says. "What did we say about minding your own?"

The lady shuffles farther in her tattered slippers. "If I can see him, then he's my problem."

They pause, and Marybeth tilts her head to the window. "You mind?" she says. "I got a feeling this one's gonna have me busy for the time being."

The old lady flails her hands. "Oh, sure. Don't mind me. I ain't nothing but a wrinkled pain in the ass."

And they walk on.

I make my way to the window that's sandwiched between steel bars on the outside and wire mesh on our end. Technically, and for safety reasons, we're not supposed to open the windows, even though it's impossible to get in or out.

Everyone around here has their quirks. Some of the patients

are ornery, some show us a different personality depending on the height of the sun in the sky, and some . . . well, some of them just are. They exist but refuse to present us with much else.

Personally, I think there's always hope—as long as it isn't misguided. A living and breathing person inhabits each and every body in here, even if we are incapable of proving it.

Every one of them has their own past, their own memories, cherished or forgotten. They have lives that few of us will ever truly know. They have friends.

They have *family*.

I glance back. Marybeth is still walking Miss Bee across the room. I turn again to the window.

Reaching over, I unlock the padlock on the crank, then turn it, opening the window just an inch. Rain dribbles from the rusted, oranging frame and drips to the dead leaves on the sodden ground.

"There. How's that?"

A light breeze ruffles the torn cloth in his hand, frayed and stained with drops of burgundy.

I stand behind him with my palms gripping the handles of the wheelchair. The lady's slippers slide across the rippled, white tile floor behind us.

I lean forward and speak at the edge of his ear. "Don't you worry now, darling. Miss Amy's gonna make this all go away."

And I see Cody's boyish smile—reflected in the crying pane of glass.

About the Author

KB Fisher is an independent author of mystery thrillers. He lives with his family in the Southeast United States and is a native of Slidell, Louisiana.

One of the most valuable things a reader can do for an author is to provide an honest review of their work. Please visit the book's review page on Amazon or Goodreads to do so.

Email: authorKBFisher@gmail.com
Website: authorKBFisher.com
X: @authorKBFisher
Facebook: KB Fisher